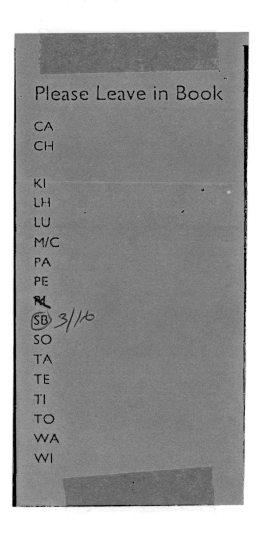

Please Leave in Book

CA
CH

KI
LH
LU
M/C
PA
PE
RL
SB 3/10
SO
TA
TE
TI
TO
WA
WI

THE FORGOTTEN

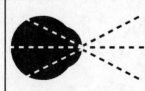

This Large Print Book carries the
Seal of Approval of N.A.V.H.

THE FORGOTTEN

HEATHER GRAHAM

THORNDIKE PRESS

A part of Gale, Cengage Learning

GALE
CENGAGE Learning·

Farmington Hills, Mich • San Francisco • New York • Waterville, Maine
Meriden, Conn • Mason, Ohio • Chicago

GALE
CENGAGE Learning®

LIBRARY OF CONGRESS CATALOGING-IN-PUBLICATION DATA

Graham, Heather.
  The forgotten / Heather Graham. — Large print edition.
    pages cm. — (Krewe of hunters) (Thorndike Press large print core)
  ISBN 978-1-4104-8029-3 (hardback) — ISBN 1-4104-8029-1 (hardcover)
  1. Paranormal romance stories. 2. Large type books. I. Title.
PS3557.R198F674 2015
813'.54—dc23   2015024119

Published in 2015 by arrangement with Harlequin Books, S. A.

Printed in the United States of America
1 2 3 4 5 6 7 19 18 17 16 15

Dedicated with sincere appreciation to
Dolphin Research Center, Grassy Key,
Marathon, Florida, and to all the
people who work with love and care to
make it such an exceptional facility,
especially Rita Irwin, Mandy Rodriguez,
Linda Erb, Emily Guarino
and Loriel Keaton.

To Jax, attacked by a shark and alive
because of DRC. I don't pretend to
know about all sea mammal centers; I
do know that this one is wonderful.

And to my very dear friend
Mary Stella, DRC, who introduced
me to Jax and Tanner and all!

PROLOGUE

"Maria."

Maria Gomez started at the sound of her name.

She'd thought she was alone.

She had been sitting in the darkness, just staring out at the night, when she'd heard her name spoken. She didn't even turn at first. She was certain she had imagined it. Her name, spoken so softly, with such affection — by him.

Because all she did was think about Miguel.

She was so numb. She knew that her children worried about her, that her friends and family worried about her, and yet she could do nothing but stare out at the night. Her balcony was beautiful; she looked out over the walled and tree-laden backyard of the beautiful home she and Miguel had built together in Coconut Grove.

In doing so, she looked out over her life.

The children had climbed the great banyan tree that grew so close to the house, just beyond the balcony. She and Miguel had hosted pool parties for Little League teams, for the Brownies and Girl Scouts. They'd hosted Michelle's engagement party and a shower for Magdalena when little Sophia had been due.

But the past was gone. The night was quiet. Only the mental echo of haunted laughter remained of the happiness that had once lived here. She knew that it was time for her to leave, too. Join the children up north, where none of them would be happy — but where they would be safe.

Miguel was gone. He had been the great force in the family. She was empty without him, empty of all the things that made a family strong. She hadn't even been eighteen when she had married him; they'd had nearly twenty-five years together. She had always trusted him.

He'd always been honest with her.

Some said that he had been a very bad man; Maria knew that wasn't true. He had gotten swept up into bad things with bad men, but he had never hurt anyone himself; he had simply been born at the wrong place at the wrong time.

It had felt like a knife in her heart when

she'd read the reports of his death in the paper; he had died as such a man might, the press — apparently desperate to be as dramatic as possible — had reported. His death had been accompanied — literally — by the same searing flame of violence with which he had lived. Doused with accelerants and burned beyond recognition, burned to cinders. Maria didn't even know if he'd been killed before the fire — she prayed he had been.

Those reporters! Even they claimed it was a heinous end, despite whatever deeds he had allegedly committed. He'd been involved in the drug trade, and everyone knew the drug trade was filled with cold-blooded killers.

But she knew that Miguel had never done anything but own land.

Most certainly his killers had known that he had gone to the American government.

That was the reason he'd been killed, of course. And the FBI man who had come to the funeral, the one Miguel had gone to, Agent Brett Cody, had been visibly distressed by that knowledge. Agent Cody had been pulled off the case shortly after he and Miguel had spoken, because other agents who specialized in the drug trade had been assigned to work with, to look after, her husband. Maria had told Agent Cody that she did not blame him for Miguel's death; after all, he hadn't gone to Miguel — Miguel had gone to him.

Miguel had been foolish; the government hadn't worked very hard for him. Protection? He hadn't been protected for a second. The men watching over him hadn't even found him until the fire had ravaged his body and rendered it unrecognizable.

She didn't entirely blame the agents, though. Those in the drug trade knew what they were up against if they tried to leave. Those who weren't in the trade didn't know that protection might not be possible — even agents who were assigned to the trade didn't always know that. No one could be watched every minute. And there was still someone out there — watching her.

"Maria."

She heard her name again. It was Miguel's voice. She missed him so badly that she could still hear him. It was almost as if she could breathe in his scent.

"Maria."

His voice seemed to be coming from behind her.

She turned. Her heart slammed to a stop in her chest, and she jumped to her feet, astonished.

There was Miguel. He was standing just inside the double doors that led from the patio back into their bedroom. He looked to be real, flesh and blood. He was there . . .

Just as quickly as it had ceased to beat, her heart took flight. They'd been wrong. The bone fragments found in the fire had not belonged to Miguel.

Because Miguel was standing right in front of her.

She raced to him, throwing her arms around him. He barely moved in response. She drew back, staring at him. It was Miguel. But . . .

Something was wrong with him. Something was really wrong.

"Miguel, what — what have they done to you?" she asked.

His eyes were blank as he stared back at her. Then, to her astonishment, he picked her up.

And he walked back out to the balcony without saying a word.

He spoke like Miguel, he smelled like Miguel, he looked like Miguel, but . . .

She was confused, but her confusion cleared in a split second when she realized his intent, and started to scream.

1

A bottlenose dolphin leaped majestically out of the water, crystal droplets raining down around it in the morning sun. It splashed as it landed, then appeared almost to fly as it raced around the lagoon, thrusting itself out of the water with the power of its fins and flukes, all the while staring straight at Lara Mayhew. The dolphin emitted a chattering sound, something delightfully akin to laughter.

Lara smiled at the sight and sound of the dolphin, a beautiful female estimated to be about ten years old and named Cocoa. Rick Laramie, the head dolphin trainer, had told Lara on an earlier visit that Cocoa was performing for her and "speaking" to her simply because she had chosen to, that she'd decided she liked Lara. That was fine with Lara. She liked Cocoa, too, and was fascinated by her. Cocoa was one of the facility's rescue dolphins. She'd been attacked by a shark and been near death when she was brought to Sea Life. Now it seemed she knew she owed her life to the facility. She was as friendly as a family pet. Today Rick was taking her for her first dolphin swim and training experience, and she was glad it was going to be with Cocoa.

Rick hadn't shown up yet, but Lara knew she was early. She was delighted just to be there, enjoying the sunlight beneath a beautiful blue summer sky, feeling the warmth of the day heat her skin. No one at the facility was up yet, in fact. It was just after six thirty. In another half hour the cooks and cashiers who ran the small café would arrive, and a few minutes after that the rest of the staff would come wandering in. The facility opened to the public for seven hours each day, but the crux of the work here was research and education, not entertainment. They didn't study dolphin disease and physiology, or perform necropsies or anything like that; they focused on training, learning more about dolphin habits and intelligence with each passing season.

Which, of course, was expensive. And why Grady Miller, one of the three founders of the Sea Life Center, had decided that, like other sea mammal research facilities, they would educate the public on dolphins, arranging for playtimes, dolphin swims and other trainer-conducted interactions. While Rick was the head trainer here, Grady was managing director. The facility had been a nonprofit research institute for years, and Grady was loved and respected by the dolphins as well as all of his coworkers. She'd seen him in the water with the dolphins; they had all rushed to him like giant wet puppies, eager to greet him, eager to have him stroke them along their backs and fins, eager for his kind words. He'd purchased the property and the docks from the previous owners — filmmakers who'd trained dolphins to perform for the camera — and continued working with the dolphins they'd left behind, simply loving and being fascinated by the creatures. That had been almost thirty years ago. He'd started with two partners. Willem Rodriguez had provided financing, and Peg Walton worked with him day-to-day. Peg had passed away a few years ago, and now Grady essentially ran it on his own. The facility was now far larger than when it had been founded, and it was thriving, with its research featured in the most influential scientific publications.

They were supported by people from around the world, rich and poor alike. Their contributors included people who

15

"adopted" a dolphin for a small donation and "sustainers" who, in return for their substantial support, were allowed to see some of the research as it was being conducted and were invited to attend a picnic-style fete each year, as well as being welcomed to various small meetings where the center's newest findings were presented. There was, in fact, a dinner planned for that evening. It would be Lara's first chance to attend such a special occasion, because there weren't many of them, and as a new employee she was lucky to find one happening so soon after she was hired. At Sea Life, every contributor was appreciated, and with nonprofit enterprises continually reliant on the philanthropy of others, it was important to always let all their contributors know how much they were valued. And tonight a few of their major supporters would be on hand. Lara didn't know much about Grant Blackwood of Eden Industries or Ely Taggerly of Taggerly Pharmaceuticals. She did know that Mason Martinez, CEO of Good Health Miami, had a nationwide reputation for his healthful lifestyle clinics and the preventive medicine practiced there. She was also familiar with Sonia Larson of Sonia Fashions.

In fact, she owned a number of Sonia's

pieces, trendy business fashions that didn't cost an arm and a leg. She was anxious to meet the woman, along with all the others, of course.

Lara's job tonight was to seat everyone and see that they were happy with the food and everyone had a good time while the trainers and scientists talked about their research and results. It hardly seemed like work.

And then there was the day-to-day here at Sea Life. Always time to walk around the lagoons and talk to the dolphins.

Lara felt she'd truly found a haven. She loved all the dolphins — but especially Cocoa.

Cocoa was in the front left lagoon that day, her usual location, though occasionally she was shifted to a different lagoon for training purposes. There were six underwater enclosures for the dolphins at the facility, front, right and left, and then two more behind each of those, with a sandbar-like island at the rear that more or less created a back street to approach the lagoons. The last two were the largest, where the adolescent males were kept. They could be rough when they played, just like teenage boys, and since two of the females had calves that were just a few months old, they were happiest away from the antics of the "boys." The lagoons were all connected via underwater gates so the dolphins could be moved around for training and medical purposes.

Each lagoon had a floating dock for trainers, medical personal and the visitors who were part of a swim program, as well as a floating platform farther out in the water.

Lara sat down on the dock. "Good morning, Cocoa!" she called.

The dolphin made that clicking sound again, disappeared for a minute, then came up near Lara in a magnificent leap and welcomed her with a showering spray of seawater.

Lara laughed. "Yes, yes, you're lovely and talented, and that actually felt very good. Love the sun, but it *is* warm. That water felt great. This is such a beautiful day," she said.

And it really was. Stunningly beautiful. The sun was shining, making the water sparkle. A breeze was drifting in off the bay, rustling the palms and sea grape trees that grew along the stone paths and by the docks. By afternoon it would be hot, and they might be caught by one or more of the torrential storms that could hit the area in the summer and into the fall. But right now, it was simply beautiful. The sky was a true bright blue; the water was like a sea of diamonds.

The move to Miami had been a good idea.

She was actually living in Coconut Grove, an area of the city that was historically artsy, with a "downtown" that was hopping until what seemed like all hours of the morning. It was a ten-minute hop over to the research facility, which was situated on a small private road off one of the bridges that connected the city with Miami Beach, which meant it was near other attractions, such as downtown Miami, the Art and Design District, South Beach, the Port of Miami, Jungle Island and the Children's Museum. While the area surrounding Sea Life was busy and modern, the facility itself had an old-time charm. The foliage was a little wild and ragged, iguanas roamed freely, and birds were everywhere. The best of both worlds.

And I so desperately needed the change, she thought.

Yes — a complete change. She had even started going by her mother's maiden name, Ainsworth. The trauma she had fled had been one thing; she was strong. The constant publicity had been another. Ironic, since media was what she had done as a congressional assistant — and was mainly what she was still doing now. Of course, her boss, Grady Miller, knew who she was and what she had fled from. He was supportive and wonderful, and she trusted him completely.

And why wouldn't she? Grady was friends with Adam Harrison, executive director of the Krewe of Hunters, her best friend's unit at the FBI. Without Meg Murray and her unit, Lara wouldn't have survived.

"Hey!" Rick called to her, heading from the service building with a cooler filled with fish. "You're here bright and early."

"I understand that this is very special. That even employees don't get free swims all that often," Lara told him, grinning.

She liked Rick; he was probably about fifty, weathered from years in the sun, slim and fit. He was married to Adrianna, another of the trainers. She had actually met Adrianna first, right here, just two years ago when she had been at her previous job, doing media for then-congressman Ian Walker. Due to a series of murders in Washington, DC, with which Walker had been involved — indirectly, or so he alleged — he was no longer a congressman.

Murders — and Lara's own kidnapping and imprisonment, naked and starving, in the dank underground of an abandoned gristmill in Gettysburg, Pennsylvania.

But she had survived, and now she was here, building a new life. Rick knew all about her past; he also knew that she'd survived mainly because of the ingenuity of a friend who worked for the FBI, and that she'd received extensive therapy since. To be honest, she hadn't felt that she'd needed all the therapy; she'd come out of the experience grateful for her life, and furious with anyone who would commit atrocities and murder for personal gain. The henchman who had actually carried out the vile acts was, she was convinced, truly certifiably crazy, but that didn't mean she was unhappy about the fact that he was going to rot in jail for the rest of his life, or that the woman whose manipulative will had set him on his murderous course would rot along with him.

"Well, Lara, you should definitely be in the water with these babies," Rick said. "There's nothing in the world like getting to know Cocoa and her buds. We bring in wounded soldiers, autistic kids — you name it. This interaction is good for whatever ails you."

"Rick," she told him firmly, "I'm absolutely fine, and I don't want people tiptoeing around me. I'm here to do a bang-up job with Sea Life's PR. Not that I'm not beyond excited to get to know Cocoa better."

"Okay, we'll start our training session on the platform," he told her. "And then we'll get in the water. No bull, though. I'll kick you out in two seconds if I don't think you're going to be a good fit with the dolphins, okay?"

"Okay."

From the platform, Rick began to teach her the hand signals that Cocoa knew. Lara dutifully imitated every sign Rick made, and Cocoa responded like a champ. She learned from Rick about the vitamins they gave to their dolphins to compensate because they didn't hunt their fish from the wild, and how they were given freshwater, too, something they usually got from their fish — and still did — but this ensured that their intake was sufficient, and they loved it. The biggest issue was trust, Rick told her. No dolphin was forced to perform or work — ever, under any circumstances.

"How on earth do they learn what a hand signal means to begin with?" Lara asked. "I mean, it's not like you can explain, 'Hey, when I raise my hand like this, I want you to make that chattering noise while you back up on your flukes.' "

Rick grinned. "We use targets, and it's a long process — except for sometimes when we work with the calves and they just follow their moms. Dolphins are social creatures, and they're curious about us, too. They like interaction, and they love learning. When the trainer blows a whistle after a task, it's to tell the dolphin that he, or she, did it properly. It's called positive reinforcement, and I don't know of any facility that uses anything else. When the dolphin hears the whistle, he knows to come to the trainer for a reward. It may be fish, like we've been using today. Sometimes it's a toy and sometimes it's a lot of stroking. Dolphins are mammals. They're affectionate. Oddly enough, a lot like aquatic dogs, but even smarter. Smart as all get-out. I love working with them. I'd honestly rather be doing what I'm doing than be a millionaire working on Wall Street. I wake up happy every day, and I get to work in paradise, with my friends and these amazing creatures. You're truly going to love it here."

"I already love it," she assured him. "I knew I would."

She *did* love what she was doing. The first week she'd started, half of her media work had been planning out her own press spin, getting the media to get past her move to Miami and the Sea Life Center and concentrate on the dolphins and the work being done here. She thought she'd handled it very well. The "news" was always fickle; a high-profile celebrity had been involved in a sex scandal, a policeman in Oregon had been accused of taking bribes from prostitutes and the world had quickly begun to forget her. In the past three weeks she had been able to work with a society that arranged dolphin interactions for autistic children, adults and children with Down syndrome and an organization involved with veterans' affairs and helping wounded servicemen and women. Writing press releases that dealt with the good things going on in the world wasn't like working at all.

It was a bit more of a challenge to politely fend off reality-show producers or convince the rich and famous that they had to go by the same rules here as everyone else. No one was allowed to just hop in and play with the dolphins; trainers always called the shots. And, of course, no one bossed a dolphin around; if a dolphin didn't want to play, it didn't have to play. Each animal could escape human interaction if and when it chose to do so. There was no drama. No one interviewed anyone without the express permission of Willem Rodriguez, who had provided Grady with the financing to buy the place a quarter of a century ago. Willem had used his business savvy in the years since then to make Sea Life what it was now: an excellently run nonprofit with a top staff of trainers and veterinarians. It was one of the most important aquatic mammal centers in the States, possibly the world.

"Ready to get in the water?" Rick asked her.

"You bet!"

Lara slid in; Rick stayed on the dock.

"You're not coming in?" she asked him.

"No, I've had all kinds of dorsal tows in my day. I'm going to teach you how to get one when you need one, though, whether you're in the water or you're on the platform, okay?"

"Okay. Thank you."

"Swim out into the center of the lagoon," he told her. "You've seen this done, so you know the hand signal. Give that signal and Cocoa will come get you. Just grasp onto her dorsal fin and go for a ride!"

Lara swam out. The day was heating up; the water was still deliciously cool. This was so entirely different from what she had left behind.

Life was good.

There was something strangely but beautifully surreal about the sight of Maria Gianni Gomez in the banyan tree.

It was almost as if she'd been posed.

Her arms were spread out almost gently, forming a casual arc over her head. Her face was turned slightly to the right.

Her eyes were open.

She was dressed in a flowing white robe. A small branch lay over her lower body, as if set there by a modest and benign hand that might have reached down with ethereal care. The great banyan with its reaching, twisting roots had grown in such a way that the center, where Maria lay, might have been scooped out to create a bed for her.

If it weren't that death was so visible in her open eyes, she could have been a model posing for any one of the sometimes very strange commercial shoots that took place in the notoriously and historically bohemian section of Miami.

Brett Cody was standing next to his partner, Diego McCullough, and looking up at the tree, studying the body where it lay.

"Ladder?" he asked Diego.

26

"One of the Miami-Dade cops went to get one. He'll be right here, along with the medical examiner," Diego said. "You got here fast," he noted.

"We're not all that far from Virginia Street," he reminded Diego. He lived right down from the mall that was more or less central to the area, almost walking distance to this North Grove area of nicer homes. "You got here pretty quick yourself."

Diego nodded. "I was at the coffee shop," he said glumly. "This is just . . . so wrong."

"She should have been protected," Brett said, a feeling of deep anger sweeping over him. But someone out there had killed Miguel — who, after all, had made his living in the drug trade, where violence was common — and now had come after his widow, it appeared.

But how?

"She had a state-of-the-art alarm system and steel bolts on the doors, and there's no sign of forced entry," Diego said.

"We need to talk to the fed who was on duty in front of the house when it happened," Brett said. "We knew Miguel's killers might think she knew too much, so we were keeping a watch on her."

"He thought she jumped," Diego told him. "She was deeply depressed, devastated, after Miguel's murder. You don't think that's possible?"

"No," Brett said quickly. Too harshly. He understood how the officer might have gotten that impression; the tree was fairly close to the master bedroom balcony, which overlooked the pool and the patio area.

But, Brett was certain, no matter what kind of an athlete she might have been when she was young, there was no way she could have jumped from the balcony and wound up where she was.

It would have been possible, however, for someone to throw her over and cause her to land exactly where she had.

"Hey, I know how you feel about this one, how much you wish you could have seen it through," Diego said quietly. "But if you want to keep the peace, don't tear into the officer on duty."

"Sorry," Brett said quickly. "I didn't mean to bark like that. And I don't blame the agent. He didn't see anyone go by, and should someone have gotten past him, the house has alarms and a top-of-the-line security system. No one broke into that house. How the hell she was killed, I can't begin to imagine. Unless Miguel has a clone running around somewhere — a clone with his fingerprints and his memories."

They were both quiet for a minute, looking at one another.

"He was burned beyond forensic recognition," Diego reminded Brett. "No DNA left, even in the teeth or the bones."

"Identified by the melted remains of his jewelry, and the fact that we saw him get out of his car and go inside, the only person in there," Brett said thoughtfully.

"Maybe Miguel *wasn't* killed in that oil-dump conflagration," Diego suggested.

Brett shook his head thoughtfully. "Those were definitely Miguel's things forensics took from the fire. And Miguel truly loved Maria. There's no way on God's earth that he would have killed his wife. Even if he didn't die in the fire," he added.

They both turned at the sound of footsteps. A uniformed police officer was hurrying over with a ladder. Dr. Phil Kinny, medical examiner, was just behind, followed by two forensic teams, one from the local Miami office of the FBI and one from the Miami-Dade homicide division.

"Let me get a quick look up the ladder first, okay?" Brett called to Phil.

"As you wish," Phil told him. "I'm here, ready whenever. I can only tell you how she died. You're the one who's going to have to figure out how she got in that tree."

29

"Thanks," Brett said.

The ladder was set carefully next to the tree; Brett nodded his appreciation to the young officer ready to steady it. Brett could have climbed the tree without it, but he was trying to maintain a level of professionalism. Once he had studied Maria Gomez in situ, photographers would chronicle everything before Phil started his exam and told them the preliminary time of death and whatever he could about the injuries that had presumably killed her.

Studying the woman, Brett felt again the terrible pang of guilt about the entire Gomez affair. He hadn't been assigned to the Barillo crime case; other agents and officers — both the feds and local law enforcement — had worked it for years. When Miguel Gomez had come to him, he'd made a point of going undercover to meet the family and find out what was going on, what Miguel had done and what he could give the authorities.

Basically, Miguel had been like a slave laborer, doing whatever his boss told him to do, letting them use his property, forced into the crimes he'd committed. He'd been minding his own business in a family where distant relatives had fallen prey to the lure of money and rewards. It wasn't always easy

30

for newcomers to trust in the United States government. Miguel's son had been approached leaving school by a couple of Barillo's toughs and warned about what happened when the "family" — meaning Spanish-speaking immigrants — didn't work together.

Nothing had happened to the boy, but Miguel had known that his son being threatened meant that he was supposed to play the game. Only later had he learned that Barillo prided himself on never going after innocent family members, and by then it was too late. He was in too deep.

He had done so for years. Then he had seen a friend who had avoided running "errands" for the family wind up in a one-car fatal crash. Miguel had realized that he might be doing as he was told, but it was impossible to know when you might do the wrong thing, even by accident, and wind up in a car crash — or worse, have one of your children wind up dead, despite the fact that word on the street was that Barillo prided himself on "taking care of" only those who were guilty of betraying the family, never wives or children.

Oddly enough, rumor had it that Barillo's own children weren't part of the family. He had two sons and a daughter. They were all seeking advanced degrees at some of the best schools in the nation.

He wanted a different life for them.

Miguel had found Brett by accident; he'd seen him in the street when the FBI had busted a small crew who had dumped five Cuban refugees off the coast in a rubber tube. Miraculously, the refugees had made it. Diego and Brett had been watching the group, and they had talked a terrified mother into identifying the suspects who had taken their life savings and then deserted them to die at sea. Brett and Diego had found the perpetrators because of her tip and taken them down. The United States Marshals had stepped in; the Cuban mother was now living safely with her family in New Mexico, all of them under new government-supplied identities.

Brett had liked Miguel, who'd stopped to talk to him after the takedown, and he'd known that the Barillo cartel had been a thorn in the side of South Florida law enforcement for a very long time, but he wasn't himself involved in the investigation. The case, and responsibility for Miguel's safety, had gone to Herman Bryant, head of the task force pursuing Barillo and his "family," a large group of Central and South American, island and American criminals whose cunning and power rivaled those of the Mafia in its heyday. Herman had a task force of two units, twelve agents, working the ongoing investigation, two of those men undercover. The Barillo family was extensive and dealt with human trafficking, illegal immigration, prostitution, firearms and drugs. Every federal, state, county and city law enforcement agency was kept alerted to their movements.

The frequent discovery of the family's victims' mutilated remains reminded them all that Barillo and his crew stopped at nothing to reach their goals, following up threats and intimidation with stunningly effective violence. The men who had infiltrated had reported back that loyalty to Barillo was all. Traitors were executed; the rule was immutable and simple.

But though Special Agent in Charge Herman Bryant was good at his job, and had managed to prevent murders, drug sales and more, so far they had been unable to crack the back of the giant beast. Bryant was a veteran of drug wars around the world; he'd dealt with cases from Brazil to the deepest sectors of China, interacting with local law enforcement agencies along the way. Brett had been certain that Miguel had been in good hands.

After Miguel's murder, Bryant had urged Maria to make an excuse to leave Miami, or to move in with her children. When she'd refused, he had kept men watching her house. He had done all the right things.

Even though it didn't really fit the Barillo methods for family to be killed — especially not with Miguel already dead.

Miguel had worn a wire the day he'd been killed.

Despite that, when he'd headed into his own warehouse before meeting with members of the Barillo family, he'd been killed. When — supposedly — he'd been early and alone. None of the officers watching had heard anything — no voices other than Miguel's — before the warehouse had burst into flames so strong and high that the conflagration had been visible miles away. Clearly his boss had suspected he was a traitor and had taken care of things in his own violent way.

Miguel had been seen entering the building; no one else had been there.

It hadn't seemed much of a question that the remnants of bone that had been found had belonged to Miguel Gomez. Melted fragments of the man's watch had been found mixed in with the charred remains along with his signet ring, the initials still partially visible. There had been no reason to doubt that the man was dead.

But there must have been someone else in the warehouse who the officers hadn't seen, who had, perhaps, been there waiting, staying when others had left for the day. Someone who was already there when Miguel first arrived and who had then set off a detonator to ignite the fire, and then had escaped unseen in the chaos.

That person had never been found, though, nor had he left any clues they could trace. The most logical conclusion had been that Miguel had been killed. After all, he certainly hadn't come home after the fire.

It must have been that person who was killed, though how Miguel's effects had come to be there was still a mystery. It would have been easy to misidentify the body, though, since there truly hadn't been anything useful left for the medical examiner to work with.

And now Maria, too, was dead. Brett had liked her. She'd been a slim, fit, energetic woman in her late forties; there had been nothing plastic about her. Miguel had loved her with all his heart. He'd told Brett once that they'd met, dated about two weeks, then eloped. So quickly? Brett had asked. And Miguel had told him, "I knew — I just knew. And it didn't matter how long we'd been together or what others thought. I knew that I would love her forever."

Maria had been wonderful. She'd had warm brown eyes and a few wrinkles, no doubt the result of her quick smile, and a great heart. From the ladder, Brett observed her and made mental notes to help in his investigation. Her head was at an angle, and he had a feeling her neck was broken. One arm looked broken, as well.

There was nothing in her hands, as far as he could see. Her face was scrubbed clean of makeup; it appeared she had been just about to go to bed when . . .

She looked so alive — except that she was dead, of course.

Instinct told him that she had seen her killer coming.

Her open, glazed eyes showed disbelief and pure terror, and he couldn't help wondering just who she had seen before she died to put that look in her eyes.

"Anything?" Diego called to him.

"Looks as if she was tossed off the balcony like a rag doll. As if she died when she hit the tree," Brett said.

"We'll scrape beneath her nails," Phil said. "If we're lucky, she got a piece of her attacker."

Brett climbed down from the ladder.

Diego set a hand on his shoulder. "You can't take this on yourself, *mi amigo,*" he said. He had been born in Miami and grown up with English as his first language, but he liked to switch to Spanish when he thought the Spanish words sounded more "real" or appropriate. *"Mi amigo,"* he had once told Brett, was warmer than "my friend," with more real meaning.

"I'm not," Brett said, but he knew that he was lying. "Diego, her eyes — you should see the look in her eyes."

"She was murdered, Brett, of course she has a look in her eyes." Diego was quiet for a minute. "We're lucky we got here before the birds," he added softly.

Brett had to agree. He'd come across victims who had been hidden by nature before. Nature wasn't gentle on a corpse.

"There's just something disturbing about her," Brett said.

"Yeah, she's dead."

Brett looked at Diego, trying not to show his aggravation at his partner's callous comment, but then he saw that Diego was staring up at the tree, obviously upset by Maria's death himself.

Diego looked at Brett. "So we're going to be lead on this? Despite Bryant and his crew

37

having been on the Barillo thing so long?"

"Bryant himself suggested to the powers that be that we take this on. I have to keep him advised, of course. He felt I deserved in on it. His team wouldn't have had a lot of the information they used to bust a number of Barillo's underlings if it hadn't been for Miguel. They were all upset when he died, and not only because they lost a source, though I know that this will really affect Bryant and the team professionally, too. They were really hoping Miguel's info could give them enough to arrest Barillo, or at least his immediate lieutenants."

"We will find who did this," Diego assured him.

Brett nodded. "Yes, we will. I'm going to speak with the agent who was watching the house."

Diego nodded back. "I'm going to step out on the street, see if I can find anyone who saw anything odd, do a bit of canvassing."

"Great. By the time we finish we can see if the forensic teams came up with anything."

"I think we know who did this — the same people who murdered Miguel Gomez."

Diego was probably right. But it was impossible to just go and arrest Barillo or his people. Barillo himself usually kept his hands clean. The man had been trained as a doctor in his native country, but he'd found crime far more profitable.

Brett followed Diego to the front of the beautiful old deco house. Some of the places around here were surrounded by big wood, stone or concrete walls. Not the Gomez home. The sides were fenced, as was the rear, but the front was open to the street.

Agent Bill Foley, who had been on duty in his car watching the house, was still by his car and staring up at the place. When he saw Brett coming toward him, his ruddy face grew even darker and he shook his head in self-disgust. He started speaking without even pausing to say hello.

"I wasn't sleeping, I wasn't on the phone, texting or even listening to music, Brett. I was watching that house. I don't know how the hell anyone got inside. I tried to reach her on the phone for a prearranged check-in, but she didn't answer. I went in and did a quick sweep and . . . no one. When I got upstairs and couldn't find her I looked out, and I thought she'd jumped. She loved Miguel. She'd been depressed. Brett, I don't know how the hell anyone got in there. If you don't punch in the alarm code, a siren loud enough to wake the entire peninsula goes off."

"Someone knew the password," Brett said. "All we can do is theorize right now. Someone had the code — somehow. I don't know. We'll check into the alarm company, make sure they don't have someone on the Barillo payroll. Someone could conceivably have come over the gate in the rear, lipped around through the foliage to the front door and then keyed in the entry code."

"I don't know how they got by me," Bill told him.

"We're canvassing the neighborhood," Brett told him. "We'll see if we can find anyone who saw anything unusual."

Diego, he saw, was down the street, speaking with an elderly man who was walking a small mixed-breed dog. Diego motioned to him and he excused himself to Bill to join his partner.

Diego looked at Brett with a grim smile. "This is Mr. Claude Derby," he said.

Brett nodded. "Special Agent Brett Cody, Mr. Derby. Thank you for speaking with us."

"Of course," the elderly man said.

Diego cleared his throat. "Mr. Derby says that he saw Miguel Gomez."

Derby strenuously nodded. "It was right around dusk last night. I was out walking Rocko here. I saw him and said, 'Miguel!

40

Thank God — we all thought you were dead.' "

"Are you sure it was Miguel?" Brett asked.

"Of course I'm sure!" Derby said indignantly. "I'm old, but I'm not senile, at least not yet! And my eyesight is probably as good as yours, especially when I was standing as close to him as I am to you."

"I'm sorry," Brett said. "What did he say?"

"Well, he didn't," Derby told him. "I've never seen anyone act so strangely in my life. He just stood there, as if he was completely unaware of me. Like . . . like a zombie."

"Like a zombie," Diego repeated.

"Did he shuffle when he walked? Was his flesh rotting off?" Brett asked.

"Don't be ridiculous!" Derby said indignantly. "I'm not a fool, and you've seen too many movies. He just wasn't right. It was as if he didn't even know I was there, that I was talking to him. I'd say he totally ignored me, but I don't think he really even saw me. It was weird. I figured maybe he was heading home, except he didn't head for the front door. I thought maybe he was going around to the side door, that he wasn't dead and the papers had had it all wrong. I figured he could be on some kind of medication that was making him spacey.

41

Anyway, I figured he'd get home and his wife could deal with him. Rocko and I, we just kept walking."

"Thank you, Mr. Derby, thank you very much," Brett said, but some of his skepticism must have been evident.

Derby wagged a finger at him. "Listen, Mr. Whatever Special Agent, I'm telling you God's truth. I'm as sane as you are, and I'm not in the habit of seeing zombies around every corner. I saw Miguel Gomez, and he was not himself, not to mention the fact that someone who was supposedly burned to ashes would have a hard time coming back as a zombie."

"I agree with you completely, sir," Brett assured him. "And I thank you for your help. I would like to ask you, though, not to speak with the media."

"Not a problem," Derby said. "Well, not for me, but I did tell my wife when she was headed to bingo, so I'm not sure who else knows that I saw Miguel by now. If you have any more questions, I live catty-corner across the street."

Brett thanked him again and looked at Diego.

"Miguel Gomez is alive after all," Diego said.

"And he killed his wife?" Brett said,

puzzled. "I just can't believe that Miguel Gomez would have killed the woman he loved so much."

"Zombies kill anyone," Diego said lightly.

Brett looked at his partner.

"Sorry," Diego said. "But you know it's going to hit the news. By now everyone at bingo knows that one way or another, Miguel came back from the dead, and if they don't know by now that his wife's been killed, they will soon. I'll go try a few more houses, find out if anyone else saw Miguel."

Being in the water with Cocoa was an incredible high. Lara couldn't remember when she'd felt quite so exhilarated. She'd done "flipper shakes," dancing, dorsal pulls, splashing and more. Now they were playing with toys.

First she threw balls and rings. Then Rick told her that Cocoa was great at diving and finding things by sight, so they often sent her down to find anything someone had accidentally dropped.

"Guests use their phones and iPads as cameras on the docks and sometimes even on the platforms," he told her. "But whatever they drop, Cocoa will find it. Not that your average cell phone still works after a dip in the lagoon, but Cocoa will bring

43

them back up. Here, I'll show you how good she is."

"You going to sacrifice your cell phone?" she asked skeptically.

"No," he assured her. "I have some little boxes that sink, same general size as a phone or a small camera. Cocoa has picked up lots of cameras, and a purse or two, as well. Here, I'll show you. Take the box. Drop it, and then twirl your hand like this —" he demonstrated "— and say, 'Cocoa, will you get that for me, please?' "

Lara did as Rick instructed. Cocoa was great, chattering her pleasure each time she made a retrieval.

"Shouldn't I be giving her a fish?" Lara asked. "She's done all her tricks, so doesn't she get a reward?"

"Do you give a dog a treat every time you see it? Or do you let it know how much you care by petting it?"

"So I should just stroke her?"

"Yes, give her a nice stroke along the back, and then, when we're finished, we'll give her some fish."

Lara tossed the boxes, first one, and then another. Rick told her to give specific vocal commands, asking Cocoa to get the big box or the little one.

It was amazing the way the dolphin

responded.

"She's brilliant!" Lara told him.

"I agree. She's my girl, but she sure likes you."

So I actually have a real friend in Miami, Lara thought wryly.

She happily tossed boxes and asked Cocoa to bring them up, and Cocoa kept complying.

Then she went down and came up with something else. It was on the tip of her nose, and she nudged it toward Lara.

"Not a box," Lara murmured. "Cocoa, what did you find down there?"

She accepted the pale sticklike thing Cocoa gave her. She looked at it, confused for several seconds.

Then she screamed and it flew from her hand.

Back into the water.

She'd realized what it was.

A human finger.

2

Brett stood glumly listening to Dr. Phil Kinny explain that Maria had died sometime between ten and twelve the previous night. She'd died quickly, at least; her neck had been cleanly snapped on impact with the old banyan tree.

"Didn't it take a lot of strength for someone to toss her that far?" Brett asked.

Kinny shrugged. "Yeah. But I've seen people do amazing things under certain circumstances. Adrenaline is something we have yet to fully explain. I've seen a tiny woman lift a three-hundred-pound man once. It was a kidnapping attempt. He was lying on top of her baby."

"But did a zombie do it?" Diego asked. Brett glared at him, and Diego shrugged. "Hey, I'm friends with the cops who were first on-site the night of the latest 'zombie' attack. They told me the guy had bullets in his head and kept moving. That's pretty incredible."

"Incredible, yes — but he did go down," Brett said. "Miguel is not a zombie. Someone died in that fire. We assumed it was Miguel, but apparently it wasn't. Because if you try to tell me that ash can reconstitute itself into a zombie, I'll tell you that you're full of crap."

"Maybe Miguel's ghost is walking around," Kinny said.

"Do you really believe that?" Brett asked.

"No. Besides, to the best of my knowledge, ghosts don't kill anyone. They're ethereal, ectoplasm or whatever."

"You're a scientist and a doctor — and you believe in ghosts?" Brett asked him.

Kinny brushed back his hair, watching as his assistants carefully removed Maria Gomez's body from the banyan tree. "It's *because* I'm a scientist — a doctor — that I said what I said. Energy never dies. Where it goes, we don't know. I'm a skeptic with an open mind, how's that? Also, I've been in rooms with the dead when I've felt something. Call me a hopeful believer. But in this case I'm with you, Brett. Miguel Gomez may well be alive. There wasn't enough left to get DNA. That warehouse burned hotter than hell itself. Everything we have is essentially circumstantial, so who knows?"

Brett's phone was vibrating in his jacket pocket. He quickly answered it to discover that it was his supervisor, Special Agent in Charge Marshall. "We've gotten a curious call. I know you're at the Gomez house, but I thought you two might want in on this. A human finger was found at the Sea Life Center. One of the dolphins picked it up."

"A finger?" Brett said. The population in South Florida had exploded in the past several decades, and with the higher population came a higher crime rate. That meant that far too often bodies — and body parts — were found in unexpected places.

He wasn't sure why he and Diego were being called to investigate a finger. Not that a finger was a good thing to find.

"You want us to check out a finger?" he asked.

"Yeah, check it out. With Miguel and now Maria dead, I think the Barillo family is sending out lots of warnings. I want you to find out who that finger belonged to, and I want to know if there are more parts to go with it. You're scuba certified, so I want you in the water. I'll get dive equipment out to you. You and Diego are on this now, too, and I want you taking lead."

Brett was silent.

He'd wanted in on Miguel's case before. He'd felt he'd owed the man because he'd brought him to the Bureau, and now Maria was dead, too. Now he owed them both.

But his boss wasn't taking him off the case, he reminded himself. He could still help find them justice. He was just taking on another case, too.

He wasn't sure about how a finger in the water was connected with Barillo, Miguel and the dead woman in the banyan tree, but he was going to find out. He had worked with dive units before, so he supposed it was a good call.

"Dr. Kinny, we'll see your full report later," he told the ME. "Right now we need to go."

Diego arched a brow at him.

"We're going diving, my friend," Brett said.

Diego looked surprised, but he only shrugged and said, "Where you lead, I follow. Only 'cause I'm paid to, of course."

"Hey, when *you're* lead, *I* follow," Brett reminded him.

"And you make a very good follower, too," Diego said with a grin. "Now lead on. I'll follow."

"It's a big city," Meg told Lara over the

phone. "Miami is a major metropolis, and that means there are murders. It's terrible and, I admit, pretty weird that a dolphin gave you a human finger, but sad to say, things like that happen."

Lara had called Meg as soon as she could. She was amazed by how quickly after her first hysterical reaction everything had changed. She had calmed down in just a couple of minutes and managed quite well, she thought.

Rick had figured out that the object was indeed a human finger at the same time she did. To her relief, she had actually thought to ask Cocoa to go back for the finger before Rick did. Once Cocoa had retrieved it again they'd called the police. Now there were police divers in the lagoon and more cops all over the place.

The finger itself was already on its way to a lab. Sea Life had been closed for the day, and the conversations she'd overheard earlier had been surreal. Some of the officers were speculating that the finger was all there was to find, that its removal had been a punishment, a lesson to do better next time, and that the owner was out there somewhere, alive and well, but minus the forefinger of his right hand.

Others were speculating about where the

rest of the pieces of the body might be.

And everyone was wondering who had lost his finger and maybe his life.

Somewhere along the line, Lara had realized that she was angry. Whoever had done this deserved to be incarcerated and maybe boiled in oil. She had survived being kidnapped by an insane killer; she wasn't going to be terrified into leaving the new job she loved because of another criminal.

It just wasn't happening, and she had told Meg as much.

"Lara, are you okay?" Meg asked over the phone. She was at her office in Virginia. It had only been a few months back that she had graduated from the FBI academy at Quantico and become an agent — a very special agent, going right from the academy to be part of Adam Harrison's Krewe of Hunters, special units dealing with crimes that crossed the boundary between everyday reality and what could only be called the paranormal. And if it hadn't been for the Krewe Lara wasn't sure that even Meg could have found her where she'd been imprisoned in the old gristmill.

"I'm okay. I'm furious that someone killed someone or mutilated him or whatever, and then dumped the remains in our dolphin lagoons. I just called you because . . .

51

because you're my best friend and an FBI agent." She hesitated. "I'm just venting. Really."

As she spoke, looking out the window from the second-floor lounge in the small house where the Sea Life staff had their offices, Lara saw that still more law enforcement officials were arriving.

"This place is crawling with cops, and I think more have just arrived," Lara said. "I think these guys must be FBI. They're in suits," she joked.

She realized that if the two men who had just arrived looked up, they would see her. She wasn't sure why, but she felt her face grow flushed.

"They really might be FBI," Meg told her. "Miami has a large field office. And what with the immigration situation and the drug smuggling, they might be looking for a missing informant or a low-level criminal who's disappeared from their radar."

Lara saw Rick standing by the newcomers and beckoning to her. "I've got to go. Whoever they are, I'm guessing the Men in Black want to talk to me."

"Hang on a second," Meg said. "Matt wants to talk to you." Matt Bosworth was both her partner and her fiancé.

"Hey, Matt," Lara said when he took the phone.

"Who's there? Can you describe them?"

"Tall, fit guy who looks Hispanic and another tall, fit dark-haired guy who may or may not be Hispanic."

"Most of our guys are fit," Matt said. "The Bureau kind of insists on it. And down there, about half the people we work with have dark hair and tons of our agents are Hispanic," Matt said. "Whoever they are, I'm sure they'll take good care of you." His voice grew more somber. "Meg and I can be down by tonight if you want us."

"I know, and thank you." She hesitated. The Krewe units came in when something about a situation was unexplainable, otherworldly. Lara had known all her life, throughout their long friendship, that her friend spoke with the dead. At times when she'd been with Meg, she'd believed *she* saw ghosts, too. Lara had never known if she really did, or if she somehow saw what Meg saw because she was with her friend. The friend whose talents had been crucial in saving her life.

Sometimes she forgot what it had been like — kidnapped and cast into a dark, watery pit. After just a few days she'd been on the edge of death; she'd been barely able

53

to move when Meg had found her.

But that had been life or death.

While this . . .

This was no threat to her.

"Really, guys. No need for you to get on a plane. I'm surrounded by cops with guns. I just called because it was so bizarre and I wanted to talk to my best friend. Trust me, Rick Laramie, the trainer who was with me at the time, was as freaked out as I was at first. But I'm fine, honestly. Don't go crazy and turn your lives upside down."

"We never go crazy," Matt told her calmly.

She smiled, because she believed that. She'd seen Matt Bosworth under pressure. He was a good man to have around at a critical moment.

"I know that," Lara assured him. "I'll keep you up with what's going on," she said. "But really, I'm good. Besides, I'm sure Grady Miller, who founded this place, will wind up talking to Adam Harrison, because they're friends. Anyway, the locals have it covered. And now I'd better go. Your fellow suits are on their way up. Tell Meg I'll talk to her soon. And thank you both for listening."

She hung up quickly and stood, waiting, as she heard footsteps coming up the stairs. Rick had been joined by Grady and the two

FBI agents.

"Lara," Grady said the minute he walked in, "I'm so sorry this happened to you."

Grady Miller was the perfect grandfather. He had thick silver hair and a lined face, but he was very fit for his seventy years. He could still swim like a dolphin himself and was often in the water with the trainers, entertaining visitors with antics only he could manage with the creatures that behaved like beloved puppy dogs around him.

"I'm fine, really, but thank you for being so concerned."

"Lara," Rick said, "these are Agents Mc-Cullough and Cody."

She wondered which man was which.

One was quick to smile and very good-looking. He reminded her of Mandy Patinkin in *The Princess Bride,* though with shorter, but still curly, hair. The other had even darker hair and equally dark eyes, and he didn't smile. He had a ruggedly sculpted face and looked as if he should have been commanding a Roman legion.

"Hello," she said, accepting a powerful handshake from each man.

"They want to know exactly what happened today," Rick said.

She glanced at Rick, frowning. He had

been there, too. "You didn't tell them?"

"We'd like to hear about it from both of you," the friendlier man said. "I'm McCullough, by the way. Diego McCullough. Strange name, I know, but this is Miami. Lots of mixes, you know?"

"Looks like a great mix to me," Lara assured him.

The other man didn't speak. He watched her — waiting. He seemed grim — or maybe even suspicious of her. He had a face with features so perfect and classic — and stern — they belonged on a marble bust.

She glanced at Rick, who shrugged, and then she said, "Rick was teaching me some of his training techniques. Part of training is play. Cocoa was fetching different-size boxes for me, and then she came up with the finger. She had it on the tip of her nose and nudged it toward me, so I picked it up. I didn't know what it was at first. I think Rick and I realized at the same time. We both screamed, and without thinking I tossed the finger back into the water, then sent Cocoa to fetch it again, and we got out of the water and dialed 911. The police came, and as you can see, they already have divers in the water searching for more . . . more body parts."

"You're sure it's the same finger you had

the first time?" the second man, the one named Cody, asked. He still hadn't cracked a smile.

The question surprised her.

"Uh . . . no, actually," she said. "I didn't inspect either of them. I just assumed she picked up the same finger the second time."

Agent Cody turned to Grady. "Sir, I know you already have some of Miami-Dade's finest in the water, but my partner and I would like to get in there, as well. One of our agents is on the way as we speak with dive equipment for us."

"Of course," Grady assured them. "We closed the facility immediately. We're at the disposal of law enforcement, so just ask for whatever you need. One of our trainers — Adrianna, Rick's wife — is out there now, keeping the dolphins occupied so the police can work."

Agent Cody headed for the door and then paused, as if remembering some form of social grace was necessary to get what he needed from people.

"Thank you," he said, nodding briefly to Lara and then to Rick. He was so brusque that she was surprised to feel a little tremor when he spoke. But of course it was impossible not to notice the waves of unconscious sexuality pouring off the man.

57

"Of course," Rick said.

Lara didn't have to speak — Cody was already gone.

The Florida Keys offered fabulous diving with excellent visibility. But here, the dolphins were in a lagoon. Much of the area off the docks was fairly deep — a good forty or fifty feet — and there were the same sea grasses and silt normally found around docks. The water was kept free of refuse, but the nature of the habitat kept it from being as clear as the local reef.

Brett wasn't sure himself just why he felt so determined to find more of the person to whom the finger had once been attached. He knew he was frustrated and angry about Maria's murder, and at least this was something active that he could do. He also knew they might not find anything; he might be on a wild goose chase.

He spent a good thirty minutes underwater with Diego. He used his underwater light as he swam by the foundations of the docks and every platform in every enclosure. The problem was, he might be looking for small body parts. Not easy. There were too many places that something that size might have ended up wedged.

The local cops, working in three teams of

two, had worked even longer than he and Diego had.

Between them all, they'd found nothing. And he'd just about gone through his tank of air.

It made sense to come up — and give up. It was more than possible that the owner of the finger was still alive and well, except for a missing finger. More people than just the Barillo family plied the criminal trades in the area. Florida had almost one thousand two hundred miles of coastline, making it ideal for modern-day criminals, drug runners and smugglers, just as it had been a haven for pirates and blockade-runners in the past. For those bent on illegal enterprise, Florida offered nooks and crannies in abundance.

Brett loved his state; he'd always wanted to work just where he was working. He considered himself well qualified, since he'd been born in Gainesville — as had his parents. His dad's parents had been born in St. Augustine and his mother's in Jacksonville. All his life, he'd heard their fascinating tales about the past; to him, the state was unique and incredibly special — though of course it faced plenty of challenges, too. He'd attended the University of Miami and worked in the Keys on weekends, and during summers he'd been hired on the charter boats that were so prevalent around the state. He knew the mentality of the Deep South stretch of the panhandle, the theme-park wonderland of the center of the state and the varied mix — Caribbean, South and Central-American, now with a growing Eastern European component — of the southern half of the state and the Keys. He'd made a point of learning Spanish and Portuguese and the Haitian patois that was spoken in some areas of Miami. Few people, he thought, knew the state and its inhabitants better, with all the quirks and oddities to be found in such a diverse population.

And he'd learned to care about people the rest of the world judged simplistically, people like the Gomezes. While Miguel hadn't shared the bone-deep goodness and tenderness of his wife, at his core he'd been a decent man caught between a rock and a hard place. He'd tried to make things right; he'd come to Brett and offered his help.

Brett surfaced and saw that the Miami-Dade teams were already up, and so was Diego, who had slipped out of his buoyancy control vest and was sitting on the dock speaking with Adrianna Laramie. She made a good match for Rick; they were both attractive in a real-world way and bronzed from their years in the sun. She'd been fully cooperative, talking to the dolphins and getting them to retrieve all kinds of anomalous objects. They had brought up bits of coral, a deflated beach ball, a pair of sunglasses and a watch. But no more body parts.

"Think we're done here?" Diego called to him.

Brett was just about to agree when he saw the CEO of the place, Grady Miller, hurrying along the dock with a cell phone.

"It's your supervisor. He wants to speak with you," Grady told them.

Diego took the phone and listened gravely, then turned to Brett. "You're going to want a new tank," he said.

"Why?" Brett asked.

"They've got an ID on our body part. And you're not going to believe it."

"Miguel Gomez?" Brett asked incredulously.

"Yup. Miguel didn't burn up in that fire. Whether he did or didn't kill his wife, he really could have been in his own neighborhood, and now he, or at least part of him, was here."

Lara spent the afternoon working on a series of press releases in tandem with a public information officer from the Miami-Dade police. She'd been going back and forth with the young officer on email for what seemed like forever when Rick suddenly appeared at her door.

"They want you," he told her.

She carefully hit the send button before looking at Rick curiously.

"*They* want me? Sorry, who are they, and what do they want me for?"

"They want you in the water."

"I'm not a trainer," she said. "And 'they' as in the cops?"

" 'They' as in the FBI guys," Rick said. "More particularly, dark and brooding FBI guy."

Lara thought about asking him which dark and brooding guy, except that she knew. It had to be Agent Cody.

"Why do they want me? I don't know what I'm doing unless I'm with you or one of the other trainers."

Rick made a face. "Well, you can thank Grady for this one. He says that Cocoa feels you're her special friend. They think that if you're in the water, she'll get into the mood and help."

Lara stood up awkwardly. She'd changed out of her suit and into dry clothing for work, but if they wanted her in the water, she would be happy to change again and get back in.

"Okay, give me five minutes. I've got to put my suit back on."

Rick nodded. "I'll wait and go down with you."

"Thank you."

Lara started to put on her suit and water shirt, but they were still damp, so it was a struggle to get back into them. She realized she must have taken longer than she realized when she heard footsteps and Rick called to her from outside the bathroom door and told her to hurry up. One final tug and she joined him.

"Cocoa did really take to you," he said as they started walking. "Maybe you're just both good-looking girls of the same age. I mean, in dolphin years, she's in her mid-twenties, too," Rick said.

"Maybe she's blonde at heart, huh?" Lara asked.

Rick grinned and led the way back down to the water.

Agent Cody was still in the water, but his scuba equipment was on the dock, which meant — she assumed, since all she really saw was his bare chest — that he was wearing a pair of swim trunks and nothing else. He was muscled like steel, but she'd expected no less. His partner was standing on the dock in swim shorts, as were the police divers. Grady was there, too.

Cocoa wasn't alone in the lagoon. Several of the "girls" — as the young females were called — were there with her.

As soon as Lara arrived on the dock, she heard Cocoa let out one of her little chattering sounds in greeting. Lara flushed; she did seem to have a bond with the animal.

"I'm not sure how I can help," she told Grady. "If the pros have come up empty and the girls haven't found anything for you or Rick . . ." She paused, aware that Diego was looking at her understandingly, while Cody was just staring at her with unreadable dark eyes.

"I had a German shepherd once, great dog," Grady told her. "He was nice to other people, but he'd only play fetch with me. Only me, no one else — not even if the best dog trainer in the world was around. Dolphins are very bright animals, and Cocoa's attached herself to you." He pointed toward her where she was floating beside the dock, eyes intently focused on Lara. "Hop on into the water, greet her, give her back a stroke, then ask her to fetch for you."

Lara sat on the dock and slid into the

water. She felt the dark eyes of Agent Cody on her all the while. Once in the water, she talked to Cocoa. The dolphin swam by Lara, allowing her to stroke her long, sleek back. Then she raced out to the center of the lagoon and did a fantastic leap before coming straight back to Lara.

"Do I need some fish?" Lara asked, looking up at Grady.

He shrugged. Rick, standing on the dock, reached into one of the coolers and pulled out a fish.

Lara swam over to him, reached for the fish and turned. Cocoa was already there, her mouth open in anticipation. Lara tossed the fish to her.

"Try now," Agent Cody told Lara.

She nodded, stroking the dolphin.

"Cocoa, fetch, please," Lara said, treading water and giving the dolphin the hand signal.

Cocoa disappeared under the water. Everyone fell silent. Not even the police divers, who had broken off to chat, spoke.

Nor did any of the other staff — trainers, educators, even the café crew — who had crowded around to watch the proceedings. Lara noted that coworkers seemed to be clustering together. Dr. Nelson Amory, head of research, stood with Cathy Barkley, his assistant, and Myles Dawson, their U of Miami intern. Frank Pilaf and the café staff stood together, while the other trainers, Sue Crane and Justin Villiers, were watching from beneath the bountiful leaves of a sea grape tree.

Cocoa returned, bringing Lara a long stalk of sea grass.

Lara thanked her and stroked her back.

"Tell her that's not it," Agent Cody said.

Lara ignored him; she wasn't about to tell the dolphin that she'd failed or disappointed in any way.

"Cocoa, thank you. And now, please, fetch again, will you?" she asked.

Cocoa went down again. This time, she returned with a pair of sunglasses that had obviously been entangled in sea grass for a very long time.

"These are great," she told Cocoa. "Thank you."

Cocoa chattered and went back down. She was obviously enjoying the game.

Agent Cody was just staring at Lara, waiting. Uncomfortable under that probing gaze, she turned around to face Grady and Rick.

"I'm not sure what you thought I could do," she said by way of apology.

"You never know," Grady said.

But then Lara felt a bump as Cocoa pushed her from behind. She heard a massive, collective gasp — almost as if all those gathered around the lagoon were actors creating a scene on cue — as she turned around.

Cocoa had something for Lara. It was balanced precariously on her nose.

And Lara had to choke back a scream, had to steel herself to remain still . . .

This time it was a human foot.

3

"It's kind of like Mike, the headless chicken," Diego said gravely.

They'd showered at the Sea Life Center and were now on their way to the medical examiner's office to see Dr. Phil Kinny, the ME, who had possession of the foot.

Brett glanced questioningly at Diego, then went back to driving as he waited for his partner and friend to elaborate.

Diego nodded at him somberly. "I swear this is no lie, Brett. You can look it up. There was a chicken by the name of Mike. Had his head chopped off, but they missed something at the brain stem. He lived for eighteen months."

"That's some kind of hoax," Brett said.

"No, it happened in 1945. I know because I thought it was a hoax, too, so I checked it out. The guy who owned Mike made money touring him around. They also brought him to the University of Utah so that researchers there could document what had happened."

"His head was chopped off and he lived?" Brett asked skeptically.

"The ax missed the carotid artery or something like that, and a blood clot kept him from bleeding out. The head was gone except for one ear. Mike even tried to peck and eat grain. It's a bizarre story. Supposedly he made the farmer like forty-five hundred dollars a month, which would be close to fifty thousand now. They fed him with an eyedropper, gave him milk and stuff. I don't remember exactly. I think he finally choked to death, but the point is, he lived for eighteen months without a head."

"So you're telling me that Miguel Gomez might have had his head chopped off and then been programmed to kill his wife?" Brett asked.

"No. I'm just saying there's something weird going on."

"I agree. But Miguel couldn't have killed Maria. I don't think that I ever saw a man and woman married so long who were still so deeply in love," Brett said. He paused for thought. Actually, he saw the same love and respect in his own parents. They'd married practically as children and were still married — and bugging him for grandchildren.

Luckily his sister had provided them with a boy and a girl, and they lived in Jacksonville, near his folks in St. Augustine.

"Miguel loved Maria. So what? Doesn't mean he couldn't have become a zombie, until someone did him in for real, then chopped him up and threw him in Biscayne Bay. All we need is another zombie story around here," Diego said.

Brett agreed. In 2012, a young man had gone crazy, stripped naked and attacked a stranger on MacArthur Causeway, claiming the older man had stolen his Bible. He'd chewed off half the face of the victim, who had miraculously survived, before being shot by police. Brett knew a few of the officers who had been among the first responders. They'd told him that the attacker had been so revved that he hadn't fallen immediately, actually growling at the officer who had demanded he cease and desist. The first bullet had done nothing; four more had been needed to bring down the attacker. The media, naturally, had seized on the event, which quickly became known as the Miami Zombie Attack or the Causeway Cannibal Attack.

They didn't need the media seizing hold of this situation — especially when years of work by a half dozen law enforcement agencies might well be at stake.

And especially when Miguel and Maria had left behind a loving family who didn't need that kind of story marring the memory of their loved ones.

"With any luck, we'll avoid the zombie stories," Brett told him.

Diego snorted.

He was right, actually. A zombie story was inevitable, unless they managed to gag the press and anyone who might have seen Miguel before Maria's death.

And now, of course, they had body parts that proved Miguel hadn't died in that fire. They were going to take some major-league credibility blows from the local, county and state police, not to mention every federal agency out there.

They arrived at the medical examiner's office on Northwest 10th Avenue. Brett sighed. He'd been there far too many times — but none quite like this. The gurneys were sized to hold bodies, but the one today held nothing but the severed foot.

The ME was waiting for them and started right in after a quick hello.

"Here's what I can tell you. Yes, the foot goes with the finger goes with the DNA of Miguel Gomez. We're dealing with body parts that have been compromised by

71

seawater, but that doesn't mean there's not a certain amount I can tell you. First, this foot wasn't in the water more than twenty-four hours — I'd say more likely around twelve to sixteen. Gomez was already dead when his foot was removed. It was anything but a precision operation. You're not looking for a surgeon. You *are* looking for someone capable of swinging a blade. That foot was removed by something like a large hatchet or an ax."

"How did Miguel die?" Brett asked.

Phil Kinny stared at him. "Brett, I'm looking at a foot and a finger. I've sent out tissue samples for analysis, in case that can tell us anything, but all I know so far is that a seemingly healthy man was dismembered after death. If he had drugs or alcohol in his system, the tox screen will tell us that. When I have anything more, I'll call you."

"How long?" Brett asked.

"I marked this as top priority," Kinny told him. "But this is Miami," he added drily. "So no guarantees."

"Thank you, Phil," Diego said.

Brett quickly echoed his words.

"If I only had a head," Kinny said.

Brett felt as if he'd stepped into a bizarre version of *The Wizard of Oz*. He understood what Kinny meant, though. Unraveling the

72

mystery of death was Kinny's passion; his determination to know the truth had helped them many times.

"Unfortunately, it's probably in Biscayne Bay — somewhere," Diego said.

"But maybe near Sea Life," Brett speculated.

"We searched Sea Life. More than a half dozen divers and as many dolphins searched Sea Life," Diego reminded him.

"But if you had the head, you could tell us more?" Brett asked Kinny.

"The brain is complex," Kinny said. He looked at the two of them. "True story — and bizarre. Police were called to a home where the husband and wife had been attacked, shot several times. The husband was found at the foot of the stairs. He'd brought in the paper, set up his cereal bowl and then died at the foot of the stairs. The wife was in bed — alive, but just barely. She came to enough to say the name of one of their sons. When she came out of the coma, she denied she'd ever said her son's name, but consequent investigations proved that he had come down the tollway, his car had been seen — and he had ditched the gun."

"I'm lost. What are you getting at?" Diego said.

"The son finally confessed. He was mad

at his father and wanted his parents' money. But here's the thing — he got to the house and shot them both in bed around 2:00 a.m. Apparently, he wasn't much of a shot, though. His mother survived, and his father . . . The kid shot him in the head. The father was doomed, but despite that, a portion of his brain was untouched — the portion that dealt with mechanical memory. He rose, got the paper and set up his cereal before dying, and without any idea at all that he'd been shot and was dying and needed medical attention."

"Mike the headless chicken," Diego breathed.

"Is that possible? Are you making this up?" Brett demanded.

Kinny looked almost hurt. "Have you ever seen me joke in this office?" he demanded.

"I've got to find Miguel's head," Brett said.

The night was beautiful. It might be summer in Miami, but as if ordered by a celestial being, the breeze coming off the bay was exquisite, Lara thought. Like many attractions in the South — and even the North in summer — Sea Life was equipped with a number of spray stations where fans were set with water pumps to send a cooling mist into the air. Now she walked out from beneath the massive roofed-but-open dining area at Sea Life to cool off in the fine spray.

As decked out as many of the guests were that evening — mostly the women, because most of the men had opted for lightweight tailored shirts and trousers — they weren't about to get their clothing or their hair wet. Lara didn't care. Her hair was down, and her white halter dress, sandals and a shawl could handle a little moisture.

Lara had discovered that Miami was most beautiful by night. Darkness hid the seedy faults of certain areas, while the lights highlighted the shimmer of the water and the many fantastic skyscrapers downtown. Lights on the many causeways and bridges created a stunning combination of dazzling colors.

So much here was so beautiful — until a body part showed up.

She gave herself a shake, trying not to think about what had happened earlier. They'd kept Sea Life closed throughout the day while the authorities had done a thorough search of the facility, but the police had assured them that they could go on with tonight's gala and open the following day.

Which was good, since they were fully

booked for every swim and encounter, many of those reservations made after word had leaked of Cocoa's discoveries.

Apparently the public was slightly ghoulish.

And since the news was out, they'd decided to bite the bullet and answer any questions honestly, giving what information they could, which wasn't much. A finger and a foot had been found in the lagoon. The police and other agencies had conducted a thorough search for additional body parts but had found nothing else. More information would be forthcoming pending the investigation.

It was easy for Lara to say that she didn't know anything, because she really didn't.

Now she looked around and took time to really appreciate everything that had been put together to make the evening special. The interns had done a fabulous job of arranging colorful plants around the open square, decorating the tables — each one held a vase filled with shells and a candle — and creating an elegant ambiance by the sea. Rain might have ruined everything, but they'd lucked out. No rain that night. Just the perfect breeze, the moonlight and the occasional sound of a dolphin calling from the nearby lagoon. Lara had worked on the menu to make sure there were delicacies for everyone. Sonia Larson was a vegetarian, Mason Martinez lived a gluten-free lifestyle and Ely Taggerly was in his early seventies and on salt restrictions, while Grant Blackwood was a forty-year-old Texan who had made his millions in the oil industry and still liked a good steak.

Rick and Adrianna Laramie were pescatarians, eating fish but nothing warm-blooded. As they said, fish ate fish, and so did their dolphins, so they had no problem eating fish, too. Everyone else — both guests and staff — ate just about anything.

Lara was proud that she'd managed to create a gourmet menu that accommodated everyone there — and cheaply. She had enlisted an up-and-coming Key West chef who had just won a cable-series cooking challenge. He and his family would enjoy a special day with the trainers and Grady Miller, and the meal would be compliments of the chef, who, as an added bonus, was featured in all their PR material.

She looked over to see what was going on in the dining area. A local jazz trio was providing free entertainment. Sonia Larson — petite, dark haired and gorgeous in a teensy-tiny black dress that probably only she could wear — was holding a wineglass in her delicate fingers as she laughed at something Ely Taggerly had said. Grant Blackwood, standing next to Sonia, let out a deep bellow of laughter. Dr. Amory was with them, being his suave and charming self. Grady Miller and the rest of the staff were circulating, making sure every guest felt special, valued. Rick and Adrianna were chatting with Kevin and Diana Valentine, locals who owned a chain of drug and convenience stores, and sponsored their special events for veterans and their families. The café staff were supposed to be guests, but she'd noticed that they were still picking up empty plates and cups when they found them. That made her smile. Everyone here loved the place.

Everything appeared to be going exceptionally well. Both Ely Taggerly and Mason Martinez had shown themselves to be interested not only in the center's general research but in what research into dolphin physiology and health could carry over into the field of human health, where both men made their living. EEG research had shown that half of the dolphin brain slept while the other half remained awake, seeing to it that they continued to surface as necessary to breathe.

She decided to take a moment longer and

enjoy the caress of the mist blower. Closing her eyes, she let the fine droplets and the gentle breeze wrap her in cool comfort.

She loved her new world, despite the trauma of the day.

There had been so many law enforcement personnel on site that she hadn't even met them all, but everyone had been nice, except for Agent Cody. And it wasn't that he'd been rude or anything. He'd just been so . . . intense. As if what had happened was a personal affront to him. Brusque. That might be a way to describe the man. Curt, or maybe tightly wound. Kind of a shame. Both he and his partner were certainly striking looking, the kind who made you look when they walked in. One had asked that she call him by his given name and not Special Agent McCullough. He'd grinned when he'd told her that his name was Diego and explained that his mom had been a Cuban immigrant at the tender age of two. She'd grown up in Miami and married the Anglo doctor she'd met when she broke her foot playing soccer her senior year of college. "That's Miami for you," he'd told her with another smile.

She'd liked that. And she liked him.

As to his partner . . .

The man hadn't had two words to say to

her that weren't directly concerned with the case. His features seemed to be composed of granite, totally immobile and incapable of expression. His eyes were almost black, they were so dark a brown, and while he ticked her off to no end, she couldn't help but feel something like a warm charge suffuse her when he gave her his intense stare.

"Stick up his butt," she muttered softly to herself.

Time to get back to work. The day was almost over. Cocoa's discovery would be the talk of the town for several days, and then something else would capture the public's imagination. And as far as she was concerned, that was a very good thing.

She opened her eyes. And started.

He was there. The agent. Not Diego, but stick-up-the-butt Agent Cody.

She wondered how long he had been standing there right in front of her.

And she wondered just how loudly she had spoken.

She flat-out stared at him for several seconds, stunned to see him.

"Agent Cody," she said finally. "Well. How nice. You're back. Just in time for the fund-raiser."

"I'm not here for the fund-raiser," he told her.

"That's a pity. The food is excellent," she said, and then shook her head. "Look, Agent Cody, this place readily turned itself inside out for you today, and we're willing to do anything to help. But tonight's event is very important for us."

"I'm not here to bother you or break up your party," he assured her.

She just stared back at him. He definitely had a blind side. It was tonight, and he was here.

And he was definitely a bother.

"I need you and your dolphin tomorrow," he told her.

"First, I'm working tomorrow. Second, I don't *have* a dolphin. I don't own any of the dolphins, and I'm not a trainer. I'm pretty new to the facility, as a matter of fact," she told him.

"I've already spoken with Mr. Miller, and he says that he's willing for you, Rick and Cocoa to participate in what I propose, as long as we record the process for research purposes."

"In what you propose?" Lara echoed slowly. She turned to look toward the dining area. Grady Miller was still standing by Sonia and Ely, but he was looking at her and Agent Cody. And when he caught her looking at him, he nodded gravely.

81

When had all this happened? How long had she been standing there in the mist?

"I'm leaving," Agent Cody assured her. "I really just interrupted you in your — your moment of whatever — to let you know about tomorrow and to thank you. You were a tremendous help today, and I'm hoping that we fare better tomorrow."

She hoped she wasn't staring at him quite as blankly and stupidly as she had a feeling she was.

"You're welcome," she told him. "As Grady told you, we're more than willing to help. Whoever did . . . *that* needs to be brought to justice. I have absolutely no idea what you're proposing. I'm sure I will tomorrow, though." There. Hopefully she sounded semi-intelligent.

"We're going to search the bay," he told her.

"For?"

"More of the victim."

She was no cop, but she knew enough to know that what he was proposing was like seeking the proverbial needle in a haystack. He was crazy.

"In all of Biscayne Bay?" she asked.

"We're researching online tonight," he told her. "We're going to track the tides and the wind patterns, try to pinpoint where

82

more body parts might have ended up, where someone might have dumped them so that the foot and finger ended up here."

Lara blinked. "Someone might have spent hours — maybe days — dumping body parts in all different places," she said quietly.

"That's true. We're going to assume that the plan was to have them end up spread out, but we also believe the killer was in a hurry to get rid of the evidence and wouldn't have taken any more time than necessary."

"I'm really sorry, but I don't know how much help I can be. I've tried explaining. I'm not —"

"You're not a trainer. I know. But Grady believes that like dogs and cats, dolphins pick who they like. Cocoa likes you. And Rick Laramie will be helping us, too. Do you dive?"

"Dive? I — No."

"You *do* swim. I know because I've seen you in the water."

"How observant. Yes, I can swim. But I'm from Virginia, Agent Cody. We didn't do a lot of diving in Richmond, not in my family, at least. If you need a diver —"

"According to Grady Miller, I need *you*," he told her. "Thank you so much, Miss Ainsworth. Enjoy your party. I'll see you in

83

the morning."

Lara watched him go, still feeling stunned. She'd only been working here three weeks. Tonight's party was taking place on the Monday of her fourth week. It was an annual event, and most of the planning had already been underway, but she'd worked hard on it after taking over, wanting it to be as special as possible.

Her days here were usually all about happiness, watching both children and adults who were thrilled to enjoy the dolphins, laughing at their antics, anxious to break the communication barrier between animal and man.

It was putting words together to fight for positive press coverage, for funding, sharing facts and figures with anyone who thought what they did here was cruel. It was writing press releases about dolphins like Cocoa, who wouldn't have survived without people's help.

But tomorrow would be . . .

A search for more body parts.

Enjoy your party.

Grady wouldn't insist that she go. He knew about her past and how traumatic today had been for her. But he *had* given Agent Cody's plan his blessing.

Maybe she'd insisted a little too strongly

that she was all right.

But if she was needed . . .

Well, hell. It would only be one day.

Right now she needed to rejoin the party and mingle. She'd discovered that she liked their sponsors, especially Sonia Larson. And it was Sonia she bumped into first.

"In Miami less than a month and it appears you've met some very intriguing people," Sonia said, nodding toward the path Agent Cody had taken when he left. "Where did you meet him? Somewhere dark and dangerous, I bet. What does he do for a living? Let me guess. Soccer player! And he's — Argentine. Oh, dear, I'm sorry — too many questions." Sonia sighed softly. "Forgive me?"

Though the woman's name was Sonia Larson, Lara had caught the faintest hint of an accent and was pretty sure that she came from a Slavic country.

Lara managed a smile. "He's not actually a friend at all. I met him here earlier today. He's with the FBI. And you're not asking too many questions at all."

"No, I *do* ask too many questions. I'm . . . awkward."

Lara looked at Sonia. Despite her beauty and vivacity, it was true. She did seem a bit awkward, as if she was uncomfortable in a

85

crowd. As if all that vivacity was an act because she wasn't sure how else to behave. She was a self-made millionaire. Her clothing line consisted entirely of her own designs. She'd begun selling in some of the high-priced shops on the beach, and around Aventura and the Bal Harbor area before expanding to other cities, other states and then around the world. But Lara suspected she was happiest and most comfortable when she was on her own, designing the clothes that had brought her such success.

"It's okay. You're fine," Lara said reassuringly. Then she smiled. "My turn. Russia? Maybe the Ukraine?"

"Close. Romania," Sonia told her. "Larson was once Lungo. My father changed it when we came to this country. I've been here since I was eight. Not everyone hears the accent."

"I worked in DC for a long time," Lara told her. "I got good at recognizing accents."

"Yours is very nice. Soft and so clear, and yet . . ."

Lara laughed. "I'm from Virginia. Richmond. Very cosmopolitan now. But I guess we still have a bit of a Southern touch."

"I like the Southern touch. Like Florida.

This is my home now. I love it — everyone is here! I meet with Russians in the morning, Venezuelans in the afternoon and Cubans or Germans, or maybe someone Jamaican or French, at night. I love the salsa — that's Brazilian, yes? Everyone comes together here. And thanks to the night life, my shoes and short skirts are popular, eh?"

"I love your clothing. I have some of your Biz-Wear line," Lara told her.

"Yes?" Sonia might be a fashion mogul, but she seemed like any normal person, pleased by the compliment. "I must bring you some things."

"Oh, that's sweet, but really —"

Sonia waved a hand in the air. "You will hurt me if you refuse them."

"Please don't feel that way, it's just that it's not really appropriate for me to accept such an expensive gift," Lara said.

Sonia waved a hand dismissively. "Just think of it as a welcome-to-Miami gift. I'm in Rio next week for a fashion show, but I'll send some things over." She smiled, then said, "And now you can't argue with me, because we have company." She lowered her voice to a whisper. "Watch out for him. His hands like to wander."

Lara turned to see Grant Blackwood headed their way.

He was a good-looking man in a rough-cut kind of way — one that he probably took great pains to achieve. He played the Texan, the cowboy, to the hilt, right down to addressing Lara as "little lady" several times. He had two homes in Florida, one on Star Island and one in Key West, a mansion in Houston and several small "cottages" around the country.

His wife was currently at their "little place" in the Hamptons.

"Ladies! How cruel of you to deprive the rest of us of your company," he said, his drawl booming, rich and deep.

"I'm so sorry, but this lady has just received a call from her chauffeur. I told him he must get me out of here and home to bed at a reasonable hour," Sonia said, followed by a yawn. "I promise you, it's not the company. It's too many flights in too few days, and I'm off again soon."

Blackwood sighed elaborately. "We'll miss you, Sonia. Until the next soiree, then."

"Always such a pleasure, Grant," Sonia said.

He turned to Lara. "What about you, little lady? How about a walk down to the docks to fill me in on anything new with our wonderful dolphins?"

Lara wasn't new to his kind of game; she'd

worked in the media after all. She was good at handling herself. But before she had a chance to put him off, Sonia leaped to her rescue.

"I think that Lara needs to be very careful about walking on the docks with any man," Sonia said.

"Why's that?" Grant asked.

"Didn't you see her boyfriend?" Sonia smiled. "He's a very handsome man — and a government man, at that."

"You're dating a fed?" Grant said, turning to Lara.

She had seldom felt put on such a spot, but since Sonia had only been trying to help her — and since she was clearly right about Grant — she phrased her answer carefully. "Well, we haven't known each other long," she said. "But he is . . . quite a man."

"I wonder if he's part Latin?" Sonia said. "He looks as if he could be quite passionate."

"Oh, yes, he's very passionate," Lara agreed drily.

"I imagine," Grant Blackwood muttered, looking over her shoulder.

As he did so, Lara knew — just knew — that she had stepped in it now. Why in God's name he was back again, she didn't know.

But he *was* back. The stick-up-the-ass agent was back. And this time he'd undoubtedly heard her.

"Miss Larson, Mr. Blackwood," he said. He looked at them and nodded, and though he said nothing else, his nod clearly indicated that they should leave.

They took the hint. Sonia waved goodbye and headed for the exit, and fell into conversation with Ely and Dr. Amory. They were lucky to have Nelson Amory, Lara knew. He'd received degrees in both veterinary science and marine biology. He was considered one of the top scientists working in the fields of marine mammal behavior and physiology.

Lara didn't even want to look at Agent Cody. She had to, of course. He was standing right in front of her, waiting for her attention.

"What now?" she asked with a wince.

"I wanted to let you know that we'll be heading out early. I need you to be at the end of the dock by seven."

"Seven. After today and tonight. No problem," she said drily.

"Thank you. And good night."

"Good night," she said.

He took a step away, but then he paused and turned back. She could almost have

90

sworn that he nearly cracked a smile. "You're welcome, by the way."

"What?"

"Feel free to use me. To protect yourself from Blackwood's advances, I mean. His Lothario tendencies are well-known. Thinking of me as your boyfriend will probably keep him from bothering you. Even if I do have a stick up my ass."

He turned and was soon swallowed up by the shadowy path to the parking lot.

4

As he drove home, Brett was surprised to find himself actually smiling.

So he had a stick up his ass.

Well, the woman he suspected was his key, however unwilling, to finding what he sought was abrasive, annoying and a pain in the backside herself. Self-assurance was an asset, however, and she possessed plenty of it. She was beautiful in a fairy-princess way, long blond hair, beautiful sky-blue eyes with a hint of green and a body that didn't quit.

Speaking of bodies . . . He couldn't really blame her for being upset at being asked to continue the search for more body parts. Most people never found even one in their lives, and she'd already been the unwilling recipient of two.

His smile faded as he thought about Miguel and Maria. He knew that it was contrary to everything in his training to feel so guilty over what had happened. It wasn't that any agent was ever supposed to forget his or her humanity, but getting too close to an informant was definitely a job hazard. Empathy was great; becoming obsessed was not.

And he had to admit it: he was obsessed.

What plagued him was the discovery that Miguel had been alive when they thought he'd been dead, and that he'd been seen by his home right before Maria was killed.

Brett just couldn't believe that Miguel had killed his wife. Even if ordered to kill her on penalty of torture or death, Miguel would have borne any pain, any degradation, even death itself, rather than do anything to hurt Maria.

Brett pulled into his garage, closed the door with the remote and sat for a minute. It was after nine; morning was going to come quickly. Hopping out, he saw that he'd locked Ichabod — the neighbors' cat — in with him. Ichabod was a great cat, mostly Maine Coon with whatever else thrown in. His eyes were orange, and his huge furry body was pitch-black.

Brett had always figured it would be cruel to keep an animal himself, since he was often away from home. But he lived in a strange cul-de-sac in an old area of West Miami that bordered the Gables and South

Miami. For being in the city, it was oddly remote. Ichabod had always been free to roam the neighborhood, and somehow he always seemed to know when Brett was home.

"You know I'm just a sucker who keeps cat treats, right?" he asked the animal.

Ichabod meowed loudly and followed him as he entered the house through the garage door.

Shake it off! Diego had told him earlier that evening. *Do something else, think about something else. Start with a clean slate in the morning.*

His partner was right. After obliging Ichabod with a handful of treats, he tossed his jacket and tie over the back of a chair, then threw himself down on his sofa. Ichabod hopped up beside him, and he rested one hand on the cat and used the other to feel around on the side table for the remote. It wasn't there; he really had no idea where in hell he'd left it. He wasn't a bad housekeeper. He was just rarely there.

He liked his old house. It had been built just off a small lake in the late 1940s, and the builders had given it a bit of retro deco styling. Rounded archways led gracefully between rooms, and the stairway to the second floor curved in a handsome C shape.

He'd been able to buy when the market had been low. He liked the house's style, and despite the busy city, he felt as if he lived in a little enclave of privacy. Greater Miami was made up of over thirty municipalities, some of them old, some of them recently incorporated. He was within minutes of downtown South Miami, downtown Coral Gables, the Coconut Grove area and downtown Miami itself.

He didn't, however, spend enough time at the house. He realized that it really needed something resembling decoration and style. It had almost had style once. That was when Bev had lived with him. She'd suggested drapes and art. But then she'd decided that living with a man who was only home to sleep — and not every night, even then — wasn't what she'd been looking for. Maybe she'd wanted to prod him into promising more, but if so, she'd failed, because he hadn't been able to.

She'd moved to the Orlando area, he'd heard. He honestly hoped she was doing well.

He realized that was the last time he'd had a woman in his house for more than a few hours.

Brett stroked the cat. "I wonder if that's why I'm obsessive, Ichabod. Yeah, I'm obsessed with this case — just don't tell that to Diego. Somehow they found one another, Maria and Miguel. They were good together. You don't get to see love like that too often, you know?"

Ichabod meowed. Brett was pretty sure it was in appreciation for the petting, not his words.

He rose and looked around for the remote, found it and turned on the television. It was already tuned to one of the national news stations.

He winced. There was no way to gag the public. The death of Maria Gomez and the news that Miguel Gomez had been seen walking around alive after he was supposedly dead and buried had made it to the big time, along with joking speculation that zombies were roaming Miami once again.

Next up — national news again — was the discovery of body parts at a dolphin facility in South Florida. As yet, no information on the victim was known. The anchor in Atlanta switched to their local correspondent, and an image of Lara Ainsworth flashed on the screen. She was cool, smooth and likable as she spoke to a sea of reporters, telling them that the facility had closed for the day but would reopen, that law enforcement had scoured the lagoons with the help of Sea Life's dolphins and that they were always willing to help in any way.

One idiot asked if it was possible that the dolphins had committed murder.

She kept her cool as she told him no, that dolphins might be aggressive at times, but they weren't capable of dismembering bodies. The picture cut to scenes of the dolphins with handicapped children and wounded servicemen and women; it was some of the best PR spins Brett had ever seen. Ms. Ainsworth wasn't only an extremely attractive woman with an easy way when she was on camera, she was damn good at her job. She'd been filmed soon after they'd gotten out of the water, he realized. Her hair was still damp, and she was in casual shorts and a polo shirt.

She cleaned up nicely, too, he thought, thinking back to the party earlier. Her halter dress had been stunning on her. He chastised himself for not noticing more, but he'd been too focused on the case. He realized, though, that part of her beauty came from her animation. Her smile was sincere and her movements fluid.

He smiled briefly, thinking of her stick-up-the-butt comment; he knew she'd been referring to him. Maybe he'd deserved it. He'd been a lucky man most of his life. He was generally well liked. Relationships — though most were merely casual — came easy for him. But this woman really didn't like him. And she was, at the moment, according to Grady Miller, the one woman he needed on his side. He'd been sure he would be best off enlisting the help of the head trainer, Rick Laramie, and Laramie would certainly be on hand. But according to the facility founder, Cocoa wanted to work with Lara. It was as if she had found a best friend. If Cocoa were human, Miller had explained, she would want to hang out with Lara to hear a new band, or enjoy a movie or an art show — or go shoe shopping.

As long as Lara came and helped, as long as everyone tried, he would be happy. He knew he was looking for a damned needle in a haystack.

But Phil Kinny had seemed sure that if he had Miguel's head, he might be able to figure out what had happened.

Brett knew the waters around Miami; he loved boating, fishing and diving, and had since he was a kid. But he didn't really understand the science of what the office techs were doing. By charting the tides and the currents, they believed they could follow the flow of body-part dispersal, using the dolphin facility as a starting point and working backward. He hoped they were right.

Restlessly, he flicked off the news. "Ichabod, you're the best company ever," he told the cat. "But I don't want Jimmy or his folks waking up and thinking you're missing. So, sad to say, out, my friend."

The cat seemed to understand him. He wound between Brett's legs and headed for the door. Brett let him out, climbed up the stairs, stripped down and headed toward the bed.

He paused, though, and went to his desk to click his computer on. Someone might have gotten back to him with some kind of a map or a plan for the morning. They would be working with the Coast Guard, and he had faith that those guys could read what they were given, but he wouldn't mind looking for himself. And while he wanted to sleep, he still felt restless.

His emails popped up, a few from fellow agents offering off-duty help. Nice. Nothing yet from the tech people, but he wasn't worried. They would work all night if they had to and make sure they had what he needed in the morning. He started to turn away from the computer when a message suddenly popped up on the screen.

He stared, stunned at first, and then disbelieving.

Miguel did it. It was Miguel, but it wasn't Miguel.

The words were then gone as quickly as they had come. Brett felt as if every hair on the nape of his neck was standing up.

He gave himself a mental shake. He must have imagined the message. He started hitting keys, slowly at first, and then more quickly, trying to ascertain if someone had hacked into his computer somehow.

Eventually he determined that had to be the case. But even though he didn't have the skills to do it himself, he would make sure the hacker got caught. They had some of the best computer geeks known to man in the Miami office, so all he had to do was take his laptop to work and let them have at it.

That decided, he rose to go to bed at last.

And it was then that his phone rang. He didn't recognize the number; it wasn't a local exchange. He thought about letting the caller leave a message, but in the end he answered. "Cody," he said briefly.

"Brett Cody?" asked a deep, slightly accented voice.

"Yes."

He wasn't sure how he instantly knew who it was; he had never been assigned to the Barillo case. He'd seen the man, of course. Barillo appeared at rallies backing certain politicians and liked to make the scene when new clubs opened on South Beach, which was fairly frequently. The beach was a fickle place; the hottest club quickly became passé when a new club opened.

For being such a powerhouse, he was a small man. Only about five-eight, gray haired and slight.

He was a mix of nationalities — born in Mexico, but with grandparents from Italy, Colombia, Brazil and Cuba — and that might well have helped him to become the kingpin that he was, in command of his multinational "family." He was known to speak at least five languages, including perfect English.

"This is Anthony Barillo," the man said.

Brett knew he should behave professionally, keep the man talking, try to get something useful out of him, but he couldn't help himself. "Then you should know, you piece of total crap, that we will chase you to the ends of the earth to see that you pay for what you've done. Maria Gomez was in-

101

nocent, someone's mother, just like your own."

Barillo didn't seem offended by his words. His tone was even, dispassionate, as he said, "Special Agent Cody, my mother was a prostitute of the lowest order. She abandoned me, and I don't know if she's living or dead, nor do I care. But that's another matter entirely. Here's the thing you must know. I didn't kill Maria Gomez. I didn't even kill Miguel Gomez. That's why I'm calling you. Word on the street is that you're out for blood. Am I an innocent man? In life, that's debatable. But in this instance, if you truly want to catch the killer of that lovely woman — yes, even I knew she was nearly a saint — you're going after the wrong person."

"Bull! Miguel was wearing a wire when —"

Brett broke off. Barillo had already hung up.

Furious, he hit Return on the call, but all he got was a recording saying he'd reached a disconnected number. He almost threw the phone across the room but caught himself before realizing the futility of the gesture. He would just have to get another cell phone, and Barillo would still be out there.

He called Diego — waking him up — to tell him about the phone call, and then he called Herman Bryant — whom he also woke up — to tell him about the call, as well.

"Man's a bloody liar. He's as dirty as a sty on Mars," Bryant said.

Brett wasn't sure just how dirty a sty on Mars was, but Bryant was famous for his strange turns of phrase. He also sounded frustrated as hell, which made sense. After all, he was head of a large task force that had so far failed in its efforts to stop the man.

Barillo always managed to keep his own hands clean, letting his henchmen pay the price of arrest. The FBI had taken down a dozen of his men. They never spoke against him. He was known to have a long arm that could reach into any prison — state or federal — in the country. "I'm surprised he bothered to call you. He's wanted on a dozen murders. What's one more?"

"I think it offended him that we thought he'd broken his own rule about not going after family, plus I think he genuinely liked Maria. Anyway, I needed to report the call to you."

"Of course, thanks. I'm glad you're in on this, Brett. You could be on the task force if

103

you wanted. You know that, right? But at the moment, I'm glad you and Diego are taking lead on the Maria Gomez case."

"Yeah, thanks. I'll keep you up on everything."

"Any time of day," Bryant told him.

They rang off. Brett knew that he had to get some rest. It wasn't easy, given his adrenaline level after Barillo's call.

His phone rang again; he stared at it. Again, a number he didn't know. He answered but didn't speak.

"Hello?"

It wasn't Anthony Barillo, though this man's voice was also accented. More of a tenor than a bass, though.

"Who is this?" Brett asked sharply.

"You lay off my father, man. He had nothing to do with Miguel or Maria Gomez. You understand? It will be harder for you if you don't quit."

Brett tried to control his temper. To a point, he did. "Listen, you gutless little tadpole. I don't know which one of Barillo's kids you are, but you just threatened a federal agent, so shut up or you just might find life getting hard for you. You were smart enough to get out of the family business, now stay smart and *keep* out of it."

"Screw you!" the caller said. "My father

didn't do it — you got it?"

For the second time that night his line went dead. He thought about letting the matter go until morning, but it wasn't that long since he'd woken the other men up, so . . . He called Bryant and Diego again, and both of them were as surprised as he was that both Barillo and one of his sons had called about the Gomezes' deaths.

After he hung up for the second time he knew he had to go to bed; the next few days promised to be very long ones.

Sleep was elusive at first. He kept playing the case over and over again in his mind. He hadn't been there when Miguel Gomez had burned to cinders. But he knew the agents and many of the officers who *had* been, and he knew that the accounts he'd heard were as accurate as humanly possible. The warehouse had been surrounded; it had been under surveillance for days before Miguel had gone in wearing the wire. There had been no other voices, so almost certainly no one else had been in there. Not to mention that only one set of charred-beyond-recognition remains had been found, with Miguel's melted jewelry right there.

But — somehow — Miguel had survived. They'd found *someone's* body, but not

Miguel's.

Maria had been murdered, too. Thrown from her balcony only minutes after Miguel Gomez had been seen in his neighborhood, behaving strangely.

At last Brett fell asleep.

At five thirty, his alarm rang. Blindly, he groped for the button to turn off the obnoxious buzzing he'd chosen because it guaranteed that he would get up.

He opened his eyes, ready to roll out of bed.

But he didn't.

He froze.

Because there was a woman sitting at the foot of his bed. Maria Gomez. Her dark hair framed her pretty face, and there was a look of infinite sadness in her eyes.

"Miguel did it. It was Miguel, but it wasn't Miguel," she said.

And then she was gone. She simply faded into nothingness.

And he was alone in his room, frozen rigid, staring at the empty foot of his bed.

"You really should get your diving certificate," Agent Cody told Lara.

She turned to look at him. They were on the Coast Guard cutter *Vigilance*. The day was just about perfect; the temperature was warm, but the breeze kept them from getting too hot. The sea was calm, and only a few white clouds puffed delicately above them. She and Rick were the only Sea Life personnel on the vessel, though Grady, Adrianna and Dr. Amory had been there to see them off before they joined Cocoa in her enclosure. Dr. Amory was fascinated by Cocoa's preference for Lara. He said he'd never seen a bond form so quickly, and he'd been doing research on dolphins' abilities for thirty years. But when they'd asked him if he wanted to come along, he'd said, "No. I don't want to distract Cocoa from her task. She'll be fine with you and Rick."

Lara wished he'd come so she would have another friendly face onboard. Not that their Coast Guard crew weren't great, because they were. But she'd been nervous about this whole thing to begin with, unsure that she had the skills she needed, and now Rick had headed aft, Diego was nowhere to be seen and she was alone with Agent Stick-up-the-Ass, who seemed to think she'd had a lamentable upbringing because she didn't dive.

The better to find body parts, my dear.

"You're going to be all right in the water, right?" he asked.

For a moment she wondered how

someone so drop-dead good-looking and presumably intelligent could be such an ass. It didn't help that he was standing so close to her that while she was busy thinking what a tremendous jerk he was, she was also far too aware of his leanly muscled body, clad only in a pair of swim trunks. She wished she was wearing more than a bathing suit herself; it was almost as if their flesh was touching. Not that he seemed to be the least bit aware of her in a physical way.

"I'll be fine, Agent Cody. We do swim in Virginia. We do, in fact, have dive shops. We have rivers and lakes and yes, even direct access to the Atlantic. It's just that not every kid in Richmond grows up to dive." She hoped she managed to sound cool and disinterested in anything but the task ahead.

"Sorry," he said curtly. He was staring out at the water, the sun gleaming down on his shoulders, those granite features facing into the wind, which seemed somehow appropriate. He turned to look at her. "Down here, it's just . . . well, it's just something most people are able to do. The reefs off the Keys are magnificent. They say there are prettier reefs other places, but I think ours compare to anything out there. In my opinion anyway. It's just . . ."

His voice trailed off, and he shrugged.

"It's something you might want to look into, living down here. It's magical. You move so easily in water you think you were born there. You hear your own air bubbles, the world is far away, and you see amazing creatures in their own universe."

"Thanks. I'll consider it," she murmured, thinking how strange his words had been. It had sounded as if he actually cared whether she liked South Florida.

They weren't more than a mile due south of the facility when one of the crew came around to join them.

"We're going to drop anchor," he told them. "You might want to gear up, sir."

Agent Cody thanked him, then turned to Lara again. "How's your dolphin doing?"

She looked overboard. Rick was still standing just down the deck and had been watching the water the whole time, keeping an eye on Cocoa as she accompanied them. She had to admit that it had been a very interesting morning so far. She and Rick had swum out of the lagoon toward the cutter, with Cocoa following, then he had talked to Cocoa before they had climbed up the ladder to the deck.

Cocoa had kept pace with them all the way. Lara was even more impressed with her intelligence, and gratified that such an amazing animal had decided to choose her as, well, a friend.

As if on cue, Cocoa surfaced, giving out her squeal.

"I believe she's fine," Lara said.

"You can manage snorkel gear?" he asked her.

It was a real question, she realized. She managed not to be totally sarcastic in her reply.

"I'll be fine," she said.

He headed to the stern, where he, Diego, Rick and one of the crew helped each other with their dive tanks.

Then Agent Cody came back over to her. "There's an embankment just that way, and we'll be close to the surface until we reach it. The depth there maxes out at about twenty to twenty-five feet, so we won't be far at any time. Do you need some type of flotation device?"

"I'll be fine in a mask and flippers," she said.

"You're sure."

"I am."

"All right. Just keep telling her to fetch. One of the crew will be with you. You'll never be out there alone."

"Thank you."

He nodded. That curt nod of his seemed

to be his trademark.

As Agent Cody went over, sitting on the hull and falling backward into the water, Diego McCullough joined her. "You okay?" he asked her cheerfully.

"You bet."

"I'm not so sure *I* would be," he said. "The dead body side of it . . . it takes time."

"I've had a few strange experiences in my life," Lara told him. "I'll be fine. And thank you, truly, for being concerned."

He nodded. Rick had already gone into the water, and now Diego followed him. A crewman came over to Lara with the mask she'd already chosen and a pair of fins. He held them out to her.

"Miss Ainsworth?"

"Thanks."

Five minutes later she was in the water. Thankfully, she had snorkeled before at Virginia Beach and on a vacation to Jamaica when she'd been younger. She knew that she was a strong swimmer and that the fins would help propel her. She loved to just have her face in the water to see everything below her while the snorkel let her breathe.

But first she treaded water and waited for Cocoa to come to her. Thanks to the events of the day before, she didn't feel in the least bit silly talking to the dolphin.

"We're going to play fetch, Cocoa. We're looking for something this size." She held her hands apart to indicate the approximate size of a human head. "Somebody killed a man, Cocoa. What we're doing can help us catch that awful person."

She wondered if human beings would ever really understand just how much other animals — mammals, especially — knew or understood. She just knew that she was on a mission, and Cocoa was on it with her.

The water was extremely clear; Lara could easily see the divers and Cocoa below her. Cocoa hadn't actually decided that she didn't like Rick anymore, but she definitely wanted to bring her treasures to Lara. Unfortunately they weren't looking for a foam wig stand or a punctured football. After an hour at that location, they moved on.

The next stop was just ten minutes away, and their efforts were repeated.

This time Cocoa found something but couldn't quite retrieve it. She chittered and squealed at Lara, trying to get her to come down and see it.

Lara tried, since the water was shallow. But when she reached Cocoa's sand- and seaweed-strewn find, a diver was at her side.

Agent Cody.

And, thankfully, he took the object and quickly bagged it in a dive net.

She'd had time to see what Cocoa had discovered, though. Only a brief glimpse, but one she would never forget.

It was a human head.

Arnold Wilhelm stood beside the tracks at the Metrorail Station and looked down at the street fifty feet below. It was his first day out in three months, and he was only there because his family had threatened to put him in a nursing home if he didn't start moving — *living* — again.

He'd taken the death of his friend Randy Nicholson hard. The two of them had been a few of the only truly old codgers left of the old days. They'd both been born at the long-gone St. Francis Hospital on the beach, and they'd gone through Shenandoah Junior High and Miami Senior High together. They'd fought in the Korean War together, had their families and remained friends since.

And then, three months ago, Randy had passed away. And while Arnold knew that he was lucky as hell — he was a man with two decent kids, five grandchildren and an ex-wife who was okay and had remarried a damned good guy — he was lonely. He and

Randy had gone to the movies together and had lunch twice a week, gone to the old Elks Club together and . . .

Hell. Randy had been better than a wife. Randy just liked to hang, as the kids said. He never wanted anything in return. He'd shared every important experience in Arnold's life.

Ah, well, that was getting old. Painful, but better than the alternative, or so people said.

But he wasn't so sure. He loved his family; he was grateful for his family. Even so, the days seemed empty without his old friend.

He glanced at his watch. The damned Metrorail didn't really go anywhere, in his opinion. It wasn't like when you went to New York City and hopped on the subway. With the Metrorail, unless you lived right by a station, you had to drive there and look for parking, or have someone drop you off, or rely on a bus — which might or might not come at anything that resembled on time — to get you there. Even when you got on it, the Metrorail only ran north-south through the city, though with some switching around you could get all the way up to Palm Beach. It did go to the Jackson Medical Complex, though, which was where he needed to go every three months for his checkups.

Because he was an old vet.

Looking far south down the track, he thought he could see it coming. He was just about the only one waiting, except for a trio of teenage boys.

He glanced at his watch and then the schedule.

He sighed. Big outing. He was traveling all by himself, a grown-up going for his checkup. Fun. He decided he would stop for coffee at a Cuban café somewhere, try to bone up on his horrible Spanish so he could better chat with the older Cuban woman at the convenience store.

"Arnold."

He heard his name and thought that his kids might be right, that his inertia really was bringing on some kind of mental-deterioration disease. It had sounded just as if Randy had called his name.

He turned.

And to his amazement, Randy was there.

"Randy?"

He'd seen the man in his coffin just three months ago.

But he was standing there, as hale and hearty as ever. Well, maybe not hale and hearty. His color was awful.

As if he'd been in the grave for three months.

115

And his face . . . Something was wrong with his face. It didn't really move. It was as if he didn't have any expression — couldn't show any emotions — at all.

"Randy?" Arnold repeated. He invented an explanation in his head for what might have happened. The family had pretended that he was dead. They'd buried some kind of an effigy. Why? Something to do with money, having money, needing money . . . They'd kept Randy a prisoner down in the basement, which would explain his awful color, while they spent their ill-gotten inheritance.

And now he'd escaped. Except that he was . . . confused, probably from being in solitary confinement for months.

"Randy, yes, it's me, Arnold."

He started toward Randy, arms out to embrace him, to assure him that he could make everything okay. He would take care of Randy, and his family would become his old friend's family, too.

He dimly heard the sound of the Metrorail as he reflected, still stunned, that he really was seeing his old friend again.

He didn't have to walk all the way to Randy, because Randy was coming at him. Coming like a bull.

Randy slammed into him and sent him

flying backward onto the tracks.

And Arnold was still so stunned that he never knew what hit him.

He was dead within seconds of his impact with the arriving train, dead long before his broken body fell to the ground far below the elevated platform.

5

There weren't many good things to be said about finding a human head, Lara thought, although at least they had assumed the man was already dead, and Agent Cody believed that finding the head meant they would have a better chance of finding the killer. Rick called Grady to let him know they'd found what they were looking for, and Grady insisted that she go home, especially given her long night at the party and the stress of the morning's discovery.

She barely saw Special Agent Brett Cody after the find. Other divers were headed to their location to continue the search, while Agents Cody and Diego headed back to shore with her and Rick — and their gruesome evidence. She gathered that more pieces of the victim were found — how many, she didn't know, nor was she sure she wanted to.

When Cocoa seemed set, following the

cutter home just as she'd followed it out to the bay, Lara sat in the galley with Rick, drinking the very decent cup of coffee one of the crew members had brought her.

"Dolphins," Rick said. "They're the most amazing creatures. I love our dolphins, and I wish people understood how much they enjoy working with us. The research we do is as much fun for us as it is enlightening for us, and even the entertainment side of things is enjoyable for them. They like people. Our guys, they're the smartest. That's why Cocoa could do this."

"What do you mean?"

"We've done extensive training with them. They recognize far more of what we say than we do of what *they* 'say' — though we do recognize what many of the sounds they make mean," Rick told her. "You'll learn more the longer you stay with us. They can actually count. They can imitate one another. You've already seen how they can find one kind of object versus another. And they know and prefer certain people, beyond a doubt. You should see the lagoons when Grady goes in. They flock around him like puppies. You could be a trainer, you know. Although you'd better not tell Grady I said that, because you're good at what you're doing already and we certainly need someone in that position."

"Well, thank you," Lara said, pleased by the unexpected compliment.

"Your work with Cocoa today was pretty amazing, though," he said.

"Well," she murmured drily, "hopefully we won't be doing this often."

"It's certainly the first time I've ever worked with the dolphins in this capacity," Rick said, then nodded toward the ladder to the deck.

Lieutenant Gunderson, who was captaining their cutter, was coming down. He nodded to the two of them and headed to the coffeepot. He poured himself a cup the way a man might pour himself a scotch after a trying day. His back was to them for a long minute before he turned around.

"Lieutenant, has something happened?" Rick asked.

Gunderson was about fifty, with steel-gray hair. He wore his uniform with dignity. He looked at them, shook his head, then let out a long sigh. "The press is at it again. Guess these days I should say the media is at it again."

"In what way?" Lara asked.

"You'll hear about it soon enough. A man was killed today. Thrown in front of a Metrorail train, body went flying down to the ground. Hope it was fast — his neck and half his bones were broken. Just happened an hour or so ago, but there were kids on the platform that saw the whole thing. They twitted or whatever it is that kids do, and the information was all over the place. Worst thing is, they described the man who killed the guy."

"How can that be a bad thing?" Rick asked. "Won't the police be glad to have eyewitness descriptions of the killer?"

Lieutenant Gunderson didn't have a chance to answer them; others were coming down the ladder, including Diego McCullough and Brett Cody.

"Mike the chicken," Diego was saying dully.

"What, another dead man rose to commit murder? You're not really falling for that zombie crap, are you? Because —" Brett asked him. Suddenly he stopped, as if realizing others were listening.

One of the Coast Guard crew said, "I'll get coffee for everyone."

"Thank you, Seaman," Lieutenant Gunderson said, nodding his approval.

Lara felt a strange tightening in the pit of her stomach. "What happened?" she asked. "What are you all talking about? Apparently it's already all over the media, so you might as well tell us."

"A man was killed when he was about to get on the Metrorail," Agent Cody explained. "There were three teenaged boys on the platform at the time. They saw the killer go after the guy. They described him to a police sketch artist, and apparently the drawing looked just like a friend of the victim's who died three months ago. So naturally the media are going on about a zombie king sending zombie henchmen out to kill for him."

"It may not be zombies, but *something* is sure as hell going on," Diego said, shaking his head and sliding into the seat next to Lara.

"Something we'll nip in the bud. I've asked that they start making arrangements to exhume the dead friend," Brett Cody said.

"Remember, we know Miguel Gomez was supposedly dead, too," Diego reminded him.

"Exhumation," Brett said. "Simplest way to know one way or another if the guy has been in his grave for three months or not."

"How did the friend die?" Lara asked. "Natural causes or . . . ?"

Brett looked directly at her. "Heart failure. Died at the hospital. And as soon as we're back, I'll be speaking with the doctor who signed the death certificate — and the funeral home where his remains were sent." He was quiet for a moment. "And those boys at the Metrorail station," he added.

"If it's just a drawing — even though it was done by a police artist — couldn't it resemble someone but not be him?" Lara asked.

Diego looked at her. "It could, but right before the murder, one of the boys was taking a selfie, and the killer was caught on the kid's phone."

"Not a clear image," Brett said.

"We haven't seen it yet," Diego reminded him.

Brett shrugged.

"I can only imagine what you and the police will be dealing with," Gunderson said. He sighed and shook his head. "Well, we're almost back, but of course we're at your disposal again any time you need us." He turned to Brett and asked, "You'll see to the proper transfer of the remains?"

"Dr. Phil Kinny, the ME, will be meeting us at the dock," Brett said.

Rick rose. "Time for us to see to our girl, Lara. Gentlemen, thank you."

She rose, too, thanked the officers for their help and accepted their thanks in return, then followed Rick when he dived cleanly from the boat to join Cocoa. Together the three of them swam back toward the gate, which had been opened for them, and into the lagoon. Cocoa swept past Lara, then came back and swam through with her. Nearing the platform, Lara found the shallows and stood on one of the slippery steps, stroking Cocoa. She watched as the cutter slid up next to the farthest platform, allowing Brett and Diego to disembark. She noticed a group waiting for them on the platform. Men in suits and white coats. One official-looking man in a dark suit immediately fell into step with the two agents; she assumed he was their superior.

They left quickly, and Lara turned her attention to what was going on at the center, which had reopened to the public that morning. Several school classes were there, and Adrianna was in one of the middle lagoons conducting a dolphin swim with special-needs children. Other visitors were eating at the picnic tables by the café.

She supplied Cocoa with fish as a reward for her efforts, and as Rick had told her, she made sure that she praised and thanked Cocoa verbally and with long strokes down her back. Then she was out of the water at last. She made it into the employee shower and back out to her office within the half hour.

Grady was waiting for her, leaning on her desk.

"You really okay?" he asked her. "You know we're thrilled to have you here. You love the dolphins, and the dolphins love you. But under the circumstances . . . if you want some time off, if you want me to call Adam or the Krewe, just say the word."

Grady was such a sweetheart, Lara thought. She walked over to him and shook her head, smiling. "A murderer's . . . work has affected the peace of our lagoon. I'm glad I can do something to help catch him, and I promise you, I'm just fine. But I *am* tired, so thank you. I think I *will* take the afternoon off."

"Okay, then. If it all becomes too much, you just let me know." He rose, set a hand on her shoulder, smiled and left.

She was gathering up some press materials to work on at home when she felt someone watching her from the doorway.

She turned.

A handsome middle-aged man was standing there. He had the look of an old Spanish aristocrat with angular features, a neatly manicured beard and mustache and dark eyes. He was dressed in a guayabera, a short-sleeved shirt made popular by the Cuban community. He looked at her, seemed to wince and then turned and walked away.

"May I help you?" Lara called after him.

No answer.

She hurried to the door. No one else was in sight, but she quickly opened the other doors along the hallway. The only person she found was Adrianna. "Did you see the man who was here a minute ago?" Lara asked.

"What man? Rick? Or Grady?"

"No. A man I've never seen before was at my door," Lara said.

"A cute one, I hope. Though I have to tell you, I think the FBI is putting *hot* on their application forms these days. I'm still madly in love with my husband — or as madly as anyone can be after twenty years — but if I wasn't, and if I weren't a good decade his senior, I'd be all over that guy," Adrianna said.

"Which guy?" Lara asked.

"Tall, dark and handsome."

"*Which* tall, dark and handsome?"

"Okay, tall, dark, *brooding* and handsome. Agent Cody," Adrianna said. "Though I wouldn't turn my nose up at either one of them."

"Well, I'm not talking about either of them," Lara said. "This was someone else — someone I've never seen before. Not a young guy, not any of the cops who were here. I think he was Cuban, definitely Hispanic, and around fifty. He seemed lost."

"I didn't see anyone. Check downstairs and if you find him, show him out — nicely, of course. This building is off-limits to visitors unless they have an appointment with one of us. Grady doesn't even like us to have visitors unless he approves first."

"I know. I'm on it," Lara promised.

Downstairs, she found their common area empty. Whoever the man had been, he was gone. She headed back up for her things, told Adrianna she was leaving and headed out. Instead of leaving through the gift shop area by the exit, she slipped out the key-operated gate to the parking lot.

It was an easy shot over the causeway onto I-95, exiting on US1 to head for her house. Without the usual rush-hour traffic she faced on most days, it just took only a matter of minutes. But as she drove, she considered the man she had seen standing at her door; she probably should have checked out the rest of the facility and made sure that he'd found his party — or the way out. They didn't employ private security at

Sea Life, since both the City of Miami and Miami Beach police were always in the area, not to mention the Florida Highway Patrol and the Miami-Dade force. The fences that surrounded the property were set with alarms, and the main entrance also had cameras. Besides, there was almost always staff on hand. Rick and Adrianna lived in a small apartment at the back of the "office building" where she worked. Grady had a bedroom in the back of his office and sometimes stayed over, and there was talk of creating housing for the interns when one of the storage sheds — an old sound studio from the property's earlier incarnation — was remodeled. That was a plan for the future, though, and would require its own capital campaign. The day-to-day running of the place was expensive and depended upon sponsors with deep pockets, like the people they had entertained the night before. She smiled, thinking about what they called the "attack cats" that roamed the property. There were three of them — Meatball, Mama and Massey — all strays that Grady had rescued and brought to the property. They ruled the place, along with a few of the resident iguanas and the peacocks that had wandered in from somewhere. They weren't far from Jungle Island, a wonderful small zoo that had once been in Miami proper rather than on the water; after Hurricane Andrew had devastated what had then been Parrot Jungle, it had reopened under a new name and in its new location off the causeway. Grady had once told her after Andrew, many of their birds had ended up living in the wild.

Lara's rental was a pretty duplex on Virginia Street. There was a gate — which she'd been advised to keep locked, so she did — a small private yard, and then the entrance to her half of the row house–style building. The gate and the wall that surrounded the property were covered in beautiful purple bougainvillea. She hadn't really brought much with her yet; most of her belongings were with her aunt in the Richmond house where she'd spent most of her childhood. Her parents had been killed in an automobile accident when she was young and Aunt Nancy had stepped up and done a remarkable job of parenting her. She would be coming down to spend a month soon, and Lara was delighted.

Though this was Florida, the building was older and had a fireplace. The mantel was the first place she'd chosen to make the home hers. She had set out pictures of herself when she was very young with her parents, their wedding picture, one of Aunt Nancy and herself and several of her with Meg. While she had come from Richmond and Meg hailed from Harpers Ferry, West Virginia, summer vacations with their families had made them the best of friends as kids. They'd even gone to college together. After that, media and promotion work in politics — finding a candidate who wasn't for sale and was motivated purely by love for the country — had been her passion.

A passion that had almost killed her. It was only thanks to Meg and the Krewe of Hunters that she was still alive.

"And now I'm out of politics, but not exactly living the quiet life I'd expected," she murmured aloud. She closed her eyes. She did love it here.

The past two days had been stressful, of course, but that didn't mean she'd stopped loving her new life.

Her town house had a small living room that led to a cute little kitchen with an entertainment room behind it. Her yard was tiny but serene, walled in and smelling of bougainvillea. Upstairs she had two small but charming bedrooms. The place was perfect for her. She'd bought a good-size television and a fancy stereo system for the entertainment room, and brought down her old Victorian desk and desktop computer, which were set up there, too. She loved noise when she was working.

She went back there now and turned on her computer. All in all, she wasn't home that much earlier than she would have been normally. She knew she didn't need to work, but she wasn't really sure what else to do with herself. The only friends she had made thus far were her coworkers. And her coworkers were still working.

Lara flicked on the television. The news had moved on, as she had expected. Not surprisingly, it was all about the man who had been killed on the Metrorail platform. The police rendering of the suspected killer came up on screen, followed by a photo of the victim, followed by one of his best friend, a man named Randy Nicholson.

Nicholson had died of natural causes and been buried three months earlier.

And he was almost a perfect twin of the man in the police sketch.

Lara had to admit, it was chilling. But, as Agent Cody had said, they could exhume Randy Nicholson's body and put to rest the "Miami Zombie Rage" that was now quickly seizing the city.

She was tempted to turn the television off

131

and force herself to think pleasant thoughts, but she wasn't sure she could manage that.

And then she glanced out the sliding glass doors into her overgrown backyard.

There was a medium-size mango tree in one corner, bougainvillea draped over the stone wall and small plants she couldn't identify lining the short path that led to a table with an umbrella and a few chairs.

She started. Standing on the path, staring at the house, was the same man she had seen standing in her office doorway.

Fear instantly seized her. She hurried over to her phone and dialed 911. When the operator came on, she quickly gave her location and explained that a man was in her walled yard, and that he could only have gotten onto the property via a locked gate, and that she'd seen him earlier at work. "I'm afraid I'm being stalked."

"We have someone on the way to your address right now. You can stay on the phone with me. Officers will be there momentarily. What is the man doing now?" the operator asked.

"Just standing there, staring at me."

"Can you describe him?"

"He looks Hispanic. Fiftyish, with a well-manicured mustache and goatee. Medium build and maybe five-eight to five-ten. He's wearing gray trousers and a guayabera shirt, beige."

She heard the buzzer from her gate. The cops had already arrived, which didn't surprise her since she was right down the street from Cocowalk, one of the area's malls, and the whole Coconut Grove area.

"They're here, I think," she told the operator.

"You can stay on with me while you let them in," the operator said.

Lara looked out the window, just to be safe, then went out to the gate to greet the two policemen waiting there.

"Someone's in your yard?" one of them asked her. "Is he threatening you?"

"No, he's just standing there. But I don't know how he got in, and he came to my office earlier today, then left without saying anything," she said.

"I'll go in with her," the second officer said to the one who'd spoken.

"Get back in the house and I'll see what's going on," the first man, whose badge identified him as Officer Dewey, said.

Lara nodded and thanked him. The second officer, badge identification Martino, followed her into the house.

"Maybe I'm being a little paranoid," she said. "He's not doing anything, in fact he looks a little lost. But I saw him before, and now he's in my yard, and the gate was locked! He might have scaled the wall, but it's pretty high, plus it's covered with bougainvillea." She realized she was babbling and stopped.

"It's okay. Better to be safe than sorry, right?" Martino asked.

"Miss? *Miss?*"

Lara dimly heard herself being called and realized she was still holding her cell phone, and the emergency operator was still on the line. She quickly thanked the woman, told her that the police had arrived and hung up. Then she headed toward the back of the house, followed by Martino, and looked out the window.

Officer Dewey was there, looking puzzled. He walked toward the back door, and she quickly let him in.

"I looked everywhere, but there's nobody back here," he said.

Lara looked at him, dumbfounded. "He was there. I swear he was."

Both officers looked at her with polite curiosity.

"I'm telling you, there was a man in my yard, staring in my back windows," Lara said.

"Well, whoever he was, he's gone now. We

can check out the house for you, if you want," Dewey said.

"Thank you." She knew they were both doubting her sanity right about now. Well, why not? The gate had been locked, the wall around her property was at least seven feet high. It would have taken a gymnast to scale it.

The officers went through the house. It was empty, of course.

Dewey asked her, "Were the locks changed when you moved in?"

She nodded. "I was here when they changed them," she said.

"And no one else has keys?"

"My boss has a set in his desk," she said.

"Any way someone could have gotten them?" Martino asked her. "You did say you saw the man at your office earlier. Maybe he *is* stalking you. Maybe he's been watching you and knew that your boss had your keys. Where do you work, and how tight is the security there?"

"I work at Sea Life. We don't have private security, but we do have cameras and alarms."

"What about you? Any enemies?" Dewey asked.

She opened her mouth to answer, then realized the truth was just too complex.

"Not that I know of now," she murmured.

"I wish we could stay with you, just in case, but we can't do that," Martino told her. "We can only see that the house is secure and then patrol frequently. We'll be close by if you need us, though."

"Do you have an alarm?" Dewey asked.

"Yes, but only for the house, not the yard."

They all stood uncomfortably for a moment. She knew they were genuinely concerned, but with no real threat against her, they had done what they could.

"At any rate, no one is here now," Dewey said. "If you're uncomfortable, perhaps you could spend the night with a friend."

She nodded. "Thanks. I'll just head back to work. A few of our staff members live on the premises. I can stay with one of them."

"We'll cruise by here a few times, and we'll ask the next shift to do the same," Martino told her.

She wasn't sure if they thought she'd imagined the whole thing or were certain that she had a stalker and he had somehow gotten hold of her keys.

"Will you give me a minute to get a few things together?" she asked.

"Of course," they said in unison.

As she packed, she called Adrianna and told her about the man in her yard.

Adrianna found Grady, who checked and still had the unmarked backup keys to her car and apartment in his desk drawer. He told her that she was free to stay at Sea Life until they got the matter settled, and she thanked him. She was definitely going to feel better knowing that Rick and Adrianna were sleeping down the hall.

The officers waited until she was ready to go, then saw her safely into her car. As she drove, she asked her built-in Bluetooth to call Meg, and the minute her best friend's voice came on the line, she immediately felt better.

"I was about to call you. So another zombie attack in your area, huh?" Meg asked.

"Yeah, the FBI is all over it — arranging to have the so-called zombie dug out of his grave," Lara said. "But that's not why I called you."

She described the day and the man to her, admitting that she might be paranoid, but it seemed she was being stalked. "Maybe it's just my past history," she admitted, a bit embarrassed.

"We're coming down," Meg said.

"Oh, please, your bosses will think you're my personal babysitter," Lara said.

"Last time we looked for you, you actually helped catch a serial killer," Meg said. "Besides, Adam is friends with Grady. He'll insist we head down after what happened today anyway. We'll be there by late tonight."

Lara glanced at the clock on the dashboard. It was nearly six. "You'll never get a flight down here tonight. And I'm heading to Sea Life. It's alarm city, and Rick and Adrianna and Grady will be there to look out for me. Listen — if Adam wants you to come anyway, that's okay, but give it up for tonight. The city is full of cops, and the FBI is already on the case."

"Agents Cody and McCullough. I know. We checked. Matt knows Cody and says he's one of the best. He doesn't know Mc-Cullough, but if he's with Cody, he's got to be good."

"See? I'll be fine."

"But they aren't Krewe! Or two of your best friends in the world who should just be helping you get through this. We'll be there as soon as we can. Listen for your phone," Meg told her.

Lara laughed. "Adam can control the airlines' flight schedules?" she asked.

"Adam can arrange for a private jet."

"Wow. Well, tell him thank you."

"Of course," Meg said. She was quiet for a minute. "I've been thinking about you a lot, and I just *know* I need to be there."

Lara hesitated. She and Meg shared a strange telepathy; Meg swore that she had found Lara when she'd been trapped in the old mill because she'd been helped by a ghost, a ghost who had become real for Lara because Meg had made him so.

A chill suddenly swept through Lara.

Was the existence of ghosts the answer to tonight's mystery?

Meg had always seen ghosts, and she herself had seen that spectral Confederate soldier. And how could a man be there and then not there, unless . . . ?

Unless he was a dead man.

"Lara, are you okay?" Meg asked.

"Yes, yes, I'm driving, that's all."

"We'll be there tonight," Meg swore.

"Just don't worry about me. I'll be with my friends, and I'll be fine."

"Okay. Just promise me you'll stay with them until we get there."

"I promise," Lara told her.

She hung up and told herself to stop freaking herself out. Even so, chills continued to sweep her until she finally came up with the right argument.

If a dead man was after her, she would be all right. Meg had always told her that the dead stayed around to help, to rectify injustice.

The sky was still bright when she finally reached Sea Life, and a lot of the staff was still there, despite the hour.

She almost felt silly.

Grady, Rick and Adrianna were about to head out to a nearby restaurant for dinner. She agreed to join them and finally began to feel better.

Along the way to the restaurant, she even tried to convince herself that everything she'd seen had all been in her imagination.

No, she had seen the man. She had never set eyes on him before she had seen him at Sea Life, but she had known it was the same man when she had seen him in her yard.

She didn't think he wanted to hurt her.

So why was he there, watching her?

Meg was coming, and Matt with her. And they had already helped save her life once.

Lara smiled drily to herself. She was educated, she was savvy — she'd been in politics, for God's sake. She was strong. She wasn't a coward, and she could handle this, whatever *this* was.

Liar.

This was creepy. Body parts turning up in the lagoon and men who simply . . . disappeared.

All right. She was starting to get scared at

last. But friends were on the way.

The idiot in front of her suddenly slammed to a stop in order to cross three lanes of traffic. She swore beneath her breath and gave her full attention to her driving. To her relief — and, she was sure, to that of the drivers all around her — a siren instantly sounded. Didn't happen all that often, but that was one jerk who was going to get caught.

She turned her radio on just in time to hear the deejay remind people that this was Talk Like a Pirate day.

A pirate phrase quickly came to her mind. *Dead men tell no tales.*

She couldn't help but think that maybe — just maybe — they did.

6

Brett was frustrated.

Their boss, Special Agent in Charge Colin Marshall, had texted them the image one of the boys had captured on his cell phone — then shared with half the world via social media — and the police sketch. While the phone image was pretty low-res, it was enough to show that the police artist had done an excellent job — especially because, Marshall had assured them, the drawing had been done without the artist having seen the photo.

It was the perfect image of a dead man. A dead man who'd attacked the man who had been his best friend in life.

Brett and Diego weren't going to be able to reach the doctor who had signed Randy Nicholson's death certificate until late that night or the next day; he was in transit back from a medical convention in California. With only so many hours left in the day, they decided that the first thing would be to see the family and request that they approve an exhumation, which would make things much easier than trying to proceed without the family's agreement. Randy Nicholson's son, Henry, was appalled that people thought his dead father had risen from the grave, not to mention that he could have killed a friend. He was incredulous that anyone could believe that it was even possible, and he was willing to prove that it wasn't. Better yet, he spoke for the whole family. He'd seen the digital photo, of course, along with the police sketch, and he agreed both looked just like his father.

But he'd been with his father in the hospital when he'd died, so as far as he was concerned, a picture wasn't worth a thousand words or much of anything else.

Brett told Henry that they would waste no time; he intended to see that the body was exhumed by the next day.

Once that was set, Brett and Diego decided to see the three boys who had witnessed the crime. The parents could have stood in their way, since the boys were adolescents, but they didn't. In fact, they offered to bring the boys in, but Brett wanted to talk to each boy individually. He wanted to make sure that their stories jibed and didn't sound rehearsed.

Brett and Diego went to see each boy in turn. Two were fourteen; the oldest was fifteen.

They talked to Thomas Clayton first. He had a little sister who hid behind her mother when Diego and Brett arrived, and his father remained in the living room as they talked, silent, but there to protect his son if need be. But despite his growing obsession with the case, thanks to his connection to the Gomezes, Brett knew how to tamp down his personal feelings and interview an adolescent. In a few minutes Thomas was talking easily about seeing Arnold Wilhelm on the platform. Ricardo Clemente, one of the other boys, had been showing them a video when they'd seen the other man — the killer they'd describe to the police. Thomas said the victim had looked surprised but also pleased, as if he'd been about to go and hug the guy. Then Ricardo had decided to take a selfie of the three of them on the platform, and it was as they'd been setting up the shot, their backs to the older men, that the killer had rushed his friend, right when the train was coming.

The boy started to cry. He'd never seen anyone die before, and Brett hoped he never had to see it again.

He and Diego rose and thanked Thomas then, and Diego offered the boy's father a card with the number of a therapist the local Bureau office recommended, and then they left.

Their next stop was the Clemente house. Ricardo and his family were from Uruguay, and his parents spoke very little English. Brett's Spanish was passable, but Diego's was very good. He assured them that the boys weren't in trouble but, on the contrary, were being a big help. Ricardo's story was much the same as Thomas's. He said he wasn't sure where the man had come from, because he'd been showing a video to his friends until he'd decided to take the selfie. When he described the murder, he turned white, clearly as shaken as Thomas had been.

The last boy was Ricky Brito. His mom was Chilean and his dad was Cuban, but both had been in the United States since they'd been kids. They told Ricky just to tell the truth and he would be fine. His story was the same, not because it was rehearsed in any way, Brett was certain, but simply because the boys had all seen the same thing.

It was nearly ten by the time they finished. Diego, who had patiently gone along with every one of Brett's plans on how to proceed, finally told him, "Brett, we've got to call it a night."

"We still have to see the doctor who signed the death certificate." Brett looked at his notes. "Dr. Robert Treme."

"And you think he's going to see us now?" Diego asked.

"His plane is due to land shortly," Brett told him.

"He'll be getting off a cross-country flight. We can see him at the exhumation. I'm sure we can make sure he's there," Diego said.

"A man he declared dead is walking around killing people. I'd think he'd want to see us as quickly as possible. His job and his reputation are on the line."

"The police spoke with him, and he's aware that we want to interview him once he's back. But if you really want to see him tonight, we'll call him after the plane has landed and reach out. But he hasn't landed yet, so can we stop for a sandwich first? I'll be no good to you if I pass out from hunger."

Brett realized that they hadn't eaten all day, but this case mattered to him, and he felt compelled to keep forging ahead. He knew their boss had put them on it precisely because he and Herman Bryant both felt there was a possible connection to the murder of Maria Gomez. Still, Diego had a point.

"Yeah, we'll eat. What's still open around here?"

"It's Coconut Grove, take your pick."

They opted for an open-air restaurant in the middle of the mall. Diego flirted with the waitress a bit, asking her if they could get their meal as quickly as possible. She promised him that she would put a rush on their order.

Brett had his phone out and was reading the press coverage of the recent murders. He shook his head. "Diego, this thing is bad. We're national news now."

Diego nodded. "Yeah, and it's not going to be solved overnight, no matter how loud the media yells."

"I know. The whole thing makes no sense. Randy Nicholson died in a hospital, with dozens of people around. He was taken to the Diaz-Douglas funeral home over on Bird. The place has been there forever. It's beyond reputable. I looked up this Dr. Robert Treme, and he's been respected in his field for a good thirty years. No complaints have ever been issued against the man."

Diego shrugged. "And we'll do the exhumation and find Nicholson sleeping peacefully in his grave. People look alike. Maybe we'll find out he had a twin. They say everyone in the world has a doppelganger somewhere."

"We thought Miguel Gomez was dead."

"Because the body had been burned beyond even scientific recognition," Diego said. "This guy died in a hospital, had a viewing at a funeral home and was buried."

"Now we just have to figure out how all three murders are related," Brett said.

"Okay, let's lay it all out in the order things happened."

"All right, we'd assumed that Miguel Gomez was burned — literally and figuratively — by the Barillo crime family. And even though it was out of character, we assumed Barillo had also ordered Maria's murder."

"But then you got a call from Anthony Barillo claiming he didn't kill Maria — or Miguel. And then another call, from his son."

"Here's the thing. Barillo is a major-league criminal, and law enforcement has been trying to get enough evidence to arrest him for years. He's never called before to claim he didn't commit a crime."

"So you think we should believe him?"

"I'm not sure. I find it curious that the

man denies a murder — when I'm sure that if he *did* kill Miguel and Maria, we'd never be able to trace it to him because he would have ordered the hit. He would never kill anyone himself. I don't think he cared so much what we thought about Miguel's death. Seems as if his motto is Live by the Sword, Die by the Sword. He *did* care about Maria. About me believing he didn't kill her."

"Go on," Diego said.

"A neighbor swore he saw Miguel — alive, even if not exactly well — going to the house. Shortly afterward, Maria gets thrown off her balcony into a tree. The next thing we know, pieces of Miguel wind up in Biscayne Bay. Then nice, gentle retiree Arnold Wilhelm is killed on the Metrorail platform, and all three eyewitnesses gave the same description of the killer, who just happens to be a dead ringer — no pun intended — for the victim's best friend." He was quiet for a moment. "So you've got two victims, each one apparently killed by someone close to them — someone who was already supposed to be dead. Setting aside the whole question of how the dead could rise . . . *why*? Why kill someone they loved? Did someone *make* them do it? *How?* What the hell is the connection? What's going on?"

"It will help when we dig up Nicholson tomorrow," Diego said. "Because then you'll know that the dead *didn't* rise."

"And hopefully Phil Kinny will have something for us tomorrow. He told me that if he had a head — Miguel's head — he should be able to tell us more about cause of death."

Diego started to speak, then stopped, looking past Brett, who turned to see what was going on. Two of Miami's finest, probably on duty, were strolling through the mall. Brett realized that they knew one of the officers: Greg Dewey. He'd helped them when they were homing in on a crack house about a year back.

Dewey saw Brett and Diego and walked over to their table. Brett and Diego stood, and they all shook hands as Dewey introduced his partner, Carlos Martino.

"You guys on duty? Or can you join us?" Diego asked.

"Just got off shift," Dewey said, pulling out a chair. The first thing he asked after he sat down was "What do you guys think about this zombie invasion talk?"

"We're trying to nip it in the bud," Brett said.

Dewey shook his head. "Man, I hope you can. There's nothing but this zombie stuff on the news — but it *is* uncanny how much that police sketch looks like the victim's dead friend. You guys running this? The briefing before our shift, they said you feds were taking the lead. Actually, I have to admit, I'm damned glad it's not us."

"We're all on this one," Brett told him.

Martino shook his head. "I hope we get this solved quickly. It's already starting to make people a little crazy, you know?"

"Who's gone crazy?" Brett asked.

"Kind of an exaggeration," Dewey said, grinning at his partner.

"Yeah, actually, it would have been nice if she'd begged us to stay awhile," Martino said, grinning, as well.

"She, who?" Diego asked.

"What are you talking about?" Brett asked, feeling more keyed up than he knew he should be. Maybe he was still spooked by seeing the ghost of Maria Gomez sitting at the foot of his bed, but he was getting worried that he was losing it.

But some kind of a sixth sense alerted him that anything could be important right now. This wasn't — or wasn't only — obsession on his part.

"We got a call tonight from a woman who was certain there was a man in her yard," Dewey said. "Gorgeous young blonde, lives

151

alone, really nice even when she was scared out of her senses. It's easy to believe some stalker might be after her. But we searched the place up and down. It's surrounded by a wall — you know those row houses just down the street? Stone walls around them and gates that lock. We got the call because we were literally down the street."

Brett wasn't surprised they'd been nearby. The Grove was a popular tourist destination. It had multi-million-dollar mansions a stone's throw from basic working class homes, and a few drug dens, too. The Grove hosted college kids by the dozen and scores of restaurants, bars, music venues and shops. Historically, it had always had a bohemian flavor, and it was beautiful, with rich trees and foliage. Tourists and locals both came to see the Barnacle, one of the oldest homes in the county, now a museum. And there were plenty of docks and yacht clubs, since it bordered Biscayne Bay. But because it was such a busy and diverse neighborhood, it could be a tough zone to work as a cop. He admired the guys who handled it well.

"So the woman seemed crazy?" Diego asked.

"No, that's just it," Martino said. "She didn't seem crazy at all. She was stunned when we didn't find anyone. She wasn't hysterical, she was scared — and absolutely certain of what she'd seen."

"And you're sure no one was there?" Brett asked. He didn't know what it meant yet, but he'd learned to pay attention to the prickly sensation shivering down his spine.

A blonde. Gorgeous.

Miami definitely had its share of beautiful women, including beautiful blondes.

And yet . . . "You're sure she was all right when you left?"

"We didn't just desert her. She was going back to work, planning on spending the night there," Martino said.

"Which house?" Diego asked. "Which house does she live in?"

"She's not there anymore," Martino said, but he gave them the address. "We waited for her to get her things together and leave."

"Where does she work?" Brett asked. He would never be able to explain the tension he felt — or how he knew what Dewey would say before he said it.

"Sea Life Center," Dewey told him.

Brett nearly broke his coffee cup, he set it down so hard. "Her name is Lara Ainsworth, isn't it?" he asked.

"Yeah, that was it," Dewey said. "You know her?" He seemed perplexed at first,

153

but then his eyes widened. "Oh, hell, how could I have forgotten? They had to close the place down when they found part of a body in the lagoon. Jeez, I feel like an idiot." He turned to Martino. "Don't know the connection, but she really *could* have been in danger. We should call in, find out if the captain wants some kind of protective detail on her."

Brett was already standing. Diego regretfully dropped the remains of his sandwich.

"We're heading out, guys. We'll be her protective detail," Brett assured him. He dug in his pocket and set money on the table.

"I'm sure she's all right. She said there are always people around," Dewey said.

"Yeah, I'm sure she's all right, too," Brett said, though he wasn't sure at all. He didn't know how any of this was connected. He'd had calls from Anthony Barillo and one of his sons — threatening calls. No information had been released identifying the body parts found at Sea Life as those of a man who'd been presumed dead over a week ago, but the Barillos had called after he had been at Sea Life to deny responsibility for murdering both Miguel and Maria.

And Lara thought she was being stalked.

He suddenly felt desperate to get to her

154

and make sure she was safe — and the hell with Dr. Treme. They could see him in the morning, just as Diego had been recommending all along.

"You know," Diego said from behind the wheel as they headed down US1, "you can make a call and have the local cops out there in an instant. Though you might want to call and alert her first. You've got her number, right?"

Brett nodded and punched in her number. He was relieved when she answered.

"Agent Cody?" she said curiously.

"Are you all right?" he asked her.

"Yes, thank you." She sounded puzzled. "You know what happened?"

"Yeah. We ran into the cops who were at your place when we were in the Grove getting some dinner. You're at Sea Life?"

"Yes. And I'm fine. I went to dinner with Rick, Grady and Adrianna. I'm in my office. I couldn't sleep, so I was working on some press releases for future events."

"We'll be there in ten minutes," Brett said. He waited, sure she would protest. She wasn't alone, after all; she was with friends.

She didn't object, though she was silent for long enough that he almost thought he'd lost her.

"Thank you," she said quietly.

"Of course." And then he said, "Don't worry, we'll see that you get some sleep. Diego and I will hang around for the night. We'll call when we get there so someone can let us in, all right?"

Diego stared at him.

Brett shrugged.

And once again Lara Ainsworth said softly, "Thank you."

It was the job, he told himself. *His* job. What they did, in the end, wasn't only catch criminals and bring them to justice, it was save lives.

And right now, they weren't talking just any life. They were talking *her* life.

She thought he had a stick up his ass. She could be sarcastic, even abrasive, but . . .

But there was something about her. The way she was confident but not in-your-face about it, the way she smiled . . .

All he really knew right then was that he had to keep her alive. If he didn't, somewhere in there he would lose his own soul.

"Coward — you're really a coward," Lara told her reflection in the bathroom mirror. She'd come in to brush her hair. She wanted to retain some sense of dignity when the FBI agents arrived.

156

After the call, she'd hurried to Grady's office-slash-apartment and found him still awake, working on his Spanish lessons via computer. He was glad to hear that the agents were coming. "I've talked to Adam. It's getting weird down here."

That's putting it mildly, she thought.

Lara nodded. "I just hate to bug him, you know?"

Grady grinned at that. "Weird is what he and the Krewe do."

"Yeah, I know."

"Anyway, I'm glad that Cody and Mc-Cullough are on their way."

So was she. But no matter what Meg had said, they might not be able to make it down that night, so it was a good thing the local agents were on their way. Like it or not, Lara was unnerved, frightened, and she needed sleep so she could do her job. And whether she thought Agent Cody had a stick up his butt or not, he was solid and practically reeked of strength and security.

With those muscles and an inner tension that seemed hotter than any fire, she would pick him in a fight any day.

Lara went back to her office and waited for Agent Cody to call again, then headed to the gate to meet him and Diego.

As always, Diego was cheerful.

As always, Agent Cody was grim.

She let them in, then locked the gate and reset the alarm.

She didn't want to sound like a crazy person and tried hard not to.

The effort failed.

"I feel guilty about getting you out here so late. I should have told you to go home and get some sleep. I'm so sorry. But this man was here today, and then he was in my backyard. And even though I know the dead man in our lagoon doesn't really have anything to do with me, with everything going on, I —"

"It's all right," Agent Cody said, cutting her off. And then he added in a surprisingly gentle tone, "Besides, you didn't call us. We called you and said we were coming."

"Were you worried about me for a specific reason?" she asked.

"Let's just say that with everything going on and you having a possible stalker, yes, we were worried," Agent Cody said. "And it's not a problem. We're glad to be here."

"Absolutely," Diego said.

She wasn't sure why, but she believed there was something else behind their words, something they weren't telling her, but what, she wasn't sure.

"Well, come on to the offices," she said.

158

"There's a nice communal area on the first floor. There's a kitchen with snacks, coffee, sodas . . . and the couch folds out to a bed. Grady has a combination office and apartment on the second floor, and Rick and Adrianna live here. Someone needs to be on the property at all times, because of the dolphins, and we don't have private security. The police patrol the area, of course, but . . ."

So much for not babbling on and on, she thought, and trailed off, but she couldn't help herself and started speaking again almost immediately.

"Well, thank you again. I'm just glad you're here. I was really unnerved tonight. And honestly, I swear I'm not a total coward. And I'll be fine as of tomorrow. I have friends coming down. They're FBI, too. You may know them. Probably not. I mean, the FBI is a pretty big organization, right?"

"You have friends in the Bureau?" Diego said. "And they're able to just come on down?"

"I guess. I hope I'm not causing them any problems. They work for a special unit."

"What unit?" Diego asked.

"It has some official name, I think, but they're known as the Krewe of Hunters."

The two agents looked at one another. She knew that the Krewe had a reputation within the Bureau. Some liked to mock them; others were in awe of their record in solving unusual cases.

"What are their names?" Agent Cody asked her.

"Meg Murray and Matt Bosworth."

He arched a brow. "I don't know Meg. I do know Matt. We were in a training class together a few years ago. He's a good guy."

"Yeah, the best," she said huskily. "I've known Meg forever. I met Matt through her." She wondered if she should just tell them what had happened to her, and how Meg and the Krewe had saved her.

Of course, they'd heard what had happened already, she was certain; the entire country and beyond had heard what had happened. But since she wasn't going by her real surname, they wouldn't know that she'd been the victim.

"So they haven't been officially assigned to the case?" Agent Cody asked. He was eyeing her oddly now.

As if she had suddenly turned another color or something, like a chameleon.

"Not that I know of." She wondered if she'd said or done the wrong thing. She hoped she hadn't made Brett and Diego feel

160

that someone else would be horning in on, even trying to take over, their case.

She led them down the winding path and around to the house. It was odd to realize just how beautiful the place was at night. Sea grape trees, palms and other flora and fauna nestled by the paths, shading them by day. A light breeze sweetened and cooled the night air. The slight movement of the water murmured in the background, and despite everything that had happened here, the place had the feel of a tropical oasis.

"Coffee?" she asked them, unlocking the front door.

"Coffee is always good," Diego said.

"And then we'll have you tell us about this man you saw," Agent Cody told her.

"Of course," she said.

The men took seats in the lounge area, while Lara slipped into the kitchen and brewed a pot of coffee. When it was done, she took it out to them, adding a cup for herself. She'd fixed a tray with sugar and cream, but neither of the agents used them. She wondered with a certain amount of humor if drinking black coffee was a job requirement.

When she sat down, her own cup in hand, Agent Cody looked at her and said without preamble, "Tell us about the man."

161

"I saw him here first," she said. "I was getting ready to leave. He was just standing in the doorway of my office. I asked him if I could help him, but he left without saying anything. I followed and tried to find him, only I couldn't. I told Adrianna about him, but she didn't seem particularly worried. Of course, Sea Life was still open to the public then."

"Was he dressed like a tourist?" Diego asked her.

"Yes, actually. He was wearing a guayabera and light trousers. I've seen dozens of tourists dressed that way — locals, too."

"Okay, so then you went home, and when you looked outside, he was in your yard?" Diego asked.

"Yes. I guess he might have been some poor lost Alzheimer's patient or something, but . . . how did he get into my yard?"

"Can you describe him?" Agent Cody asked.

"Of course. Fifty plus. Medium build, medium height. Dark eyes and dark hair. I thought he looked like the pictures you see of Spanish conquistadors — minus the helmet, of course."

The two agents looked at one another as if startled by her description.

"Don't even go there," Diego said.

"How could I?" Brett said, his voice sounding deep and scratchy. "We know the man is dead. The DNA on the body parts matched. Not to mention what remained of his face."

"What are you two talking about?" Lara asked. "You're really frightening me."

"Nothing. It's just that your description sounds like the description of the man we found," Agent Cody said.

She felt as if she'd been bathed in a bucket of ice. "You mean the man whose body parts we found?" Her voice sounded odd and stilted.

"Lots of people look like other people," Diego said, turning to Brett. "Hey, I'm half Cuban. I can look like a conquistador. Hell, that description could match Anthony Barillo or a dozen of the men working for him."

Agent Cody's voice sounded thick when he spoke. "Yeah, I've been afraid that it might have been Barillo or one of his men, frankly."

"That description fits half the older Hispanic men in the city," Diego said. "There *is* one guy I've seen, though, does a lot of Barillo's dirty work. I can't think of his name, though. But I kid you not, that description fits hundreds of people."

His explanation made sense, but Lara found that she barely heard him, because Brett Cody was staring at her as if he'd just discovered something important about her.

And he had.

"Washington, DC," he said. "You were a media assistant to Congressman Walker. Your real name is Lara Mayhew."

She stared back at him for a long moment before nodding. She supposed it had been just a matter of time before someone figured it out. The killer's rampage and her own rescue had been national news after all. And these men were FBI.

"Yes, my last name is Mayhew," she said. "I've been using my mother's maiden name."

"What the fu—" Diego quickly cut himself off.

Lara barely noticed him. She felt as if she'd locked eyes with Brett Cody. She couldn't turn away. And yet the look he gave her didn't make her want to shrink away or hide; he wasn't looking at her with pity, anger or suspicion. He seemed to have an empathy for her that was somehow reassuring.

"You're a survivor," he said quietly.

"I survived — but I wouldn't have made it without Meg and Matt."

164

He nodded at that. "Few of us survive alone."

"Agent Cody," Lara began.

"Brett. You call him Diego. So call me Brett. I don't really have a stick up my ass, and I'm sorry if I've acted as if I do. This case is kind of a personal one for me. Diego says I'm obsessed. I guess I am. I feel guilty. We haven't released the information yet, but the body parts we found belonged to a man named Miguel Gomez. Miguel came to me for help. He'd been pressured for years and forced to help a drug cartel down here run by the Barillo family. I turned him over to the agents — all of them top-notch — who had been working the case for years. We'd thought that he died in a fire, but we were wrong. According to the witness, he showed up and may have killed his wife — before someone killed him and we found his body parts."

"Brett . . ." Diego murmured.

Lara realized that Brett had just told her more than the authorities were telling anyone. She was surprised and pleased — more so than she wanted to be, in fact — to realize that he seemed to trust her implicitly.

She turned to Diego. "I was in politics for years," she said drily. "I'm a pro at keeping my mouth shut."

"I have to ask this, so please don't be offended," Brett said. "Is it possible that you might be a little bit paranoid — perfectly natural, after everything you've been through — or are sure you saw that man twice? I mean, maybe the first time you saw him, he was just a lost guest. But couldn't you have imagined him the second time?"

Lara nodded, smiling drily. "I can understand why you might suspect that I'm losing it, but I'm not. I saw the man. I saw him as clearly as I saw you. He was in the doorway of my office, and later he was in my yard. Staring in at me through the sliding glass door."

"Did you suspect at any time that he meant to harm you?" Brett asked.

She puzzled over that for a minute. "I don't — I don't think so. He just kept staring at me."

"It sure as hell sounds like the ghost of Miguel Gomez," Diego said, causing both Lara and Brett to turn and stare at him.

Was he seriously talking about a real ghost?

Lara didn't mean to, but she shivered visibly as Diego's words echoed her own thoughts. "A ghost?" She lowered her head for a second, thinking about Meg, who definitely saw the dead. Could she be seeing them, too?

"I was just thinking about your Krewe friends. Don't worry. We'll find out what's going on here," Diego said. "Tomorrow we dig up poor Mr. Nicholson, prove he's in his coffin and start searching the city for look-alikes."

"Is there a computer we can use?" Brett asked Lara.

"Of course. There's a house computer just over there," she said, pointing toward a comfortably arranged grouping of wicker furniture.

"Would you mind logging me on?" Brett asked.

Once he was online, he pulled up a newspaper article featuring a close-up of a man.

Lara stiffened, as cold as Arctic ice as she read the clipping. It was Miguel Gomez's obituary. And the face looking out at her from the computer screen was the exact same face she had seen earlier that day.

Twice.

Brett Cody turned to look at her. "Is that the man?" he asked.

She stared at Brett. And she didn't know how he knew — or even how *she* did — but they both knew there was no doppelganger running around the city.

She'd seen the ghost of Miguel Gomez.

"That was him," she said at last.

"Obviously the man has a twin who's trying to reach you. Maybe he's afraid to go to the authorities, maybe he thinks you can help him somehow, since you were the one who found his brother's remains," Diego said.

"Even if Miguel had a twin — which I'll bet you cash money he doesn't — how would he know that when we haven't released an ID on our dead man?" Brett asked.

"I don't know, but what other explanation could there be? A real ghost? I won't discount the idea, though . . ." Diego let his words trail off and he shrugged. "Or maybe Lara is loco? Sorry, Lara. I'm just trying to cover every possibility. But, I mean, it has to be another man."

"I'm not crazy," Lara assured him. "I swear to you, despite all the therapy I probably still need, I'm not crazy. I saw a man — who looked just like this man — here today, and then later in my backyard."

Brett looked at Lara and nodded slowly. "I promise you," he said softly, "we will find out exactly what's going on." She was surprised by the crooked smile that twisted his mouth as he spoke. "I swear," he added softly.

7

Randy Nicholson had been buried in one of Miami's older cemeteries on Southwest 8th Street near 37th Avenue. It was a large cemetery, stretching for many city blocks, and one of the most beautiful in the city, in Brett's opinion. While the City of Miami Cemetery was the oldest and housed many of the city's original rich and famous, along with some Confederates and Yankees who had survived the Civil War, he'd always preferred this one, which traced its origins back to 1913. There were beautiful angels and cherubs, and impressive mausoleums throughout, along with trails and trees that created a parklike yet still solemn atmosphere. It was perfectly manicured, not at all forlorn and overgrown, as so many older cemeteries were.

The exhumation was carried out smoothly; there was only one funeral happening that Wednesday morning, and it was taking place in a section far away from them.

Nicholson's headstone was courtesy of the United States Marine Corps; it was the headstone he had requested, according to his son. Henry Nicholson seemed like a decent guy, and he'd done everything they'd asked to help the process proceed. But no matter how respectful people tried to be, there was just something inherently disquieting in digging up a human grave. At last the cement sarcophagus that was a cemetery requirement was removed and the coffin was set on a gurney for its journey to the morgue.

One of the workers came over to speak with Brett and Diego. "You get used to how coffins feel," he told them. "This one — it don't feel right."

Brett wasn't sure why, but he had a sinking feeling that the man was right.

When they reached the morgue, Phil Kinny was waiting with his assistants. Brett and Diego were in the autopsy room where the coffin was opened, while Henry Nicholson, who had asked to accompany them and hear their findings, waited outside.

There was no body in the coffin, only a sack of sand. The only indications that a person had once lain there were a few strands of hair and a couple of fiber strands, and the satin lining still bore the impression of a body.

But the coffin held no occupant.

When Henry Nicholson heard the news he lost his cool completely. "No! No!" he shouted. When he ran toward the autopsy room, determined to see for himself, Diego and Brett had to scramble to catch him. The man moaned incoherently, tears dampening his eyes as he sank to the ground.

"My father is not a zombie!" he screamed. "My father is not a zombie!"

In the end, though unaccustomed to dealing with the living, the ME gave him a sedative.

Henry sat quietly after that, only speaking again when the agents dropped him off at his house. Before he got out of the car he stared straight at Brett. "My father is not a killer," he insisted softly.

And Brett could only tell him, "There's something else going on here, because I don't believe that your father is a killer, either."

Brett Cody and Matt Bosworth had obviously gotten on well during their past acquaintance, Lara reflected as she watched them laughing over old times. And seeing Brett joking around that way, he suddenly seemed more human to her. Though if she were being honest, she had to admit that the process had begun even before Meg and Matt had arrived just after one in the morning.

Brett and Diego had suggested that she get some sleep, but she had known there was no way in hell she could sleep, not to mention if she wasn't there to let Meg and Matt through the gate, they would have to wake Grady, and that didn't seem fair.

And so they had sat in the lounge area, and she had done her best to explain why she'd ended up in Florida after what had happened to her when she had quit her job with Congressman Walker and the ordeal she'd been through before heading south. In turn, they had told her more about the Greater Miami area, the violent drug wars that had gone on during the eighties, and how they were doing their best to prevent anything like that happening again.

"Things have changed over the years," Brett explained to her. "Our offices across the country have hundreds of agents working on cyber crime, things like identity theft that take place without violence on the internet. But there are also always going to be those who are still into real-world criminal enterprises like drug smuggling and — especially here — stealing everything a refugee has, promising to get him to these shores. Some of them even make good on their promises, but others have no intention of risking being caught with illegal human cargo. They leave their trusting victims at sea."

"And then there are crimes like this," Diego said. "Senseless crimes — like the murder of Maria Gomez, who never killed anything bigger than a palmetto bug in her whole life."

"Even Miguel only got caught up in it because he was afraid not to," Brett added.

"And now there's Arnold Wilhelm, a retired war vet, harming no one," Diego added.

It was right around then that Meg had called; the room had gone oddly silent for a minute, and Lara had jumped when her phone rang. Now she realized that Matt and Brett knew each other better than she'd expected, and all four agents shared an easy camaraderie that she found herself envying. Between them, Brett and Diego quickly brought Matt and Meg up to speed.

As they spoke, Brett checked his emails and informed them that there would be a task force meeting including key state, county and city officers the next day. By then the exhumation would be complete, and hopefully Phil Kinny would be ready to tell them more about Miguel Gomez's death. Matt told him that they had been assigned to the case through the director's office and told to follow Brett's lead as agent in charge.

Brett smiled and shrugged at that. "Your unit does as it chooses, I guess."

"We aren't here to step on toes," Matt said.

"You would be welcome to stomp all over my entire body if it got us some answers," Brett assured him.

It was nearly 2:00 a.m. when they finished talking. With Matt and Meg staying at the facility, it was overcrowded as far as sleeping arrangements went. Since Brett and Diego had an early appointment at the cemetery, Matt and Lara escorted them to the gate, and she made sure to lock up and set the alarm once they were gone.

As they headed back in, Matt paused on the walkway, looking around. "Interesting," he said.

"What's that?"

"This place has great security as far as it goes, what with the gates and alarms, but that's a big bay out there. What's to stop someone from coming here by boat?"

"Nothing, I suppose," Lara said. "But our whole purpose is to study and protect marine life. Have you ever heard of anyone trying to steal a dolphin? Honestly, Matt, I don't think anyone is after Sea Life. I think it was pure accident that Miguel Gomez's . . . body parts wound up here."

"This whole case . . . . I've never seen anything like it."

Back inside, they discovered that Grady had woken up, and come down and met Meg, and the two of them had enjoyed extolling Adam Harrison's virtues. Rick and Adrianna came down then as well, and despite the hour they had more coffee before finally determining that they all really needed to go to bed. Though Rick and Adrianna offered to give up their spot, Matt quickly said that he'd slept on the plane, so he was happy to catch a few z's on the sofa, and Meg would bunk in with Lara.

It was morning before Lara had a chance to speak with Meg and Matt alone, taking them for a tour of the facility and introducing them to the other members of the staff. Finally, the three of them sat on the platform by Cocoa's enclosure and fed her fish.

"This place is wonderful," Meg said.

It was really good to have the two of them

there, Lara thought. Meg was a lithe, fit five foot ten, with raven-dark hair and deep, penetrating blue eyes that somehow communicated both confidence and cordiality. Matt was a bruiser — smart, fit and built like a tank. More than that, she knew they'd both had enough training to tackle almost any situation.

"It *was* wonderful," Lara said. "I mean, it still is, really. I love what I'm doing. I love Cocoa, and the other dolphins and the sea lions — and even the cats and birds, the lizards and the squirrels. But Cocoa just had to give me that finger. And then . . . the rest."

"You can't let what's really good in life be ruined just because there are evil people in the world," Meg said.

Lara looked at her friend and smiled. Meg had known her whole life what she wanted to do. As a child, she'd lost a member of her own family to a murderer, and even then, Meg had played a role in seeing that the man was caught.

Because she saw the dead.

"I saw him," Lara told her in a rush. "The man whose body parts we found in the bay, I saw him — after he was dead. They haven't released this yet, but his name was Miguel Gomez, and Brett Cody wasn't

176

surprised that I'd seen him — it was almost as if he expected it. Diego was talking about doppelgangers and twins, but Brett was staring straight at me and I knew — I just knew — that he believed me."

"Maybe he sees the dead, too," Matt said.

"All of a sudden?" Lara demanded. "You knew him before — did he see ghosts? Can you go your whole life delightfully oblivious and then suddenly start seeing ghosts of the dead?"

Meg smiled at that. "You've seen the dead before. You saw the Confederate officer who helped us save your life," she said softly.

"You described him so clearly that I believed he was there."

Meg shook her head. "No, you saw him. Maybe you've always had the ability. Maybe there just wasn't a ghost out there who needed to reach you. Until now."

Lara groaned inwardly. Once she'd been so passionate. So determined to create a world where good people wound up in power, where candidates were elected on merit, not because their campaign contributions were large enough to feed entire countries.

She still dreamed of seeing good men and women in power; she still meant to write the speeches and white papers that could help put them there. But she was also in love with dolphins and sea life in general, and she'd become passionate about ecology, and that was all part of the bigger picture. Politicians owed a decent world to those who would come after them.

"I'm going to suggest you open yourself up to this ghost and find out what he has to say," Matt told her, then added softly, "I came into all this paranormal stuff kicking and screaming. Most of us do — unless we grow up with it and consider the dead as friends. After all, most of them are just as good in death as they were in life."

"What about evil?" Lara asked, feeling a little silly. "There are evil people, too, so there must be evil ghosts, right?"

"I've heard about a few from some of our fellow Krewe members," Meg said. "But the good is there to outweigh the evil."

"If only," Lara said.

"If only?" Matt asked her.

"If only good outweighed evil in life the way you say it does in death," Lara said.

"Then, we just have to make sure it does, right?" Meg asked her. "And," she added, staring out at the sparkling water, where Cocoa, determined to get their attention, was doing a backflip, making the water spray and dance like diamonds beneath the blue sky and dazzling sun, "we have to take every minute we can to appreciate everything that's so amazing about this world."

Cocoa swam over and stuck her head out of the water to look at them. Lara stroked her back and watched the delight on Meg's face as the animal slid beneath her hands. She gave Cocoa a fish.

"Meg will stay here with you," Matt said, rising. "I'm heading over to the local office. Adam will have sent down our assignment paperwork by now. I'll be back by the end of the afternoon."

Lara turned to Meg. "You don't have to babysit me. I have work to do. And I'm sure you have a job to do, too."

Meg smiled at her. "Right now, my friend," she said, "*you* are my job."

Brett stared as Phil Kinny spoke, almost smiling.

He didn't consider himself completely ignorant when it came to the human body and medical matters, but Kinny had left him and Diego far behind when he started talking about neurotransmitters and other features of the brain.

"Layman's terms, please, doc," he begged at last.

179

Brett was glad that the head was turned away from him; he wasn't sure he could have stood there like a hardened professional if what was left of Miguel's face had been staring at him while he tried to grasp what the ME was saying.

"Okay, first, we only use about ten percent of our brain power, give or take. But the brain is divided into sections that are responsible for different chores when it comes to our bodies. You're heard about people with bullets in their heads surviving for years?" Kinny asked.

"I don't personally know anyone with a bullet in his head," Brett said.

"Wait, *I* do — and so do you," Diego said.

"Yeah? Who?"

"David Archer, NYC office," Diego said. "They can't take the shell out — too dangerous. He gets scanned or X-rayed or whatever every so often to make sure it hasn't moved. He's not in the field anymore, works a desk now. Great guy, though."

"I knew he was shot taking down an Eastern European human trafficking operation," Brett said. "I didn't realize he'd been shot in the head, though."

Diego nodded. "Yep. And he's basically fine."

"Yes, depending on where the bullet is,

depending on the damage it caused, a person can live a pretty much normal life even with a bullet in his brain. I'll try to explain more clearly what I think happened to Gomez, though I can't say I understand all the science behind what I think happened myself," Kinny said.

"Just give us whatever you've got. We're pretty desperate," Brett said.

"All right, an anatomy lesson, more or less in layman's terms," Kinny said. "The human brain is an amazing thing. Think of it as a computer for a few minutes. The frontal lobes are associated with what we call executive function — thinking things out, consciously controlling our behavior, our ability to reason, and also our capacity for abstract thought. Then we have the cerebral cortex, a layer of neural tissue that covers everything. It's pretty thick in human beings. While our brains may be smaller than those found in some animals, they're larger in proportion to our size. Understand?"

"So a blue whale has a bigger brain than ours, but it's much smaller in comparison to the many tons it weighs, right?" Diego said.

"Something like that, but I digress. None of that matters in regard to my theory as to what happened to Miguel Gomez," Kinny said.

"Mike the chicken," Diego said.

Kinny arched a brow. "So you know that story?" he asked.

Diego nodded. Brett looked from one of them to the other, then asked Kinny, "So the chicken story really is true?"

"Absolutely," Kinny said. "So, in a nutshell, you have the frontal lobe, parietal lobe, temporal lobe and occipital lobe. We perform many different functions, and each of those functions is associated with a particular part of the brain. Even when someone is clinically brain dead, he may still move, react to stimuli, process nutrients, often even breathe without artificial help. In short, I believe, based on what I saw in my autopsy, that parts of Miguel's brain were still functional even though other parts had been destroyed. In a very real way, he remained alive, at least technically speaking. Just as we breathe due to the programming built into a part of the brain that requires no conscious thought, so we perform other functions."

Brett frowned, trying to digest the science.

It was actually easier to believe that Miguel's neighbor had seen a zombie.

"So someone managed to kill part of Miguel but not all of him. Then they somehow programmed him to kill his wife before finishing him off?" he asked incredulously.

"I've given you the science, and I've sent a sample of his brain matter out for toxin testing. The man wasn't shot, but I believe he was injected with some type of toxin that killed just the part of the brain that made him who he was," Kinny said. "I can give you a technical explanation, use medical terms like *cerebral cortex, neurotoxins* and the like, but I mentioned before that the brain is like a computer, so think of it this way. Miguel had no internet connection going. He was essentially dead from the time his brain was damaged. This is probably the most insidious murder I've ever come across, and I'm guessing it was some kind of experiment, since this isn't something there's a lot of medical documentation on."

"Not your typical mob hit," Diego said drily.

"Not a typical hit in any way," Brett said. He hesitated. "I don't know a lot about this, but what about voodoo or Santeria?"

"I know some people who practice Santeria," Diego said. "They sacrifice chickens, but they don't turn them into Mike the chickens."

Brett shook his head. "I know that what

we think of as voodoo comes mainly from Hollywood, but to many people — especially in New Orleans and Little Haiti here — it's a very real religion. Papa Doc used it to support his regime of fear in Haiti. He had a devoted group of voodoo priests who could supposedly make the dead rise. From what I understand, they used poisons that caused their victims to appear to be dead, and yet they weren't. Even physicians couldn't tell the difference. Then the priests used mind control when they brought them back to 'life' as zombies. Many people believe that the Tonton Macoute, his private militia, was made up of those zombies."

"It's actually a crime to make a zombie in Haiti now," Dr. Kinny said.

"From what I understand, Papa Doc and the voodoo priests use a powder made from the poison of a puffer fish," Brett said.

Kinny nodded gravely. "It's only really been about the past thirty years or so that science has begun to explore the creation of 'zombies' and admit that such things really are possible."

"So we're looking for a homicidal voodoo priest?" Diego asked.

"Or a mad scientist," Kinny said.

"Funny," Diego responded.

"I'm not trying to be funny. I'd say

someone who has studied the human brain — and the creation of so-called zombies — is at least in on this. And I'll pretty much guarantee you that the poison the tests find will be puffer fish toxin, whether real or synthetic," Kinny said.

"We were never intended to find the body," Brett said. "And if it hadn't been for that dolphin, we never would have. We would have gone on believing that Miguel was burned to cinders in a fire and that his neighbor must have been mistaken about the date or hallucinating or something." He let out a long breath and turned to Diego. "We have to find Mr. Randy Nicholson," he told him.

"That will go a long way to proving my point," Kinny said.

"And I'm betting Nicholson's body ended up in the same condition — even if not the same place — as Miguel's," Brett said.

"Damn," Diego said. "This is a big city and a hell of a long coastline."

Brett looked thoughtful for a moment, then said, "It's curious. They kept Nicholson alive a long time. He was supposedly buried three months ago. Miguel only died recently."

"Maybe the killer gets rid of his victims once they're of no use to him anymore,"

Kinny suggested.

Brett was silent for a minute and realized that Diego and Phil Kinny were looking at him, waiting. "Say you're right, which you probably are. The question is, why? Why is he doing this? And why kill these particular people? It was easy for us to accept that someone wanted to murder Miguel Gomez, but why Maria, much less Arnold Wilhelm?"

"Maybe he killed them just because he could, testing how far he can push his . . . minions," Kinny suggested.

Brett turned to Diego. "Time to see the good Dr. Robert Treme and find out why he signed a death certificate for a man who wasn't dead."

A group called Just Say Thanks was coming in on Sunday. Lara had been in contact with the events coordinator several times. She had just spent another hour with her on the phone now, assuring the woman that they were open and ready for the group's visit. Meanwhile, Meg was bent intently over her Bureau laptop.

Just Say Thanks had been founded by a wealthy household-appliance inventor who hadn't served in the military but who was grateful to those who had the courage he didn't. It was largely funded by about twenty wealthy people across the country, though they accepted donations. Their mission was to help wounded veterans, and especially those with PTSD, by getting them out into the world. Lara had been thrilled when they made contact, and Grady had even offered to underwrite their visit. Lara had done a half dozen press releases for the event, but now she continued contacting the media. Sea Life liked to welcome vets and went all out for them. The employees even lined up to applaud as the soldiers went by. It was a nice touch. Not nearly enough, but nice.

She emailed a small piece for the next day's paper, then turned to look at Meg, who was so deeply involved in her work that she could have been back in her own office in Virginia. She didn't even notice Lara.

"Hey, sorry to interrupt," Lara said softly. "But . . . what are you doing?"

Meg turned to her. "When you were on the phone I was cyber-conferencing with Matt, Diego and Brett. Here's a shock to the system. Someone is making zombies."

"What? Zombies aren't real. They're horror movie stuff."

"No, not zombies like in the movies," Meg said. "Real zombies. Slaves with no free will, basically. The whole thing comes from

Haiti, and it involves voodoo and drugs, and now it's here in Miami. A conservative estimate for South Florida says close to half a million people here are Haitian or of Haitian descent." Meg smiled. "I've been on the computer a long time, and now I'm full of statistics. Miami's Little Haiti is a small area. It runs, roughly speaking, from Northwest 79th Street to Northwest 86th Street, and from the bay over to 2nd Avenue. It's got a fascinating history. It used to be a small agricultural community called Lemon City, founded around 1850. There were lemon groves everywhere, and supposedly there are still a lot of lemon trees in people's yards. It's a poor area, with its share of crack houses, but the median income has been rising, and the local businessmen are fighting to protect their investment and keep drugs out of the area.

"The population has grown a lot more mixed since the 1980s, but it's still primarily a Haitian and overall Caribbean community." She shook her head. "It's not the safest neighborhood, though. The trip advisory sites all say to be careful, even though the design district and a lot of tourist attractions are just to the south."

Lara nodded. "I've been there."

"What? Already?"

Lara laughed. "I took a city tour when I first moved down."

"Well, at any rate, you can still find voodoo priests and priestesses there," Meg said.

Lara leaned back. "Okay. So how do you guys go about that? Do you just walk down the streets and ask people where the voodoo priest lives?"

"Don't be silly."

"What, then?"

"We use the internet, just like everybody else, ask the local cops at the task force meeting. To tell you the truth, I suspect there will be a voodoo shop on every block, though." She was quiet for a long moment, studying Lara. "I'd hate to be handling the press on this one. I can just see the headlines. 'Real Zombies Roam Miami.'"

"I admit, I'm glad I don't have to spin this one," Lara said.

"Listen," Meg said, "I've got some time, and since you know the area, how about you go with me, and we drive around, see what we can see?"

"It's nearly lunchtime anyway, so give me ten minutes to finish up here and I'm all yours."

Forty-five minutes later, Meg and Lara stopped at a place called The Haitian Princess.

As Meg had suspected, they'd had no difficulty finding voodoo shops, and they'd chosen this one at random. Lara knew she could take a long lunch, but she didn't want to be gone *too* long. Still, she was eager to go inside and see what the place was like.

A tour group was just leaving when they arrived. Lara was glad; she didn't want to share the place with a large group. The neighborhood itself had a few sketchy housing projects not too far away, but she was with Meg. And Meg was armed and knew how to use her weapon.

But Lara didn't think about any of that once they entered the shop. It was magical. There were beautiful carvings everywhere, freestanding sculptures along with African masks and paintings adorning the walls. A large table held gris-gris bags and a wide variety of herbs. Religious talismans and statues of the Virgin Mary and various saints were displayed in handsome cases. A sign over an archway advised that there was an altar in the back for the faithful.

They had just stopped by a tightly packed bookshelf when they were approached by a tall African-American man in a handsome white suit.

"Welcome," he told them. "May I help you?" Then he smiled, his eyes on Meg.

"Ah, you're a police officer, here to ask me about zombies."

Lara's eyes widened. How did he know?

But Meg only smiled and introduced herself as she pulled out her badge. "FBI," she said. "And yes, we're here to ask you about zombies."

Lara followed suit and introduced herself, then said, "We're hoping to learn, to gain insight, as Meg told you."

The man smiled at her. "It's all right, miss. I am an ordained priest, with a wonderful flock of the faithful here. Good people, gentle, working people. I am called Papa Joe, and you are welcome to call me that, as well. Voodoo, like any religion, may be twisted by poverty, fear and greed. My shop has been full since the media began talking about the so-called dead man who murdered his friend. I am more than happy to help you, though I'm not sure I can. Neither I nor any of my followers know anything about zombies, and we certainly don't create them."

"We never thought you did," Meg assured him. "But we think that someone here in Miami has resurrected — no pun intended — some of the practices that were popular under Papa Doc's regime. What we were hoping to talk to you about is the history of

191

voodoo generally, and we're curious whether you've seen or heard of anyone with a particular interest in zombies."

"History?" Papa Joe said, his eyes brightening. "Ah, yes. I'm happy to tell you the history of voodoo. It is quite possibly as old as the continent of Africa. We believe that our spirits walk the earth with those of our ancestors. We believe in one great god and many saints, a pantheon based in Catholicism from the time when Europeans came to Africa and began the slave trade around 1510. And voodoo with the slaves to the islands of the Caribbean and the shores of the North American continent." He paused for a moment. "I was a boy late in Papa Doc's rule of Haiti, when we all feared the Tonton Macoute, his private army under the control of his devoted voodoo priests. I saw men who looked at the world with sightless eyes, as if they had no souls. How much of that was a result of fear of the priests and Papa Doc himself, and how much came from brainwashing — or the promise of power and the adrenaline rush of brutality — I don't know. I do know that Papa Doc reigned through fear. My parents walked with their heads down. We were helped out of the country when I was a boy, and I thank God and my ancestors continually that they brought me here."

Lara smiled; she found herself liking Papa Joe. "Did you ever hear of anyone — anyone specific, I mean — coming back from the grave?"

"Back then, of course. We heard about it frequently. There were always stories going around, rumors — as was intended. The men I saw, though, I don't think they were truly dead. Many things can cause a trance-like state. Maybe they were using certain drugs, maybe they were using hypnotism. I heard about one particular man who came back, though. His family buried him, and then he showed up at his house a week later. He even talked a bit at first. Then he died again, and they buried him again. I think someone used the zombie poison on him, and because he wasn't truly dead the first time, he miraculously came back. But I never heard of anyone who was known to have been buried and then came back with his mind intact, or who lived more than a week at most. If you want to know more, I can point you to the right books."

"That would be great," Lara said.

He led them to a shelf of books on the history of voodoo, its use in the United States and abroad and more. They made several selections, thanked him again and prepared to leave.

"If I can help you more in any way, let me know," Papa Joe told them as they left.

"Thank you," Lara and Meg said in unison.

"I'll do some asking around for you, too," Papa Joe promised. He shook his head. "Naturally, my flock is disturbed. Whenever talk turns to zombies, especially zombies right here in Miami, the spotlight falls on we Haitians. So you never know. Someone may have heard something."

Lara got behind the wheel, and Meg had her head in one of the books before they were even out of the parking lot.

"Whoever is doing this has taken zombie poisoning to a level unseen since Papa Doc's days," Meg said after a few minutes.

"I don't know. I mean, Miguel Gomez . . . maybe. They didn't have a positive identification on the body, and his neighbor said he'd seen him. But Randy Nicholson . . . The man died in a hospital. There was a viewing at a funeral home, which almost certainly means he was embalmed. He was buried."

"Except that he wasn't in his grave," Meg said. "Matt told me."

"So you think the hospital staff was in on it?" Lara asked doubtfully.

"Hospitals aren't perfect. The body could have been whisked away. Or maybe it was managed properly there and they were fooled by the effects of the poison, and something went on at the funeral home. Maybe someone paid them off not to embalm the body." She turned to look at Lara, speculation in her eyes. "Meanwhile, we need to learn everything we can about Miguel Gomez."

"I'm sure the Bureau has a massive file on him," Lara said.

"No, we need to know what you can find out."

"What *I* can find out?"

"It's evident that he's trying to reach you."

"I don't know if —"

"You have to embrace your ability to see ghosts, Lara," Meg told her. "That's all there is to it."

8

Dr. Robert Treme was a cardiologist with an array of diplomas and certificates on his office wall to prove that he'd gone the distance. He was about sixty and appeared to have embraced his vocation, since his build suggested that he did just the right amount of exercise for his age and ate well, watching out for his own heart. He wasn't defensive when he met with Brett and Diego, he was puzzled.

He had a file before him, which he readily handed across the desk to them. "I gave copies of all this information to the police, as well. I have a list of the nurses and personnel who were on the floor at the time of his death, including the orderlies who took the body to the hospital morgue and the morgue attendant. The nurse on duty called a code blue, naturally. Nicholson was seventy-eight, and when he flatlined, I happened to be at the hospital, just finishing rounds. We performed all the proper resuscitation techniques to no avail."

"He died from congestive heart failure?" Brett asked. When Treme nodded, he went on. "And he *was* dead? You're sure of it?"

Treme nodded gravely. "I have been practicing medicine for forty years. The man was dead. No pulse, no heartbeat. I don't know who that was on the platform, but it wasn't Randy Nicholson. If you doubt my words, you and the police are welcome to question everyone in the hospital at the time — including his family. I left them alone with him to say their goodbyes before he went down to the hospital morgue."

"The man isn't in his grave," Brett informed him.

"Then, you need to be looking into body snatchers," Treme said with certainty.

"Was he tested for brain waves?" Brett asked.

Treme leaned forward, irritated for the first time. "He'd had a bad heart for several years. He didn't help it any by living on red meat coated in salt. He was in the hospital for congestive heart failure, and his heart gave out. He didn't have Alzheimer's disease and he wasn't being tested for mental acuity or a brain injury, so no, he wasn't tested for brain waves. Believe me, he wasn't breathing. He didn't have a pulse. He was in his room for over an hour after death so his family could say goodbye, and then he was in the hospital morgue before going to the funeral home. The man was dead."

"Is there any possibility — any at all — that he was in a state that simply resembled death?" Brett asked.

For a moment Treme betrayed a hint of uncertainty. "If he wasn't dead, it was an impeccable imitation of it." He rose, apparently finished with the interview. "Gentlemen, if Mr. Nicholson's body was not in his grave, I suggest you look to the funeral home. From the time I signed his death certificate, the hospital and the funeral home became responsible for the body. He had a viewing, so his body definitely made it as far as the mortuary. I really don't see how I can help you further."

It was a dismissal, and Brett nodded at Diego to indicate that it was time to go. That was it — all they could get at the moment. And it did sound as if they would have to move on and find out just what had happened after the death certificate had been signed.

While Meg had kept her nose in the books most of the way back, she was interested in learning more about the facility when they returned.

"I noticed last night that the place is locked and there's an alarm. And a fence runs all around the property, right to the water. What's next door on the left?" she asked.

"The land is owned by a museum, but they haven't built there yet. They're fenced, too. And actually, they have full-time security."

"What about on the other side?" Meg asked.

"County property. Apparently an old guy used to sell bait and rent fishing boats from there. But when he died, the property reverted to Dade County." Lara made a face. "It will probably be sold and turned into condos."

"The way of the world," Meg said. "So conceivably, anyone could come through from that side."

"If they were willing to get wet, yes."

"And what about the dolphin lagoons?"

"The lagoons themselves are fenced, with gates that are opened when there's a major storm. There are thirty dolphins here, and they've been released ten times. Every single one has come back, because they all choose to," Lara told her proudly.

Meg smiled at that. "Good to hear."

"I don't think this place is in any danger," Lara said.

"I don't think the dolphins are in danger. *You're* my worry," Meg said. "But back to the lay of the land. When you're open, people can enter the facility proper via the parking lot or through the gift shop, right?"

"Exactly," Lara agreed. "And if you follow the path to the left, you get to the docks, and if you keep going you end up here, at the offices. If you head straight, toward the water, you come to the education building. To the right of that you have the café, and past that, more lagoons. Cocoa is usually in the first lagoon, because she's one of the main performers." She smiled, realizing it sounded as if she were talking about a niece who was doing exceptionally well in school.

"I'll have to meet your Cocoa," Meg said. "And the rest of the staff. So far I've met your boss, Grady Miller, who reminds me a lot of Adam, and I bet he's just as good to work for. And I've met Rick and Adrianna, who seem lovely. What about the rest of the staff?"

"Come on, we'll take a walk and I'll introduce you. I can tell them I'm just checking to see how plans are going for Sunday. We're hosting a group called Just

Say Thanks. They bring in military vets to interact with the dolphins. I've been told the effect on the vets is amazing."

"I'm glad we'll be here for it," Meg said.

They left the office, and Lara headed toward the education building first. They waited outside the door of one of the classrooms and watched as Myles Dawson, their intern, enthusiastically lectured a visiting summer-camp group on the work they did. He showed a short video demonstrating that young dolphins were quick to learn behaviors from their trainers, just as they did from their parents. He talked about how dolphins learned both visual and verbal commands, and could even comprehend several commands combined sequentially. He also showed that dolphins were able to discern symbols and match like to like. He finished by saying, "These incredible creatures have been man's friend for years. The tales of dolphins saving people from shark attacks are true. And remember, here at Sea Life they're top dog, so behave yourself and follow all instructions when you're interacting with them today, because you'll get sent to the corner before they will."

His words were greeted with laughter, and then the group filed out, smiling and ready for their adventure.

"Hey, Myles, I brought a friend to meet you," Lara called to him. "Good class, too," she added.

Myles grinned at that. A nice grin. He had longish brown hair and warm hazel eyes, and Lara knew that he liked to flirt, but she also appreciated the fact that he kept it within friendly limits.

"Thanks, and hi, friend of Lara," he told Meg, offering her his hand. Then he turned back to Lara. "I heard your friends from the FBI were here. I've got to admit, I was afraid everything going on here would kill business, but it looks as if we're already pretty much back to normal. Some people are asking about what happened, but that will go on forever, I guess."

"I'd say that the accidental publicity definitely put us on the map," Lara said. "Though maybe not the way we'd like to be."

"This place is wonderful," Meg said.

"It really is. I had this great idea that we put Lara in a bikini and have her ride across the lagoon on a dolphin's back. That would really bring them in. But the bosses didn't go with idea. They're all about dignity around here, go figure."

"Funny, funny, thank you," Lara told him.

"I doubt that my coordination level would be up to the task anyway. Meanwhile, Meg and I have been friends for years, and as you know, she and her partner, Matt, are both with the FBI. They'll be hanging around, with Grady's blessing."

"Glad to have you — feels nice and safe," Myles assured her. "Come on, I'll take you back to meet Dr. Amory and his lovely second, Cathy Barkley."

He led the way to the office behind the classroom, rapping at the door as they entered to herald their arrival. Dr. Amory was busy at his computer while Cathy was sorting through a stack of files. They both looked up, smiled pleasantly and stopped their work to meet Meg.

"Glad to have you here," Dr. Amory said to Meg, standing to shake her hand. "And if you want any information on dolphins, come by any time."

"Seriously, any time," Cathy said. She was in her mid to late thirties, thin, and she wore wire-rimmed glasses and a very studious expression. She explained that she kept medical records on the dolphins and other inhabitants of Sea Life.

"I just love to talk about sea mammals. They're so incredible. Dolphins' life spans vary," Cathy said. "In the wild, luck is a huge factor. Everything depends on how pristine their environment is, the availability of food and whether they run into a predator — or a motorboat. Here, where we can control the environment and provide medical care when necessary, two of our dolphins are in their late forties. In the wild, twenty to twenty-five years is pretty much the norm, and only about one percent of the entire population anywhere makes it to fifty."

Lara thanked Cathy for talking to them about the dolphins and then said that they had to move on so Meg could meet the rest of the staff. They said their thank-yous, then headed over to the café, where Frank Pilaf was at the grill, and Juan Jimenez and Rosa Estancia were taking orders, bringing out food and picking up after those who didn't pick up after themselves. Rosa, a warm and effusive woman, greeted Meg with a hug and a kiss on the cheek. Meg looked a little surprised, but then Juan and Frank did the same. Rosa refused to let them leave until they were armed with bottles of ice-cold water.

"That was quite a welcome," Meg said once they were out of earshot.

"You get used to that down here," Lara said. "It's the Latin influence. Everyone hugs and kisses everyone else."

They paused for a minute at the front enclosure, where Adrianna and Rick were hosting the afternoon show and three of the dolphins were doing a synchronized leap out of the water, delighting the crowd of campers and other visitors. After a minute Lara nudged Meg, and they walked over to the showers and storage area on the far side of the left-hand lagoon. Sue Crane and Justin Villiers were there, collecting the towels the trainers used after their swims.

Sue was in her late twenties, Justin somewhere around thirty. They both had brown hair, but Sue was tiny with a perfect little gamine face, while Justin was very tall and skinny; they made quite a pair when working together.

"Good to have security around," Sue said after Meg had been introduced.

That made Justin frown. "You don't think we're really in danger here, do you?" he asked Sue.

"I wasn't suggesting we're in danger — except from Lara stealing our jobs. You're amazing with Cocoa," Sue said, shaking her head.

"No fear there — I'm much better with words. And Cocoa's the only one of the dolphins who even seems to notice me,"

Lara said.

"Dolphins are really a lot like dogs," Justin said. "You know how dogs seem to know if a person is okay or not? Well, dolphins are the same way. So, Lara, if Cocoa says you're good people, we'll keep you."

After Sue and Justin left to handle the dolphins for the next encounter, Lara turned to Meg. "That's it for full-time staff. We have local college and high school students who come in as volunteers to help out sometimes, but they're not here on an everyday basis, and there's a vet who comes when we call him."

"Everyone seems terrific, and this is a great work environment," Meg said.

"I think so," Lara said. "Were you expecting otherwise? There's no suspicion that anyone from here is involved in what happened."

"It's still good to know who everyone is." Meg paused, then asked, "Now, what about Miguel? When am I going to meet him?"

Lara tilted her head questioningly. "*Miguel Gomez?* Meg, I'm still not sure I really saw a ghost. And even if I did see him, I have no idea how to introduce you to him."

"You saw him in your office doorway, right?"

"Right."

"Then, let's head back there. He probably won't show when there are so many other people around, but you're one of the last to leave, right?"

"Usually, yes."

"We'll make sure that you are tonight," Meg said, then shrugged. "And if he doesn't show up here, maybe he'll come to the house again tonight. If he does, we won't be calling the police on him."

The Diaz-Douglas Mortuary Chapel on Bird Road had been around as long as Brett could remember; Diego also knew the place well, since his great-uncle's wake had recently been held there.

While he and Diego were heading to the funeral home, Matt Bosworth was on his way to the cemetery where they had exhumed Randy Nicholson's empty coffin that morning. He was going to begin interviewing the employees. Someone, somewhere, had to know something, and the cemetery was a convenient place to start.

"It's a pretty smart deal they've got going," Diego told Brett. "When people want their service slanted toward the Anglo side, Douglas handles arrangements. When they speak Spanish, Diaz steps in."

They'd done their homework on the business. It had been founded in 1940 by the current Douglas's grandfather, then passed to his father. When the current Douglas had taken the reins, he'd joined up with Diaz, whose family had been in the funeral business in Cuba before coming to the United States.

The parking lot was almost completely empty, but it was early for viewing hours. The outer reception area was furnished tastefully in beiges and browns, with comfortable couches and chairs offering places for mourners to sit. The end tables all held large boxes of tissues, and there were three stations dispensing bottled water in sight.

As they stood for a minute, letting their eyes adapt from the bright daylight to the dimmer artificial light in the room, a very pretty Latino woman in a blue high-button suit approached them and immediately offered her hand, "Geneva Diaz," she said, and then, without waiting for them to introduce themselves in turn, went on. "Let me bring you right to my husband and Mr. Douglas. We received a call from your office, advising us that you were on the way."

Signs along the hall told mourners whose wake was being held in each room. They passed by a door that said Staff Only. When they'd come in, Brett had noticed a sign pointing toward the "receiving entry," and he was pretty sure that this door led to the embalming room.

Geneva Diaz rapped on the office door before entering. The room held two desks, one for each partner. A nameplate identified the desk to the left as belonging to Richard Diaz, while the second belonged to Jonathan Douglas.

"Gentlemen, we've already been apprised of this strange situation," Douglas said, stepping forward. He was a tall man who seemed somehow colored by his occupation, gray in color from his hair to his skin. His face had bloodhound cheeks and wrinkles, and he looked as if he wore a perpetual mask of sympathy and sadness. "We've gathered everything we have for you. I can't tell you how appalled we are."

Diaz was a younger, shorter man, with bronzed skin, sharp dark eyes and handsome features.

"We can't begin to tell you how upset we are by this situation. We have a reputation for providing exceptionally fine service at a family's most terrible time, and this is just . . . unheard of. Sit down, please."

He indicated two chairs in front of Douglas's desk, then perched on the edge of it while Douglas returned to his seat.

Brett lifted his hands. "We're aware of your sterling reputation, gentlemen," he said. "So how could this have happened?"

Douglas indicated a file. "Here are our records. We made arrangements for pickup from the hospital. When Mr. Nicholson arrived, I met him at Receiving myself and had him brought straight to the embalming room."

"So he *was* embalmed?" Diego asked.

Diaz glanced over at Douglas, and it looked as if he were uncomfortable. "The family requested that he not be." He sighed. "There are laws that deal with embalming, but generally, in a case such as this, the family has a right to refuse. Sometimes funeral directors won't even tell you that — especially if there will be an open casket at the viewing, but Mr. Nicholson's casket was closed." He shrugged uneasily. "Strange, we still call it a viewing when the casket is closed. *Wake.* I guess that's the right word. Or *visitation.* At any rate, his service was held here the night Mr. Nicholson arrived, and he was buried the next day."

"So no embalming and no open casket. Interesting. Where was the body held overnight?" Brett asked.

"It was refrigerated. But I can assure you,

the body was in that casket when it was taken for storage after the viewing."

"Can you explain how we opened an empty coffin, then?" Brett asked.

Both men stared back at Brett, looking both embarrassed and baffled.

"No," Douglas said at last. "I accepted the body, so I know it arrived. He was bathed and dressed in the clothing the family gave us. Then he was placed in his casket and we closed the lid. The entire coffin was kept in what we call the cool room overnight. At ten the next morning, he was transported via the cemetery's hearse to the cemetery and lowered into the ground."

"No one saw the body after it was placed in the coffin on his day of the arrival and the lid was closed?" Diego asked.

"No. There was no reason to open it," Diaz said. "But we are willing to accept responsibility if we are found negligent in any way."

"Except that we weren't," Douglas said. "Whatever happened must have happened at the cemetery or on the way to it."

"But wasn't the coffin sealed then?" Brett asked.

"The coffin *was* sealed at that point. But burial practices at the family's cemetery of choice — as in most local cemeteries these days — require the coffin to be placed in a cement container before burial. That way, if a coffin breaks and there's any leakage of . . . well, leakage, it's contained by the cement. But that sarcophagus isn't added until later, once the family is gone, so for some period of time the casket was available to someone looking to . . . steal the body. As I said, the cemetery sent a vehicle to pick it up — no motorcade, again at the family's request — so anything could have happened along the way." He paused, shaking his head. "However it disappeared, I'm certain that it didn't happen here," he said. He pushed the file folder toward Brett. "All our records, including the names and numbers of all our employees, are here. You've met with the family already, I understand. They are, naturally, threatening to sue us, so I'm hoping, as you can imagine, that you'll be able to discover just what happened."

"How is your security?" Brett asked.

"Well, we have the usual alarms, of course. Customarily, Carl Sage, our head mortician, is here until quite late, sometimes as late as midnight. I haven't embalmed a body in years. Jill Hudson is our best cosmetician, and she works from ten until six. Whoever leaves last at night checks the locks and sets the alarm. Either Richard or I come in sometime between seven and eight the next morning."

"How many keys to the facility?" Diego asked.

"Five," Diaz answered. "Jonathan and I have keys, as does my wife, Geneva, whom you met. And then Jill Hudson and Carl Sage have keys, as well."

"Security tapes?" Brett asked.

"Only in the viewing rooms," Diaz said. "And Mr. Nicholson's coffin was never open in the viewing room," he added regretfully.

"We'd like you to arrange for us to see everyone who works here tomorrow morning at ten," Brett said, rising.

Douglas was upset as he also stood. "Agent, let me assure you again, we work to impeccable standards here. Whatever happened to Mr. Nicholson's body, it happened after his body arrived at the cemetery. You need to investigate and find out what went on."

"Mr. Douglas, if you truly want us to find out the truth and, I hope, clear your establishment, you'll help in any way you can."

"Of course, of course," Diaz said, standing, as well. "We'll have our people here, as you asked."

As he drove out of the parking lot a few minutes later, Brett turned to Diego and asked, "Well?"

"Funeral homes have been in trouble before, but the cases I've heard about had to do with dumping the bodies to use the coffins again. We found Mr. Nicholson's coffin in perfect shape."

"What about Douglas and Diaz?" Brett asked. "What's your impression of them?"

"We've learned a lot about how to spot a liar, and they both seemed to be telling the truth," Diego said. "What about you?"

"I think they're telling the truth, too," Brett said. "But . . . there are all their employees."

"Okay, say one or more of the employees are creating zombies," Diego mused. "How would that connect to Miguel Gomez walking into a warehouse that went up in flames — and somehow getting out alive?"

"Maybe they're not creating zombies, just supplying a body when one is needed," Brett said. "Okay, so here's my theory so far. It's not much, but it fits the facts. This isn't about drug cartels, crime lords or anything else we customarily deal with. Someone out there wants to play God, wants to push every boundary and find out just what he's capable of doing. The Barillo family may be involved — because someone died in that warehouse, and we know it wasn't Miguel Gomez. But Gomez worked for Barillo, and Gomez showed up after his supposed death, behaving strangely, the night his wife was killed. So whoever was involved in reanimating Randy Nicholson's undead body was almost certainly also involved with the reanimation of Miguel Gomez's body, which means he may also be involved with the Barillo family.

"Okay, what else do we know? We know that Nicholson made it to the mortuary from the hospital, because Jonathan Douglas just said that he saw the body. So now we're looking for someone with the connections and the ability to reanimate the supposedly dead. I just wish it was as easy to find him as it was to figure out he exists."

"It really does sound as if we're looking for a mad scientist," Diego said gravely.

Brett frowned. He wanted to disagree, but he really couldn't.

Grady Miller left that afternoon for a meeting with an association of marine-mammal-park owners. Cathy Barkley had left early for a dental appointment, and Nelson Amory and Myles Dawson left at exactly five. A few minutes after that, even the café staff were gone and the gift shop had closed. By six that night the trainers — other than Rick and Adrianna — had cleaned up and taken off for their homes. Lara knew, because she watched them all go from her office window. Rick checked in with her before going out to lock the gate.

"Meg and I are here for a while, Rick," Lara told him. "Some of the other agents are headed back here to meet up with us. I'll come and tell you when we're going to leave."

"Sounds good, but I'll still lock up for now."

"Thanks," she said.

Meg, who was curled in a chair, looked up and thanked Rick, too.

When he was gone, Lara — who had picked up one of the books they had bought that afternoon — looked over at Meg and said, "Did you know that Papa Doc is estimated to have killed over thirty thousand people?" She set the book aside and rose to stretch. "I've read enough history to make my flesh crawl, but I haven't found anything resembling a recipe for creating a zombie."

"I'm not sure there is one," Meg said. "I think it's a combination of factors, starting with someone who has a suggestible mind.

The toxin is part of it, but mind control through fear, that's a part of it, too. And Haiti, especially under Papa Doc, was the perfect cauldron, poor and with a dominant religion that already focuses on the use of herbal substances to put people in a trance, and erase the boundaries between dreams and reality. The thing is, from everything I've read, if puffer fish toxin is used, even if the dead come back, before long they die. The interesting thing is, Randy Nicholson supposedly died months ago, but stayed 'alive' long enough to commit a murder *after* the more recently dead Miguel Gomez killed his wife."

"Well, Miguel *did* die," Lara reminded her. "And I imagine Randy Nicholson will die, too. Unless he's dead already."

"Right," Meg said. "The thing is, will they ever find his body? Or has the killer improved his methods and made sure that we'll never find him?"

Lara shook her head. "I don't know. Did you find out anything from Matt?"

Meg grimaced. "Yeah, I found out that so far no one has found out anything." She forced a smile. "It's all right to go down to the water, isn't it?"

"Of course."

"But you're not supposed to go jumping

in to frolic with the dolphins, right?"

"No, not without their trainers and permission and all that," Lara said. "But we're certainly welcome to sit out on the docks, and it's beautiful this time of evening."

"Right when day turns into night," Meg told her.

They headed out and wandered down to the docks. Cocoa immediately came to the water's edge, clicking out a welcome. Lara slipped out of her shoes and hurried out to the dock, where she could sit and stroke the dolphin when she went by.

Meg stayed back, sitting on one of the benches where visitors sat to watch the shows. As Cocoa went back and forth, entertaining her at first and then just hanging around near her, Lara took in her surroundings. It was still light, since they were on daylight savings time, but there was a different feel to this time of day. The dead heat of the sun had slipped away, especially by the water. The air was cool at last, and that night a soft, sweet breeze was blowing. Looking out, she saw that the water was as calm and smooth as glass. The sky had gone a soft blue, with puffs of clouds that moved along like dancers in a show.

Cocoa rose in the water, letting out a

strange sound.

And Lara felt someone settle next to her.

She was afraid to turn and see who it was. She wanted to believe that it was Meg, but she knew it wasn't. She lowered her head for a minute, praying for courage and inner strength. Then she looked to her side and saw him, the man who had stood in her office doorway and later appeared in her backyard.

Miguel Gomez.

He was there, seemingly solid, and yet she knew he wasn't real. He spoke, saying, "Please" very softly, and with the trace of an accent.

She couldn't respond right away; she couldn't help being afraid.

"You were the one who made sure they knew the truth," he said into the silence.

She managed words at last. "What is the truth? I want to help — I do — but *you* need to help *me* understand."

Miguel looked out over the water, sadness in his eyes, as if he knew that was where his body had been. Where parts of it still remained.

"I loved my wife, and I didn't kill her," he said brokenly.

"I believe you," she said softly. "What happened?"

"I went into the warehouse. I was careful, because I knew someone would be there. One of the Barillo family. I didn't see anyone, but he came up behind me. I felt . . . pain. Then . . . then I knew nothing, until I was looking at Maria's body . . . I was dead, I knew I was dead, and Maria was gone, as well. People said I did it. I hear what goes on. I know someone said he saw me there, but . . ."

His voice trailed off just as Lara started to speak, and then he was gone. He was there — and then he wasn't.

She felt a presence behind her and turned quickly, thinking that Miguel had returned.

But it wasn't him. In the dying sunlight she saw the dark form of Agent Brett Cody, tall and broad shouldered and just standing back, waiting. She wondered if he had seen her talking to someone who wasn't there.

And if he thought the kidnapping that had nearly cost her her life had in fact cost her her sanity instead.

He walked slowly down to the platform and reached down to help her up. When she met his eyes she was surprised to see him looking at her with a strange understanding. His hand on hers felt strong, and as the gaze continued, she suddenly felt as if she knew him far better than she should.

And that he knew her just as deeply.

She didn't realize that she was still holding his hand until Meg hurried over to join them. "Lara? Are you all right?"

She really didn't begin to understand how Brett Cody's nearness seemed to give her strength, but somehow it did.

"I'm fine," she said.

"I saw him. Miguel. I saw him here with you," Meg said.

She knew that they were waiting for what she had to say, hoping he had said something that could help them solve the mystery.

She realized that Matt must have just arrived, because he was standing just behind Meg, and she saw Rick and Adrianna in the distance, walking toward them in the growing dusk.

"Did he say anything useful?" Brett asked.

"He said that he didn't know from the time someone hit him from behind in the warehouse until he was in his house. He knew he was dead, and he knew that Maria was dead, too. He said he knows people think he did it."

"Hey!" Rick called to them.

"Hey," Lara echoed as he and Adrianna joined the group. "I'm going to head out with these guys. I just need to run up and get my things. Will you lock up when we leave?"

Adrianna smiled. "Of course. You were saying good-night to Cocoa, huh? If you have some time tomorrow afternoon, you can do a training session with her and me if you want to."

"That would be great," Lara said.

Rick turned to Brett. "Have you found out anything yet about what's going on?"

"We're working on it," Brett assured him.

"You guys aren't worried about being out here alone, are you?" Lara asked Adrianna.

"No, honestly, we're not. Once you're gone, we'll set the alarms. You don't think we should be worried, do you?" Adrianna asked.

"No, no, of course not," Lara said. "Right?" she asked, looking at the others.

"I don't believe that this facility or anyone here is in any danger," Brett said. "But if you're at all worried —"

"Lock and load. I have a licensed Colt," Rick said. "We're good. I have the cops on speed dial, not to mention our alarm buttons, which are everywhere, just in case we need them. We don't have security personnel here, but our alarm system calls the police with the push of a button, and they can be here within minutes."

"Okay, then," Lara said. "I'll be right back."

Meg followed her back to her office. "You really okay?" she asked.

"Fine, honestly."

"You seem anxious to leave."

"I just talked to a ghost. That's not a normal day at the beach for me."

"Okay. You look rattled. I'll drive your car. Matt has our rental and Brett has his own car, so they can follow us."

"I'm good to drive, and I know where I'm going," Lara assured her. "But I'll be happy to take you with me."

Meg studied her. "I guess you are all right. Let's go, then."

Lara *was* all right, and she proved it. She drove smoothly and competently to her house; the traffic had died down, so it only took a few minutes. Matt was right behind her, and when they'd parked and were approaching her duplex she said apologetically, "I haven't really been here long enough to do much with the place, so . . ."

"I've been in my house for years and I haven't done much with it, either," Brett said. "And don't worry, we're not expecting you to cook for us. We'll order some dinner — or am I the only one who's starving?"

"Dinner sounds great," Matt said.

223

Brett suggested Chinese and everyone agreed, so he took requests and ordered once they were inside. After that Lara asked what people wanted to drink, and they all opted for iced tea. Apparently everyone wanted a clear head in case Miguel showed up again.

Lara went to get the tea, and when she finished she found them all in the family room. Meg and Matt had taken the wicker sofa with its overstuffed cushions, which left her and Brett the matching chairs facing it across the coffee table.

Brett started the conversation as soon as she sat down, turning to her and diving in without preliminaries. "I have the feeling you were pretty unnerved today. Talking to a dead man."

She wasn't sure what to say. He was the one who had pulled up the picture of Miguel Gomez and asked her if he was the man she'd seen, so obviously he wasn't fazed by the idea of people talking to ghosts. But he was right: *she* was.

"I —"

"It's all right," he said flatly, looking from her to Meg and Matt. "Because I think I'm seeing a ghost of my own." He met Lara's eyes again. "Miguel has decided that he needs to communicate with you." For a long moment he was silent, and then he said, "And apparently, Maria Gomez has decided that she wants to speak with me."

9

Strange how life was so often all about perception, Brett thought.

He had been living with a tension unlike anything he'd known before, as if his muscles had been twisted like burning wire and then hardened that way.

But later that night, sitting on the back porch of Lara's apartment, he sat back and realized that he should have been thinking like Sir Arthur Conan Doyle's Sherlock Holmes.

When you have eliminated the impossible, whatever remains, however improbable, *must be the truth.*

He'd respected Matt Bosworth from the time he'd met him, and he'd heard the news when Matt joined the Krewe. He'd also heard the snide remarks people made and the nickname Ghost Posse, but he knew that despite the attitude behind the asides, the Krewe were called in whenever something "different" came up — and when others failed.

And that night, because the Krewe were there and because Lara had been so open about her own experiences, it was all right that he read strange messages on his computer and that Maria's ghost had shown up in his bedroom.

They ate Chinese food out of the cartons and talked about the case and its similarity to past cases Matt and Meg had worked. He was sitting close to Lara, and when she looked at him now and then, he could feel the strange connection that he couldn't deny was growing between them. He frowned when Meg and Lara talked about visiting the voodoo store. He wasn't worried that they'd gone to the store or talked to Papa Joe. He had met a number of people who practiced voodoo through the years — good people, all of them.

It was Lara's involvement in the case that bothered him.

Then again, he was the one who had gotten her involved so deeply.

Neither Miguel nor Maria made an appearance during dinner. But he learned exactly what had happened to Lara, the truth behind all the press surrounding her abduction and the Walker scandal, and his admiration for her grew. She'd endured so much. She'd been kidnapped by a serial killer, held prisoner under god-awful circumstances, and yet she had survived. And now this.

Perception. It was everything, really.

He had thought of Lara as an extremely attractive woman. Any man would have found her appealing, even in a city where beautiful women could be found in abundance.

But now . . .

Now he also saw her as strong. Now . . .

Now her smile turned his insides molten.

He didn't want to leave her — not even with her best friend, not even with agents he trusted.

And now he felt even more determined to solve this case.

It was growing late, and despite the fact that he was actually working and his line of work didn't adhere to an eight-hour day, he needed to sleep, and that meant he needed to leave.

At last he regretfully stood. "Tomorrow is going to be another long day. I've got to get home. Thank you, Matt and Meg, for your help. And thank *you,* Lara. You've been great through all of this."

She smiled, rising. "Thanks. Is home far?"

"Not even five miles. If you ever want a brisk walk in the blazing heat, I'm in South Miami, just past the Gables." As soon as he said the words, he wondered what had gotten into him.

Matt stood, too, and said to Brett, "We'll be at Sea Life in the morning, and I'll meet you at the cemetery around one. I'm going to try to find connections between all these people — the staff at the funeral home, the dead we know about — and the Barillo family. I know the local task force is working it, but I also know your Special Agent Bryant isn't getting anywhere and his informants aren't giving him anything useful, so since Meg and I are here, we're going to help if we can."

"All help appreciated," Brett replied. "And I can't help but thinking that this might be an unwitting conspiracy."

"What's that?" Lara asked.

"What I mean is that a number of people might be doing things that are illegal without any idea how their efforts are being combined for a much larger — and deadlier — end," Brett said. "Someone may be supplying whatever drugs and poison are being used. Someone else may have been bribed or blackmailed into supplying a body. A third person may be sharing the know-how without any idea that someone is actually using it. So the more connections we can make between any of the players, the better."

"In other words, if we start at the end of the string, it may lead us to another string, then another, and eventually they'll lead us to the spool of thread," Meg said.

"So is there any indication that Miguel or Maria Gomez knew Randy Nicholson or anyone at the Diaz-Douglas funeral home, or anyone at the cemetery?" Lara asked.

"No. Miguel might not even have known anyone else involved. Except the Barillo family. Because I know they're in on it somehow," Brett said. "There's no other way things could have gone down that way in the warehouse unless someone in the Barillo family was involved. No one else would have known he would be there."

"What about his family?" Matt suggested.

Brett shook his head. "No, Maria loved her husband, and Miguel made sure his children and grandchildren were far away after he contacted the FBI — even when he caved and started working for Barillo, he wanted his children and grandchildren living elsewhere. They're out in the Midwest, and they've agreed to stay where they are until we've gotten some answers. They're not happy about it, but they understand it's a safety issue."

He told them all good-night at the gate, wishing he felt entirely sure that Lara would be all right even as he told himself it was foolish to want to stay. As an agent, he'd quickly learned that no man was an island. They depended on one another. Trusted one another. They had to. He was usually pretty good at it; it was pure ego to think he was the only one who could manage any particular task.

But this was different. Still, he managed to leave, his fingers lingering on Lara's as she shut the gate, his eyes meeting hers. "Good night. You're in good hands," he told her.

She smiled and nodded. He thought that maybe she was wishing he could stay, too.

Or was that just wishful thinking on his part?

He got into his car and drove home. As he neared his house, he saw that a car was parked in front of his neighbor's house, and there were men just sitting in it.

Watching his house.

An assassination team? he wondered.

He told himself for the second time that night that no man was an island. It was late, but he sat in his own car down the street, lights off, and felt for his Glock and his phone. He dialed Diego.

Diego answered right away, instantly alert, even though Brett was sure he'd been sleeping.

"Men in front of my neighbor's house," Brett said.

"I'm on my way. Should I call for backup?"

"No, this time of night, you should only be five minutes. I'm parked down the street, and let's leave the line open."

"On my way."

Brett set the phone on the seat next to him. He didn't get out of the car — he would be an easy target if they spotted him — just sat, watched and waited.

A moment later the other car's driver's door opened; a man stepped out and walked around, then opened the passenger-side door. He reached in to help a second man out.

It was Barillo. Even in the dark, Brett knew. He'd seen video and pictures of the man often enough.

The two men walked over to where he was parked. So much for hiding in the shadows, Brett thought.

"Agent Cody," Barillo called.

Brett drew his Glock and stepped out of

232

the car. Barillo lifted his hands. The younger man at his side did the same. They weren't holding weapons, though Brett was certain that one of them, at least, was armed.

"What?" he asked, Glock aimed at the older man.

"There's no need for that," Barillo said to him. "I came in person to tell you that you don't need to be afraid of me."

"I'm not afraid of you," Brett said.

"Then, you're *estupido*!" the other man said angrily.

Barillo nudged him, and the man went silent.

"I'm here to tell you I don't murder women," Barillo said. "And I didn't kill Miguel. You need to look somewhere else and find out what is going on. I came here in peace. I'm old. I'm done with my old ways. Do you understand? If you want to catch a killer, you need to look elsewhere. I came in person to tell you. That's all. Good night, Agent Cody."

Barillo turned around and headed back to the car. Brett watched him go. The man was in his mid-sixties, though he looked at least fifteen years older. When his name was said, people imagined a tough virile man who could take down half an army.

That wasn't the Barillo Brett had seen tonight.

I'm old, he'd said.

He was more than old, Brett thought. He was also sick.

The Barillo car drove away and disappeared down the street. As Brett stood by his own car staring after it, he saw Diego round the corner in his beloved old BMW.

Diego slammed to a stop and jumped out of the car. "Gone?" he asked.

Brett nodded. "Barillo and a younger man, maybe forty, forty-five," he told Diego. "Oddest thing. I was afraid of an ambush when I stepped out of the car, but he came out to tell me 'face-to-face' that he didn't kill Maria *or* Miguel."

"I wonder why it's so important to this guy that we believe he didn't kill Miguel," Diego said. "Or why he's so focused on you."

"Maybe he knows that Miguel came to me. We have informants, they have informants," Brett said. "I've never seen the younger man. Some lieutenant, probably."

"Must be, since he keeps his kids out of the family business."

"What a good father," Brett said.

"Do you think it was a ploy, something to get us off his tail?" Diego asked.

"No," Brett said thoughtfully. "I actually don't. He seemed sincere."

"Lots of criminals seem sincere — the same way murderers find Christ just before they go up in front of a parole board," Diego said.

That was true enough, Brett knew. "Come on in. Might as well get out of the street."

At his door, Brett keyed in the alarm code and they went inside. "Want coffee or something?" he asked.

"Coffee? I'm still dreaming of getting something called sleep for part of the night," Diego told him. "I'll take a water, though."

Brett grabbed a bottle of water for Diego and made himself a cup of coffee. It wouldn't keep him awake once he lay down to sleep, he knew.

The two of them sat on the stools at the kitchen breakfast bar.

"You know what struck me as odd?" Brett asked.

"Besides dead men going around killing people?"

"Barillo himself. He's a shell of a man. Quite frankly, he looks weak in every way. How does a shriveled little man like that command such an empire? I think he has something, Diego, some kind of disease. I wish I knew what it was."

Diego shrugged. "Heart disease? Cancer?"

"I don't know, but it was interesting. The man with him was twice his size and plainly hostile, but Barillo shut him up effortlessly."

"Like *The Godfather*. There can be only one don until the don steps aside."

"Well, I doubt it will be one of the sons," Brett said. "According to Bryant, there are three kids. Jeremy is going for his law degree. Apparently he'd like to go into politics, but I think his father's reputation will put an end to those ambitions. Then there's Felipe. Smart kid — he's in anatomy or something premed like that. Anthony Barillo himself has a medical degree, not that he uses it now. Maybe everything Felipe does is to impress his old man, who knows. Then there's the daughter, Cecelia. She's about thirty and already has master's degrees in two fields, I forget what, and she's going for a third. It really *is* like *The Godfather*. He's a major crime lord, but he wants his kids to be above reproach — like Michael Corleone. Of course, Michael wound up being the one to take over the family. Maybe Barillo's kids are starting to feel the pressure, too. The man who called me the other night said 'my father.' The guy tonight was too old to be either of the sons, though. Maybe it was his brother."

"Barillo's brother?"

Brett nodded. "Now that I think about it, it could be his youngest brother, Tomas. There were originally four brothers, but one died of natural causes and one died in a shoot-out. Tomas is the youngest, and Bryant thinks he's being groomed to take over, not that Barillo has loosened his grip by a millimeter."

"Sounds almost like a royal dynasty. When Anthony Barillo is gone, it will be like, 'The king is dead, long live the king!' No wonder poor Bryant has been at it so hard all these years. They have to root out the whole dynasty if they're going to have a real effect." Diego yawned.

Brett remembered that he'd roused his partner from a sound sleep and shook his head. "You want to just sleep here?" he asked.

"No, that's okay. I'd only have to get up early and go home to shower and change." Diego indicated the old AC/DC T-shirt he was wearing. "They'll frown on it if I come to work like this. I'll take off and see you in a few hours."

"Thanks for the backup."

"You'd have my back, too, *amigo,*" Diego said.

Brett saw him out to his car, and he didn't head inside and lock up until Diego was out of sight.

It was disturbing that Barillo had come to his house. Despite the job, agents didn't usually fear for their own lives unless they were in armed pursuit; it just didn't pay for criminals to attack them. Law enforcement never came after you with greater ferocity than if you killed a fellow officer.

He set his alarms and double-checked that his Glock held a full clip before going to bed. His head was filled with questions and theories as he tried to sleep — and in the middle of every one he found himself thinking about Lara Ainsworth Mayhew.

He thought about her eyes.

And then her body.

Her smile.

And the way he had felt when she was so close to him in her swimsuit, nearly touching, when they'd been in the water and on the boat.

She was still on his mind when he finally fell asleep.

He woke with a jerk, dreaming about Lara in a way he shouldn't have, but his dream vanished as he came instantly alert, almost as if someone had poked him. Instinctively

238

he reached out, ready to grab his Glock, though with the alarms set it should have been impossible for anyone to get in without him knowing.

There was no danger. Even as he noticed the shadowy figure at the foot of his bed, he knew there was no danger.

Maria Gomez was back, looking at him with eyes filled with sadness.

Looking at him . . . and asking for his help without speaking a word.

When she did speak, she said nothing new.

"Miguel did it . . . It was Miguel, and yet it was not Miguel."

"I know, Maria," he said, wondering if he was imagining things because he'd gotten so damned obsessed with this case. "Maria, I know he loved you. He never would have hurt you — not if he was himself."

The ghostly woman shimmered in and out of focus. And then she said, "Please. Please . . ."

The first pale sliver of morning light seeped through the drapes. For one minute more, she was there.

And then she was gone.

Lara thought it would be impossible to concentrate on her job, but throughout the morning she worked on the plans for the

Sunday event, sending out emails to their members, replying to veterans who wanted to know what to expect, addressing their special concerns.

She thought that Meg would be bored to tears, but she wasn't; she was on her laptop the whole time, wrapped up in what she was doing.

At about eleven-thirty they were interrupted when Lara received a call from the front; Sonia Larson was there to see her.

"One of our sponsors," she explained to Meg. "A major sponsor — she loves the place and donates heavily."

"Tax write-off?" Meg asked.

"Well, it's a tax write-off for everyone, but I've seen Sonia at the lagoons. She really does love the dolphins."

"You *are* talking Sonia Larson the fashion queen, aren't you?"

Lara laughed. "I think she's more like a goddess. You'll see."

Meg did.

Sonia walked into Lara's office loaded down with bags bearing her company logo. She smiled with genuine pleasure on being introduced to Meg and apologized because she didn't have anything for her. "But I have a feeling this one shares," Sonia said, beaming at Lara.

Among many other things, she'd brought Lara a slightly daring bikini and matching lace-edged cover-up in a rich blue with just a hint of green.

"Matches your eyes perfectly," she said.

"This is lovely. And I thank you so much. But I'm not sure I'm supposed to accept gifts like this," Lara said. "And aren't you supposed to be in Rio?"

Sonia waved a hand in the air. "You're not going to believe this, but they had to put the show back a week. It's one of the biggest in the world, but Jean Paul Genet — the host, you've heard of him, yes?"

Lara and Meg had both heard of him — yes! He had a makeup line, a perfume line, a clothing line and now he was designing yachts and cars.

"Well, anyway, the man got sick. So they have postponed the show. It's all right with me. My schedule is my own. So I'm here and able to bring you a few presents."

"And you'll be here on Sunday?" Lara asked. "It would be wonderful if you can. The soldiers would be so thrilled."

"I *will* come," Sonia promised her. "But you wear the bikini I brought you and they'll be more thrilled with you."

Lara smiled. "Well, thank you. But we're required to wear our regular wetsuits, and

I'm not even sure I'll be in the water at all. I'm media. The trainers are the ones who'll work with the vets and the dolphins. You're a celebrity. They'll love seeing you."

Sonia smiled. "I understand about the suit. And if you think I will do some good by being here, of course I'll come. But for now I have a doctor's appointment and my chauffeur is waiting."

"Is anything wrong?" Lara asked, worried.

"No, no. I have an irregular heartbeat, so I see Dr. Treme for regular monitoring. I had to cancel my next appointment, but luckily he was able to fit me in today."

"Treme?" Meg said.

"He's the best down here," Sonia said. She blew kisses. "I must go, but I will see you on Sunday."

As soon as Sonia left, Lara looked at Meg, frowning. "What's bothering you about Dr. Treme?" she asked.

"He's the doctor who signed Randy Nicholson's death certificate."

"Should we stop her?" Lara asked nervously.

"No. He's probably not guilty of anything. The man flatlined, and an entire group of medical personnel thought he was dead."

"But . . . ?"

"I'll call Matt and Brett," Meg said.

242

"Perfect," Lara said, jumping up.

"Where are you going?" Meg asked her.

"To stop Sonia. I'll get her to postpone, tell her I could use her help thinking about next season's gala," Lara said. "Just to be safe."

Meg nodded. "A conspiracy of the unwitting," she murmured.

Diego, Matt and Brett stood in the offices of the Diaz-Douglas funeral home, along with the entire staff. They went over the events that had followed the arrival of Randy Nicholson's body at the mortuary. Every employee seemed equal parts stunned, scared and mystified. They'd been there for thirty minutes, and all they'd ascertained so far was that yes, the body had arrived. Many of the employees had seen it, but since the family hadn't wanted embalming or an open casket, there had been no need for anything beyond cleaning and dressing the body, then laying it in the silk-lined coffin his children had chosen. That meant, as Mr. Douglas had explained, most of them had no actual contact with it.

"All right," Brett said. "Who prepared Mr. Nicholson for the coffin?"

Carl Sage lifted his hand. "I cleaned and dressed Mr. Nicholson," he said. "I laid him in the coffin, and I sealed the coffin. And I can tell you, when I did so, Mr. Nicholson was in it. Two of our ushers, Mike Bitter and Victor Menendez, helped me set it in place for the service. We also saw that it was transported from the funeral home to the cemetery. I'm telling you, they did not take the body, and neither did I."

"What about the night the body stayed at the mortuary?" Brett asked.

"I was here until quite late, as usual, but I locked up when I left," Carl said.

"Anyone else? After closing, I mean," Matt asked.

"We were all here for a while," Carl said. "The ushers leave first, but Mr. Douglas and Mr. Diaz were here for a while. And Mrs. Diaz," he added. "When they left, I locked up and then went to my office."

"May I see your office?" Brett asked.

Carl looked at his bosses. Both men nodded grimly.

It was odd, Brett thought as Carl led him, with Diego and Matt, with Diaz and Douglas following, through the employees-only area, that while he'd attended many autopsies, he'd never been behind the scenes at a mortuary. They passed by the embalming room, where several bodies were in various stages of preparation.

244

Somehow, he found this place sadder even than autopsy. In an autopsy, doctors worked to discover cause of death. To speak for the dead.

While here . . .

The soul was gone, but every pretense was taken to pretend the dead weren't really gone. A makeup set on a tray sat by a stainless-steel gurney holding the remains of an older woman.

No amount of makeup would change the fact that she would never look like herself again. The internal spark that had made her who she was had fled.

They moved past the embalming room and stood in the doorway of Carl's office. The small room held a desk, a computer, filing cabinets — the usual accoutrements of any office, although this one also held a collection of books on embalming, and the reconstruction and cosmetic preparation of bodies. There was also a thick book of Florida statutes on proper and legal burial procedures.

But it wasn't the office itself that interested Brett. It was the fact that the office was at the far end of the hall, near the funeral home's receiving bay. But if the office door was closed, the bay doors could easily be opened and closed — and someone in the office would be none the wiser.

"Do you keep your door shut when you're in here?" Brett asked Carl.

"Yeah. I turn on my music and do my paperwork," Carl said. He seemed puzzled by their question.

Matt walked to the end of the hall and the receiving doors. Diego closed the office door.

"What's going on?" Diaz demanded.

"There are only five people with keys?" Brett asked him.

"Yes, I told you. Myself, Jonathan, my wife, Carl and Jill," Diaz said. "Why?"

"Because I think someone opened that door and let somebody in, somebody who took Randy Nicholson's body from the mortuary," Brett said.

"That's just not possible." Douglas sounded genuinely indignant.

"I think it's time we stopped cooperating and called our attorneys," Diaz said.

The only way Lara could legitimately think of to stop Sonia from going to her appointment was to come up with something else for her to do, so she told her that Meg was crazy about her designs and really wanted to take her to lunch. It was a bit hard to persuade Sonia to agree, but in the end she agreed to reschedule her checkup for a second time. Given her semi-celebrity status, Dr. Treme's office was more than happy to oblige.

Lara raced back to brief Meg on her "role," and then they joined Sonia outside. Her chauffeur drove them over the causeway to South Beach.

The area had a character all its own, a faded elegance left over from the days of Sinatra and Al Capone, who had both spent time here. The hotels had weathered through the years, and the local kids had come in droves to ride waves that really weren't there. High-class restaurants and nightclubs had been replaced by coffee shops and bagelries. Then a boom had hit. The old deco hotels had been recognized as the treasures they were, painted and spruced up, and high-end restaurants and clubs had made a comeback.

The problem with the beach now was parking, but they didn't have to worry about that, since Sonia's chauffeur would drop them off, then come back for them when Sonia called.

They opted to stroll along Lincoln Road Mall and choose a restaurant at random. Options were plentiful, along with shops, a movie theater, a bookstore — and dozens of dogs. The open-air mall was known for being pet friendly. All three of them were dog fans, and they stopped to compliment so many dogs that Lara was afraid she would be gone so long that she would miss a full afternoon of work.

Sonia finally chose a restaurant, and of course she knew the owners. They were shown to a special table and offered a select champagne. Lara and Meg demurred — they were working — but encouraged Sonia to enjoy.

Sonia, meanwhile, was delighted with the whole event. "Lunch with girlfriends! This is something I never get to do," she told them.

As they ordered and ate, Lara thought she understood why. Sonia was approached several times by people who wanted their pictures taken with her.

Sonia explained that she always tried to be obliging when people recognized her. "I met Versace once when I was young. People loved him because he was always so available. He lived on the beach. He had breakfast at the News Café. He was a man of the people, and I want to be the same."

Lara realized that she really liked Sonia. The woman was a bundle of sincere energy. Glancing at Meg, she knew that her friend was thinking the same. While Meg had always been hell-bent on her law enforcement career, Lara had intended to save the world through politics. Their friends hadn't often been fashionistas.

It wasn't until they were almost ready to leave that Lara noticed Ely Taggerly having lunch with three other men in a dark corner of the restaurant. Ely was nodding vehemently as he spoke, making some kind of point. He was clearly aggravated. Lara hadn't seen him angry before, but then she'd only seen him at Sea Life, and the facility seemed to have a calming effect on everyone.

It wasn't until Ely shifted in his chair that Lara realized one of the men he was having lunch with was Sea Life's own Nelson Amory. Amory, too, looked annoyed.

"Look who's here!" Sonia said, noticing the men at that moment, and before anyone could stop her, she hurriedly swept through the restaurant to their table.

As Lara quickly rushed to get ahead of the temperamental woman, intent on averting a potentially disastrous encounter if she could, she saw that the other men at the table were two of their other benefactors, Grant Blackwood and Mason Martinez.

"Good afternoon, gentlemen," Lara said

breathlessly as Sonia came up behind her. "How nice to see you all together. Are you planning a new line of vitamins for dolphin health?" she teased.

"No, no, of course not," Dr. Amory said, rising. Lara was certain that he was drawing out his answer because he was thinking up a lie.

"We're all planning on being at your Sunday event," Grant said. By then, all four men had risen.

"And in the meantime, I'm trying to squeeze more money out of them for research," Dr. Amory said.

They were lying — she was sure of it — but why lie to her? Maybe one of them was trying to persuade Dr. Amory to leave Sea Life and work for him instead?

Maybe later she would walk down to the education building and ask Dr. Amory straight out.

"Well, keep squeezing," she said cheerfully.

"He's pretty good at it," Ely told her, smiling benignly.

He always appeared to be the perfect gentleman, but Grady had told her once that even though they always saw him as kind and smiling, he was hell in a boardroom. He'd built his pharmaceutical company from nothing, and his scientists had done a lot of groundbreaking work with diseases like Parkinson's and Alzheimer's.

He'd made a small fortune on his drug patents, and he'd told her once that all drug companies changed things up just a little now and then to keep their patents in force. "After the money and effort we put into developing them? We don't like to see the generic showing up two seconds later."

As nice as he'd always been to her, though, she felt uneasy now, certain that she and Sonia — who was smiling and chatting, she noticed, completely oblivious to the undertone Lara had picked up on — had interrupted something they shouldn't have.

"Who is that pretty young woman waiting for you?" Grant asked, slurring slightly. A glance at the table showed that it had probably been a three-martini lunch for him.

"My friend Meg," Lara said. "She's with the FBI, but she's down here for a while."

"Well, isn't that too bad?" Blackwood said with a laugh. "Anyway, I think she's getting impatient. You fillies oughta mosey along."

"We're not fillies, Grant," Sonia said. "You show some respect."

"Yes, ma'am!" he agreed, grinning.

Sonia rolled her eyes. "We'll see you on Sunday — enjoy your lunch," she said.

251

"See you Sunday," Lara echoed. They rejoined Meg at the table, where she had waited.

"Meg, you didn't join us," Sonia said.

"I was afraid to make us any later. Lara has to be back at work," Meg said, standing and tucking a receipt into her wallet, having apparently paid the check while they were talking to the men.

But Lara also knew exactly what her friend had really been doing.

Watching. She had realized that Lara felt disturbed.

"Just as well. Blackwood is a douche," Sonia said, looking at Lara as if for confirmation.

"I'm not saying a word," Lara said.

Sonia laughed. "Let's go, then. I'll call Henri and we'll head back. This was delightful. I hope we can do it again."

"That would be nice," Lara assured her.

"Absolutely," Meg agreed.

Twenty minutes later, back in Lara's office, Meg closed the door and turned to her. "Okay, tell me about them — all of them."

"You met Dr. Amory, and all the men he was with are big supporters of Sea Life. Grant Blackwood is a Texan pain in the ass who tries to pick up just about every woman

252

he meets, even though he's married. A lot of women are flattered and fall for his line, and they don't care about his wife because he's not just rich, he's filthy rich. Ely Taggerly is the founder and CEO of Taggerly Pharmaceuticals. And the last guy was Mason Martinez, the health guru. You must have seen him on at least one of a dozen of his infomercials for vitamins or exercise equipment."

"Yeah, I thought I recognized him. So they were with Amory because he was trying to hit them up for money?"

Lara shrugged. "So he claimed."

"But you didn't believe him?" Meg asked.

Lara shook her head. "He looked guilty. I think maybe one of them was trying to hire him away from Sea Life. He's a brilliant man. He has doctorates in marine biology and veterinary medicine. He's done all kinds of research. Before he came here he was with the military. They still use dolphins in some missions. The animal-rights activists aren't happy about it, and I think maybe he came here precisely because we're all about learning what the dolphins themselves need." She frowned. "Why? Are you suspicious of him for some reason?"

"I'm always suspicious of everyone," Meg said. "And pieces of Miguel Gomez's body were found in this lagoon."

"Dr. Amory would never be guilty of that. I can't believe he could kill, and even if he was capable of murder, he wouldn't want his dolphins in a lagoon that was contaminated in any way."

"Still, it's an interesting situation," Meg said. "I think I should find out a little more about Dr. Amory *and* your sponsors."

"I know Dr. Amory well, and the others I'm getting to know, and I don't think any of them would —"

Meg cut her off. "I believe you. But remember what Brett said about an unwitting conspiracy."

"But there's no reason whatsoever to suspect anyone at Sea Life," Lara protested. "Those body parts don't mean anything. The ocean is huge!"

"Precisely," Meg said.

10

Arnold Wilhelm's cause of death was no mystery. Three teens had seen him thrown in front of an oncoming train, which had knocked him to the ground below like a rag doll. As to Miguel Gomez, Dr. Phil Kinny was still inspecting slides and studying lab reports. He wasn't quite sure what some of the chemical combinations he'd discovered were, but the end result was that while the cognitive section of the brain had been destroyed, the part that controlled rudimentary memory movement had apparently been fully functioning for some time between his first "death" in the warehouse and his actual death.

"If I only had another specimen to compare him to," Kinny told Brett, before quickly apologizing. "I'm sorry. Miguel Gomez was a human being, and I'm not trying to take that away from him. I *am* trying to help solve his murder. To that end, if we were just able to find out what's happened to Randy Nicholson, I believe I could make further strides. In the meantime, I have our best neuro experts conferring with me on this."

Brett couldn't help but feel as if he had burst into a twisted version of *The Princess Bride*. A man could be mostly dead but not completely dead. Then *The Princess Bride* segued into a horror version of *The Wizard of Oz*.

If I only had another brain . . .

He and Diego had spent the day at the funeral home with Matt, and then the three of them had gone to the cemetery. Brett was growing more and more certain that Randy Nicholson's body had disappeared from the funeral parlor, and not on the way to the cemetery or after its arrival. They'd found too many witnesses to attest to the coffin being sealed before being encased in cement. Diaz and Douglas had lawyered up, but under the circumstances, until they found direct evidence rather than plausible theory, there were no charges they could bring against the mortuary anyway.

The only thing in their favor right now was the power of social media. Randy Nicholson's family was more than happy to vent their grievances online, and it was bound to have an effect, which might force Diaz and Douglas to be more forthcoming. After all, who wanted to bury a loved one out of a funeral home that didn't actually get the dead into the ground?

By the end of the afternoon he'd traipsed over more ground and spoken with more people than he could count, and that was even with dividing the question-and-answer sessions with Matt and Diego. And none of it had turned up anything useful. He was convinced that someone at the Diaz-Douglas Mortuary Chapel knew more than they were saying; however, unless someone cracked under the pressure and gave him a clue, there was nothing he could do except keep investigating.

At six o'clock Matt suggested that they call it quits, at least for dinner and a breather. Just as Brett was about to agree, he got a call from Lara.

"Brett, Papa Joe just called me. He wants to meet — with me, I mean, and I told him about you, so he wants you there, too. And Meg, of course. He asked us to meet him at a little place called La Petite Bar. He doesn't want to make a big deal out of it, so he's going to come with a selection of jewelry to make it look as if he's trying to sell something to us."

"Papa Joe, who owns the voodoo store?" Brett asked.

"Yes. He says he may have some pertinent information."

Brett was thoughtful for a moment. "I'll come get you and Meg, and I'll ask Diego and Matt to follow at a distance, then pull surveillance from outside or even inside, whatever they think will work. Where are you? At Sea Life?"

"No, we're at my house."

"Okay, I'm on my way."

He filled the others in as they headed for their cars.

"This guy obviously feels he's taking a chance," Brett said quietly. "I don't want to put a spotlight on him."

"He could be guilty of something," Diego commented.

"I don't think so," Brett told him. "He called Lara more or less out of the blue. We have absolutely nothing on the man, no reason to connect him to this case or anything else. I think he's just trying to do the right thing."

Diego shrugged. "I saw an article about him once. He's a leader in the Haitian community, works with youth groups, that kind of thing. I'll go with your faith in the man — with some careful reservations."

"Careful reservations are always good," Matt said.

They had two cars, Brett and Diego's Bureau vehicle, which Brett took, and Matt's rental. Diego and Matt would hang behind in the rental.

Brett called Lara back, and she and Meg were waiting by the gate when he arrived. He watched her as she walked to the car. She had dressed in jeans and a knit pullover. Casual wear, not designed to be provocative. And yet she moved with such natural elegance that not even a hazmat suit could be less than seductive on her. When she and Meg reached the car, he thought drily that there was no way he could be seen with these two women and not be noticed.

Meg stopped before getting into the car. "I was just thinking, I should ride in the backup car, too. There are people who might be watching you — just because of everything that's going on — who know that I'm an agent. Thanks to Sonia Larson, some of those same people think Brett and Lara are a couple. It's more natural for the two of them to be out together."

"She's got a point," Diego said.

"All right," Brett said. "We'll make your apologies to Papa Joe."

As Meg headed back to join Diego and

Matt, Lara slid into the passenger seat.

She was wearing a light perfume, subtle rather than the overwhelming scents so many women chose. It immediately insinuated itself through his system and intoxicated his senses.

Yep, beyond a doubt, he was now totally infatuated with her. He felt a raw longing unlike anything he'd felt in a very long time. If ever.

It wasn't just her looks. Not just her eyes, her voice, her scent.

Maybe it was chemistry.

He couldn't help but wonder if she could tell how he felt it or if she still thought he had a stick up his ass.

He forced himself to focus on the matter at hand. "Lara, you don't have to do this. I could just take Meg with me to meet Papa Joe."

Lara shook her head. "No, I have to go," she said. "Miguel came to *me* for help."

Whatever she felt about him, he could tell that Lara had been touched by this case just as he had. He'd been obsessed from the get-go, of course, because he'd known both Miguel and Maria. But now it seemed that she knew Miguel, too. And she probably felt that she would never sleep well again if she didn't do everything she could to help bring a killer to justice.

He knew he could stop her, *should* stop her.

But knowing how she felt, he couldn't bring himself to do it.

He studied her wide eyes and determined features, and he nodded.

It wasn't much of a drive to the small family-owned restaurant where they were due to meet up with Papa Joe. La Petite Bar was just between Biscayne Drive and 2nd Avenue, on the border between the Design District and an area of Little Haiti that had yet to be fully reclaimed from drugs and poverty. The place was busy, with clientele of all colors, and judging by the conversations he overheard, they were of all nationalities, as well. The sign out front had proclaimed the best Creole food this side of New Orleans, and as he looked around, Brett figured it had to be true.

A small woman had met them at the door, and seeing that Papa Joe had yet to arrive, Brett told her that they were being joined by a third person. As she led them to a vinyl-covered table in the back he glanced over his shoulder and saw that the others had scored a parking place right out front. Once he sat down he checked out the menu. The prices were reasonable, and the place smelled great. While they waited for Papa Joe they ordered sweet tea to drink.

He leaned in toward Lara once their server was gone and said softly, "I shouldn't have let you come. In fact, my supervisors would probably ream me out for this. This is the most bizarre case I've ever been on, and I don't know just how dangerous it may get. If Papa Joe were to come in here with a gun and start shooting, I'm not sure I could throw myself on you quickly enough to save you — or guarantee that the bullets wouldn't go right through me."

To his surprise, she smiled and set her fingers lightly on his hand. "Actually, I let *you* come to *my* meeting."

He felt her touch, just as he felt her eyes. The restaurant grew warm. He smiled in return. "Well, then, thanks for inviting me."

"You knew you had to let me come," she said seriously. "I'm your connection."

"Yes."

"An acknowledgment," she said quietly, and smiled. "I *am* helpful to you."

He nodded, meeting her eyes.

She drew her hand back. "I really don't think anyone is going to come in here with a gun, although . . ." Her smile deepened. "Now I can't help thinking about what would happen if you did throw yourself across the table to protect me. I'll bet you're fast."

"I can move pretty quickly, yes. Not as fast as a bullet, though."

"I keep thinking about what you said about an unwitting conspiracy. This crime family — the Barillo crime family. Miguel worked for them because he'd been threatened? Is that how it happened?"

Brett nodded. "More or less. A couple of Barillo's men approached his son at school. He knew what that meant. Barillo never would have touched his kid, but Miguel didn't know that, so he gave in and did what Barillo asked him to."

She opened her mouth to speak, then paused. "He's here," she said, and waved.

Brett turned as Papa Joe, dressed in a lightweight suit, approached the table. Brett recognized him, having seen him on the news a few times, representing the community.

Papa Joe evidently knew the hostess. He spoke with her for a minute and then approached the table, shaking hands with them as he sat and producing a small felt satchel from his pocket. He sat down, smiled and started to talk — the niceties before any business deal, except this time he wasn't extolling the value of his merchandise.

"There is a man I know. He will be on the corner of 2nd Avenue when you leave here, carrying a looking-for-work sign. Pick him up and drive with him, and he will tell you a story that you need to hear," Papa Joe said, his head bowed as he unwrapped several necklaces that he took from the satchel. He met Brett's eyes for a moment. "You're Cody, right?"

Brett nodded.

"Word on the street is that you care," Papa Joe said. "This man has a story like those you're investigating. Except that it happened to an immigrant. An illegal, probably. One of this city's forgotten people. I'll let my friend Pierre tell you the story. His English is good enough. I think you'll find what he has to say illuminating — and, I pray, helpful."

Brett thanked him, then, as their waitress appeared at the table, reached for one of the necklaces, a handcrafted rendering of St. Francis. "I think Lara would like this one, Papa Joe. She's such an animal enthusiast."

Papa Joe smiled, then ordered the Cajun-spiced fish and chips. Brett and Lara followed suit. The waitress left them.

"We can't just walk away right now. Can

you tell us anything else?" Lara asked. "And what do we owe you for the necklace?"

"Consider it my gift. You may feel free to pick up the dinner check," he said. "Meanwhile, since we will be here a little while, I will tell you my friend's story after all. It will save time when you meet him. Pierre came here on a raft with a group of other Haitians, including his wife and several of his brothers. They were among the lucky ones who survived the journey. He was given work by a man who found him Dumpster diving at one of the hotels on Biscayne Boulevard. He went to work for the man he knew only as Mr. Z, dropping bags. Literally dropping paper bags where he was told to leave them. He never looked inside them. He felt lucky simply to have a job, because he was illegal, living off friends who had made it here before him. He got his older brother, Antoine, a job working for the same man. This goes on for a few months when suddenly Antoine has a heart attack and dies. The man promises to take care of his burial. There's a funeral."

"Where?" Brett asked.

"Pierre doesn't remember. The man took care of everything for him. He drove Pierre and his family to the gravesite, he saw a coffin go into the ground."

"And then?" Lara asked.

Then their food arrived and they started talking about jewelry again.

The waitress left. Brett continued to look through the necklaces while eating, and Papa Joe went on.

"Pierre was walking down the street one day when his brother came walking toward him. His dead brother. Pierre said he knew right away that something was wrong. He'd seen things like it as a child. He realized that Antoine had become a zombie, and worse, that his own brother was coming at him with a baseball bat in his hands. His brother had been a very good player, but he wasn't looking to play now. Pierre could tell that his brother didn't recognize him, that he meant to hurt him. But when he swung the bat, his swing went wild. And then he fell.

"When Pierre touched him, he was certain that Antoine was dead then. Really dead. He ran, ran to his wife. A man who was living with them went back with Pierre, but the police were there and the body was gone. He tried to follow the news, because he couldn't go and identify his brother, since he is afraid of being deported. But as you can imagine, the death of an illegal immigrant was not important to the TV sta-

266

tions. There was a brief mention the day the body was found, then . . . nothing." Papa Joe stopped speaking and stared at Brett. "You will get justice for Antoine, and you won't let Pierre be deported. I swore for you that you will not let that happen."

He didn't have the right to swear such a thing, but if this man could help them, Brett would do whatever it took to see that he somehow gained legitimate residency. Even if he didn't know the right people, he knew people who did.

Brett nodded. He leaned back, slipping his hand over Lara's as their waitress approached to see if they wanted anything else. He asked for the check while praising the food.

"You all come back," she said.

"I always bring my best friends and clients here, Miss Marie," Papa Joe assured her.

Brett paid the bill, leaving a generous tip. He made a point of fitting the necklace around Lara's neck once they were out on the sidewalk as Papa Joe cheerfully said that doing business with them had been a pleasure, and to please call or come by the store any time.

On the way back to his car Brett slipped his arm around her shoulder, just as if they were a real couple, and she leaned against him. He breathed in the scent of her and reminded himself to stay alert, because danger could be anywhere.

When they got to the car, he was surprised that she smiled at him when he opened the door for her.

"What?"

"Not so bad for a guy with a stick up his ass," she said.

He couldn't believe it, but he was pretty sure he blushed.

"Go figure, huh?" he said lightly, walking around to his own side. In the car, he quickly pulled out his phone and dialed Diego, who assured him, after Brett told him what was happening next, that the others would keep following at a distance.

"Watch for our guy," Brett told Lara as soon as he hung up.

She nodded.

As they headed toward 2nd Avenue and their rendezvous with Pierre, they entered an area where skimpily clad prostitutes plied their trade. He was glad that Lara was watching for Pierre, because it was hard for him to search the diverse crowd while driving.

"I think that's Pierre," Lara said suddenly, pointing.

He followed the direction of her finger and

was certain she was right as he spotted the man carrying a sign that said Looking for Work and standing right where Papa Joe had said they would find him. Brett pulled over to the curb and waved the man over. Quietly he said that Papa Joe had sent them, and Pierre jumped in.

"Drive, please," he said, his English clear, but slightly accented.

Brett quickly pulled back onto the street.

"I am Pierre Deveau," the man told them. "Thank you for listening to me. There was nowhere — nowhere for me to go."

"No. Thank you for speaking with us. *Merci. Merci beaucoup,*" Brett said. He looked at the man in the rearview mirror.

Pierre was perhaps in his forties, lean and wiry from hard physical work, with strong features, large brown eyes and graying dreadlocks. He nodded solemnly. "We came for freedom, for better . . . At least my children do not drink mud for water. But my brother . . ."

There was a sadness in his voice. Clearly he had cared deeply for his brother.

"Please, talk. Papa Joe told us a little of your story, and we believe you," Lara said.

Pierre began to tell his story. He talked about coming over — about fearing death in the rough, shark-filled waters between the island of Hispaniola and the Florida Keys. When they had finally arrived, they had been lucky. They had reached Islamorada, a small city spread out over several islands, where they had found people to help them. Then they made their way to Miami and found a room in a small apartment that a countryman — who was in the United States legally — rented and allowed his illegal friends to live in. It was a rundown place, but it was better than what they had left behind.

He and his brother had found odd jobs and manual labor easily enough; people didn't ask for your papers when they needed yard work done or something heavy hauled away. They paid cash. Then he had begun working for Mr. Z, and eventually he'd gotten Antoine a job, too. He admitted that he suspected they were doing something illegal, but all they had to do was deliver bags to certain places.

But then his brother . . .

He'd seen his brother die. And he'd been grateful to their boss, who had offered to arrange a quiet, private funeral and promised that no one would find out that Antoine and Pierre were there illegally. There had been a priest, they had been at a real cemetery, and Pierre had seen his brother's coffin go into the ground.

"Do you have any idea where this graveyard was?" Brett asked.

Pierre shook his head. "They brought us — my wife and me and our children — in the back of a van. No windows. We drove for about half an hour from our apartment. I don't know what direction we went. Antoine received the words of a priest. I threw the first handful of dirt on the coffin. The man led us away."

"What was the man's name?" Brett asked.

"Just Mr. Z or Boss Man. I don't know what the Z stood for, but mostly he liked to be called Boss Man. And he liked it."

"Can you describe Boss Man?" Brett asked.

"Medium tall, medium size. He wore good clothes, and he liked jewelry. Maybe forty years or a little less in age," Pierre said.

"But not old?" Brett said.

"No. Not old. And he was white, I think. Maybe Hispanic," Pierre said.

"Could you describe him for a police artist?" Brett asked.

Pierre shook his head emphatically. "No. No police. Besides, I do not wish to die like my brother."

"Pierre, I can make sure you're safe. I can

271

take you somewhere right now," Brett offered.

"No. I have a wife, and a son and a daughter. I can't go without them, and . . . we aren't real. I mean, we aren't legal."

"We'll get your family right now, too," Brett promised. "I'll make sure that you're protected by the police. No one, not even Boss Man, will be able to get to you. We need your help. And when everything is over, I'll make sure that you can all stay here legally."

Tears sprang into the man's eyes. "Papa Joe said so, but I did not dare believe. It cannot be."

"It can," Brett swore to him.

"I've heard such things before. Friends . . . the police make promises, but they are not immigration," Pierre said.

"Just say the word, Pierre. And give me your address," Brett said softly.

It took a full thirty seconds for Pierre to respond, but he finally gave them his address. Brett called Diego and passed it on, asking for backup.

By the time they reached the run-down projects where Pierre lived, the building was surrounded by police cars.

As they entered and went down a long hallway toward Pierre's apartment, Brett

272

sensed people watching silently through peepholes. Half the residents were undoubtedly terrified of arrest, he thought.

Pierre's wife and children certainly were, but Pierre quickly spoke to her in his native patois, his words so fast and clipped that Brett couldn't hope to follow them. Within minutes they had packed up their few belongings. But then Pierre turned stubborn; he'd apparently realized his bargaining chip. He insisted that Brett also help the couple living with them.

Brett winced, doubting his own power, but Matt, standing next to him, said, "Do it. I've already called Adam about Pierre and his family. If there's any trouble, Adam will step in. That's a guarantee."

Brett nodded to Pierre, and the young couple who also lived in the tiny apartment came along, too. No doubt everyone watching assumed they were being arrested and turned over to *La Migra,* Immigration, and that was fine with Brett. Boss Man was unlikely to go after them if he thought they were in police custody.

It was almost midnight by the time Pierre, his family and their friends, Mali and Jacques Brigand, were settled in a safe house. Brett and the others all drove back to Lara's house at that point, though he knew he and Diego should have simply gone home.

But Matt, Diego and Meg were talking about pizza, since they'd missed out on dinner and were starving.

"I need pizza," Diego insisted. "I can feel my belly button touching my spine."

"Then, pizza you shall have, if I have to use my badge to force Papa Giuseppe to stay open past closing," Meg said with a grin.

Brett realized they weren't just feeling hungry, they were feeling exhilarated, because at last something seemed to be going their way.

They needed Pierre. Needed him badly. They needed him to identify "Boss Man," and they needed him to find out where his brother's body had supposedly been buried, because that could link them to Boss Man. Police and municipal records should let them know where Antoine had ended up after his second death, though that was undoubtedly the city's potter's field.

Antoine's body might be the missing piece Phil Kinny needed to solve the puzzle of dead men walking.

If nothing else, Pierre could give them a good description of Boss Man, who might be working for the man at the top or might

274

himself be the puppet master who managed to kill and kill again with complete impunity.

They ordered pizza, and Matt and Diego drove to the restaurant to pick it up. Diego wolfed down half a pie and then told them that he had to call it quits for the night. "Agent Cody may not need sleep, but I sure as hell do," he teased.

After he left, Meg begged forgiveness and said that she was going up to bed, because she was exhausted, too. Matt waited, saying that he would lock up and see that the alarms were set once Brett went home.

Lara followed Brett to the door, where he paused and looked down at her. "Thank you," he said. "We wouldn't have gotten this break in the case without your help."

She smiled and stepped closer to him. He wanted to touch her, not to talk anymore. Wanted to touch her face. Pull her closer still. Wanted to kiss her. He focused on her mouth.

"You know, it's really late. I can just make up the sofa," she said, breaking the spell.

Matt was tossing out the paper plates, ready to follow Brett out and lock the gate when he left.

Brett felt ridiculously young and awkward, which was foolish. He'd never been the love-'em-and-leave-'em type, but he'd had relationships over the years, a few of them serious, one he'd thought was the real thing, but most of his dealings with women had been pretty casual. With Lara, though, he could already tell that there was something different.

"No, but thanks," he said softly. "I really need to go home. Clean suit for tomorrow and all that."

She lowered her head for a few seconds and then looked back up at him, smiling. "Too bad. I feel really safe when you're around. I mean, I feel safe with Meg and Matt, too. I just mean, if you ever want to stay here . . . you'd be welcome."

"Thanks. Before this is over, I may take you up on that." Even as he spoke, he wondered if she'd meant her words the way they'd sounded. The way he hoped she'd meant them.

She was even closer to him now. He wanted to forget talking, forget that other people were in the house. He wanted to escape the case by pulling her close, holding her, feeling her heart beat, warming himself at that fire within her . . .

Okay, and also by ripping their clothes off and . . .

"Gotta get going," he said.

She stood on tiptoe, her body touching

his, and kissed his cheek. "Thank you," she said. "For trusting me, working with me, or letting me work with you, really. Helping."

Temptation almost overwhelmed him. He stepped back, burning.

"I'll see you tomorrow," he said, and called out in a voice that was far too husky, "Hey, Matt, can you come out and lock up the gate?"

He turned and hurried to his car. He was careful driving home, watching to be certain that he wasn't being followed.

He was just as cautious when he reached his house.

But he had no nocturnal visitors.

As he lay awake, trying to focus on the case and not on the feel of Lara Ainsworth Mayhew against him, he wondered why no one had come after them.

Was it because whoever was pulling the strings was smart enough to stay away from the FBI to avoid having the entire Bureau, plus local law enforcement, come after him, quite likely ignoring a few laws along the way? Or were they still so far from figuring it all out that the head of the web wasn't even worried about being found out?

Or maybe the head honcho wasn't aware yet that they had found Pierre and were getting closer to cracking this case wide-open.

Maybe they should all stay together, turn wherever they chose to set up camp into a real stronghold.

Of course, he could just be making all that up to rationalize his desire to stay as close to her as he could.

Because he wanted to sleep with Lara Mayhew.

No.

He *would* sleep with Lara Mayhew. And he was pretty sure she knew that, as well.

He was smiling when he fell asleep.

11

Adrianna poked her head into Lara's office. "Hey," she said.

"Hey," Lara echoed, looking up from her computer.

"Is your friend still hanging around?"

"Meg? Yes. Is there a problem?"

Adrianna smiled. "No. In fact it's kind of nice to know that there's an armed agent on the premises. But that's not why I'm here. A two-spot opening for an eleven o'clock dolphin swim just opened up. You know we frown on employees jumping in without making prior arrangements, but I checked with Grady, and he said I was welcome to ask you and Meg to take the slot."

"That sounds great. I know I'd love it, and I'm sure Meg would, too. She went downstairs to make coffee. I'm surprised you didn't see her."

"I didn't even pop my head in the kitchen.

Anyway, just give me a buzz on the walkie-talkie."

"I will."

After Adrianna left, Lara drummed her fingers on her desk, surprised that she'd actually accomplished quite a bit so far that morning. Everyone was still talking about zombies and the grisly discoveries Cocoa had made in the lagoon. And even the mere thought of the lagoon made her think about Brett Cody. Made her think about what a difference time and getting to know someone could make. By any rational standard she didn't know him that well, and yet she felt as if she did. She'd thought he was nothing but a rigid robot, good to look at, but as personable as a rock.

And now . . .

And now she'd nearly asked him to crawl into bed with her. She blushed at the thought of what she'd said last night.

And how he had simply walked away.

She gave herself a mental shake as she heard footsteps coming her way. Meg entered the office with two cups of coffee, and Lara passed on Adrianna's offer.

"Of *course* I'd love to swim with the dolphins."

"I knew you would," Lara said, and

reached into her drawer for her walkie-talkie.

She let Adrianna know that they would be down as soon as they changed. Digging through her locker, she found an extra bathing suit for Meg, then suggested she leave her gun and ID there. Meg was hesitant about that, though, so Lara told her that there were computer-combination lockers down by the water, which seemed to satisfy her.

"Have you ever done this before?" Lara asked.

Meg shook her head. "No. I'm so excited, I feel like a little kid!"

Adrianna never took more than six people into the water with the dolphins at a time, and the other four were already there when Lara and Meg got down to the water. They were joining a family for the swim, Mr. and Mrs. Latrobe from Lansing, Michigan, and their two teenage daughters. Cocoa was in the side lagoon with Destiny, an older dolphin who had been at Sea Life for years. The girls were obviously in awe.

"First thing we've done this whole vacation where they've really been excited," Mrs. Latrobe told Lara and Meg as they gathered on the platform. "Dolphins just make people happy, I guess."

Lara agreed.

The encounter began with a speech that Lara never tired of hearing. Adrianna talked about the founding of the facility and its goals, as well as the dolphins themselves. When it was time to get in the water, Lara realized that as wonderful as it was, she had been spoiled by her session with Rick when she'd had Cocoa's total attention.

Lara was certain that Cocoa turned on the extra charm for her, but she knew the dolphin was also the ultimate performer. She shook hands — in her case, a flipper — danced and towed their entire group. Alongside Destiny, she also spoke and retrieved toys, delighting the watching crowd. The Latrobe family all had pictures taken of the dolphins giving them kisses.

The Latrobes were talking excitedly as they left, and Meg looked to be in total awe.

As the others walked away, Lara heard Adrianna using her whistle and calling for Cocoa. She turned to see what was happening and realized that Cocoa had done one of her fabulous flips — right over the underwater fence and out into the bay.

She didn't seem to be trying to go anywhere. She simply kept doing her tail dance for them.

"What is she doing?" Lara asked, walking

over to join Adrianna.

"I don't know. I've never seen her or any of the other dolphins act like this."

Seeing Lara, Cocoa began to squeal loudly.

"Cocoa!" Lara called. "Cocoa, come on."

Adrianna dived into the water, swam over to the fence and called to Cocoa from there. She turned back to Lara when the dolphin continued to ignore her. "Come in, will you? Maybe you can work your magic."

Lara dived in and swam to Adrianna's side. The trainer seemed puzzled and said, "Talk to her. Try to get her back in."

Lara did her best. She spoke softly, she urged, she pleaded.

Cocoa squealed back at her, but she didn't come back in.

"Try moving away," Adrianna said at last.

"All right, Cocoa. I've got to go," Lara said, swimming away.

At last the dolphin responded, making a huge leap and sending crystal droplets of water flying everywhere.

She raced past under the surface and emerged in front of Lara, who gave her a fin rub and thanked her. When they returned to the dock, Adrianna followed and gave Lara several fish to feed her, and then a few to feed Destiny, who came over to see what was going on.

"Okay, I have to leave now," Lara said as she gave Cocoa a last stroke and a last fish. Cocoa still seemed on edge, and she squealed and did another fluke walk. "I'll come back soon," Lara promised.

"I hope she'll be all right," Adrianna said. "I have to tell Rick about this."

"If I can help, let me know," Lara said.

"You know we will," Adrianna said.

Lara went to join Meg by the lockers at that point. As they headed back to the office and the showers, Meg said, "I was watching, and I'm sure as hell no expert, but it looked to me as though that dolphin wanted you to follow her."

"Maybe she wants another outing. I think she had fun the day we went out to look for — The day we went out with the Coast Guard. And found Miguel's head," she added. Not saying it didn't change what happened.

"Can't she jump that fence any time she wants to? Can't any of them?" Meg asked. "If they want to go exploring, I mean."

Lara stopped and looked at Meg. She knew what her friend was thinking. "You think that whoever made a zombie out of Randy Nicholson has really killed him now, and cut him up and dumped him in the bay."

"I think it's quite possible," Meg said. "I'll mention it to Matt. Or to Brett and Diego, since they're the leads on this. I'm just used to going to Matt first, since I'm working with him."

Lara smiled. "And living with him."

Meg smiled back. "Trust me, it's pretty great living and working together. Not everyone could, but for us, it works." She was quiet for a moment. "He's still a little in awe of *us,* though."

"Matt? Why?"

"The way our minds work in sync," Meg said. "Even at a distance. When you were kidnapped and needed my help, I knew it. Not many people have that kind of ability."

Lara laughed. "I think more people believe in ESP than in ghosts, but maybe all that kind of stuff is related somehow. Who knows?"

Meg grew serious. "Not me, but I do know that when it comes to this case, someone knows what he's doing, playing with the greatest computer ever, the human brain." She paused for a moment. "That's what the Krewe does, in a way. We push the boundaries, too, looking past this world and into the next, so to speak, even seeking help

285

from the dead. It's a little less extreme to think that a dolphin might help, right?"

Lara looked at her friend and nodded. "Can you imagine the headline? 'Dolphin Saves Miami from Zombie Attacks.' "

"Maybe it's not so far-fetched," Meg told her. "Speaking of which, I wonder how the guys are doing on finding Antoine Deveau's body."

Brett loved computers. You could find almost anything somewhere on the internet, and the Bureau had hundreds of employees nationwide who were the most talented geeks in the world. If the information had been recorded, the Bureau's geeks could find it.

And in this case, all they had to do was hunt down the day the body had been found, find the autopsy report and then look up where the body had been buried.

The geeks in the Krewe's Virginia office were handling the search. Once Adam Harrison had been called in to help get the ball rolling on Pierre's application for legal residency for his family and entrance into the Witness Protection Program, he'd put all his resources at their disposal, geeks included. That left Brett, Diego and Matt to work with Pierre himself while his family and friends remained in the safe house, heavily guarded.

Pierre had already worked with a sketch artist. The problem was that Boss Man seemed to have different color eyes each time Pierre saw him. Mostly he had a mustache and a beard, but not always, and they weren't always shaved in the same style. He usually wore glasses, too, but not always the same frames.

Even so, staring at the sketch, Brett told Diego and Matt that the drawing resembled the man who had accompanied Anthony Barillo to his house.

"We can bring him in," Diego offered.

Brett shook his head. The resemblance could just as easily be a coincidence. "I can't say it was him with Barillo. And if we bring him in before we're sure, before we have evidence, we could blow the whole case."

"We can keep him in mind, at least, in case we find some hard evidence, then move on him," Diego said. "Unfortunately, an empty grave isn't evidence."

"Let's start by hoping the records will direct us to the right potter's grave," Brett said.

"It's a plan," Matt agreed. "And if not, we'll keep digging till we find the right one."

Brett grinned; he liked the man. He was always willing to go the extra mile.

Brett knew they wouldn't find Antoine in the grave where Pierre had seen him buried, but the killer might be "storing" other bodies there, and there was always the possibility of catching him in the act.

They visited every cemetery within an hour's drive of Pierre's apartment, just in case he'd been mistaken about the length of the drive, but he didn't recognize any of them. Frustrated, Brett went online himself and tried historical cemeteries, which brought up several they had already seen but also some new possibilities. On the third page of listings he found a blog dedicated to an old cemetery down in Florida City, close to the Everglades and the gateway to the Florida Keys.

It was a small place, mostly reclaimed by nature, just on the edge of the national park. The road to it clearly hadn't been repaved in years. But when Brett started driving down it, Pierre suddenly perked up.

"Mais oui!" he cried. "I remember this — bouncing before we reached the graveyard."

The gravestones were scattered, some still standing, others tipped over, even broken. A few were military issue from World War I, a few more from World War II, and they even found a small stone marker that showed the deceased had fought in the Civil War.

"I hadn't realized there were that many people living around here that long ago," Matt said.

"There was a military base on the Miami River years before anything approaching a city existed down here," Brett explained. "They were down here fighting the Seminole wars, which raged for years and years. Sherman got his start down here. Zachary Taylor fought down here, too. Miami itself was incorporated in 1896."

Matt laughed. "I doubt this place is in Miami."

"No, but it *is* in Miami-Dade County," Brett said, looking around. They were surrounded by high grasses and, except for the little hummock that held the cemetery, the land here was marsh. The Everglades themselves were much the same. The "river of grass" was a mix of marsh and river and hummock, and it was often difficult to know where one ended and another began. It was much the same here, but on a smaller scale, a place being overtaken by nature, the heat of the day broken by a cool breeze moving through. He could hear the forlorn calls of different birds. To the east, buzzards were circling, and he imagined that they had probably homed in on road-kill somewhere on US1.

Pierre wasn't paying any attention to the agents. He was moving through the thickly overgrown gravestones, head down, searching.

Suddenly he stopped dead. Brett tensed, nearly drawing his Glock. Then he realized that Pierre had stopped because an adolescent alligator was sunning himself on a large concrete-slab marker.

"Leave him alone," Brett said. "He'll leave you alone."

Pierre nodded and pointed. "There. I remember that tree. They buried my brother beneath it."

Diego groaned suddenly, looking at Brett. "I'm digging, right?"

"I'm not even sure who we call to get the proper permits to work here," Brett said. He knew, of course, that he *should* call someone. He was talking about digging up a graveyard after all.

But he didn't want to wait. He didn't want permits and word getting out and a big show.

"Hey, I'm digging, too."

"There are three of us, and the ground will be soft," Matt said.

Diego shook his head and started walking

to the car. "I know you," he told Brett. "The shovels are in the car, right?"

Brett grinned and nodded. "It pays to be prepared."

That night, Brett, Matt and Diego traipsed into Lara's duplex covered in mud that they'd tried to remove, though without much success.

Matt and Diego took turns showering in the guest bathroom, Diego first, while Brett used the shower in Lara's bathroom. He'd suggested that he and Diego could go home to clean up, then come back to discuss their day. Lara had been about to insist that was ridiculous, but Meg had beaten her to it, saying that she was anxious to share information and didn't want to waste time. She'd pointed out that pizza and lasagna were already on the way, and that they could borrow clean clothes from Matt. That had turned out to be unnecessary, since both men kept a change of clothes in the car.

Lara went upstairs to her room to leave a clean towel for Brett. She knocked, and when she didn't get an answer she went in to leave it on the bed, only to discover that apparently he'd found one on his own.

He was coming out of the bathroom in his jeans, his chest bare, drying his hair. She tried not to stare at that broad expanse of tanned flesh, feeling a rare moment of sympathy for "breast men," the ones who couldn't quite raise their gaze to meet a woman's eyes.

She forced herself to focus on his face, more than a little alarmed by the trembling she felt. She couldn't help being suddenly plagued by the realization that it had been forever — it didn't just seem like it, it was — since she'd been in a relationship, even a casual one. She had been so focused on her career that she'd hardly even noticed a man in a sexual way.

And now . . .

She wasn't desperate, she assured herself. Brett Cody was damn close to perfect.

"Sorry," she murmured, feeling herself blush. "I was just . . ." She held up the towel in his direction.

"Thanks. I'll be down in a few. It's been a productive day. We've located the grave we believe belongs to Pierre's brother, Antoine, and we have the paperwork to exhume him tomorrow," he said. "It will really help Kinny to have a second victim. Makes me wonder how many others might have died. How many experiments there might have been."

She tried to pull her mind back from the

place where it had gone. But he made that impossible as he moved closer to her, smiling and taking the towel.

"I guess I used your towel. My apologies."

She shook her head, unable to speak. His sleek, still slightly damp chest was mere inches away.

She was in very sad shape, she thought.

"We had an interesting day, too," she said.

"Oh?"

She backed away. She'd come on to him pretty strong the night before and he had walked away. She had to be careful here, keep herself under control.

"Yeah, I'll . . . I should wait and tell everyone all at once. I'd better get back downstairs. I think I heard a call from the gate. Meg's probably brought in the food, and Diego's probably done showering, maybe Matt, too . . ."

She was babbling. She was a media expert. She never babbled.

"See you downstairs," she finished in a rush.

She stared at him for another few seconds before she actually left. He was towel drying his hair, looking like anything but a tough-as-nails FBI. He looked like a male model.

She turned and hurried down the stairs,

almost crashing into Meg and Diego, who were heading to the family room with the food. "I'll get plates," she said.

"Got more paper?" Meg asked.

"We'll use the real ones. I hate paper in my lasagna."

Brett and Matt appeared simultaneously a few minutes later.

Brett was wearing a T-shirt featuring a band called Bastille. Lara loved the group and imagined he did, too. He had the T-shirt after all. She lowered her head, smiling, wondering what he was like at a concert. When she'd first met him, she would never have imagined that he ever listened to live music.

"About time you got down here. I'm famished," Diego said when the other men appeared. He looked at Meg and shook his head. "Brett never seems to care about eating, and you know as well as I do that regular meals are a job requirement."

As soon as they'd all filled their plates, they started talking about the day. The men began by talking about their trip to the historic cemetery.

"So . . . all that digging and you found nothing," Meg said, passing the lasagna around for seconds. "I mean, I know you didn't expect to find Antoine's body, but I hoped maybe there'd be evidence, a clue of some kind."

"No, nothing," Brett said.

"Are you sure you were in the right place? A cemetery like that, in the middle of nowhere, how would Boss Man or anyone else even know it existed?"

"The gators seem to know it okay," Matt said, reaching for a dinner roll. "We saw several."

"I don't know how Boss Man knew, but he did, and Pierre confirmed it was the right place," Diego said.

"We found the gravesite. It was pretty obvious where the dirt had been dug up. But not only was the body gone, the coffin was, too. So . . . no prints, no scraps of fabric or strands of hair that might have gotten caught on it," Matt said.

"I want to get back out there and look around some more," Brett said. "I think it might actually be a body dump for more of our forgotten citizens, and maybe for more of Boss Man's experiments. We'll bring dogs — maybe ground-penetrating radar — and see what we can find. But first, tomorrow we're going to look for the body of Pierre's brother where it was buried after his second — and final — death." He turned to Lara. "You said you and Meg had an interesting day, too. What happened?"

"I had my first dolphin swim," Meg said. "And when it was over, Cocoa behaved very strangely."

Brett smiled at Lara. "She didn't throw you over for Meg, did she?"

"No, nothing like that," Lara said. "She went over the fence."

"She wanted to escape?" Diego asked.

"No, I think she wanted Lara to follow her," Meg said. She hesitated, glancing at Lara, then addressing Brett. "She went out with you guys and Lara and Diego, and she found what you were looking for. I think she knows there's more out there — and she may even know where."

"How could a dolphin know —" Diego began.

"You had her looking for human remains before," Meg said. "Dolphins are smart. If you rewarded her for finding body parts once and she knows more are out there — if she can smell them or whatever — why wouldn't she think you'd reward her again for finding them?"

"We could go out," Brett said, and looked at Lara. "If you're willing."

Was she willing? She didn't know. She would never forget the discovery of Miguel Gomez's head.

Or the other pieces of him, for that matter.

But, she realized, she was never going to feel right until they found out what was going on. She frowned, thinking about lunch the other day, and seeing Dr. Amory with Ely Taggerly, Grant Blackwood and Mason Martinez. She'd been instantly suspicious.

And she would look at everyone, view any innocent meeting or association, with that same suspicion if this wasn't solved.

"I'm fine with going out again," she said. "You'll need to speak with Grady and Rick first, though. Rick will know what to do if it turns out that's not what Cocoa wants."

"Great. I'll do that. I have no idea if we'll find a body at all, and even if we do, there's no guarantee it will be Randy Nicholson's."

"If you find anyone who had the same drug in him, won't that help tell you what you need to know, even if you never find Randy's?" Lara asked.

"We need every piece of evidence we can find," Brett said. "And then," he added grimly, "we need to put all the pieces together and find out whose money is behind these murders."

"Money?" Lara asked.

Brett nodded. "It takes money to pull off something like this. Despite Anthony Barillo making such an effort to tell me he's not guilty, he's got the bucks — and the muscle — to make things happen. Money to hire thugs. Money to create the drug they're using. Money to hold funerals and steal bodies."

"Why do any of it, though?" Lara asked. "Even if he creates a whole army of zombies, what does he think he'll do with it? And the victims so far were no threat to anyone. So . . . why?"

"Knowing why would help a hell of a lot," Diego said. "But knowing *how* will help, too. I keep hoping that Dr. Kinny will come up with something. That's why it's so important that we find the bodies."

"Here's something that may or may not mean anything," Lara said. "Talking to Sonia Larson today, we found out that she sees Dr. Treme. The same Dr. Treme who signed Randy Nicholson's death certificate."

"He *is* one of the most highly regarded cardiologists in the area," Diego said.

"So maybe it's nothing," Lara said. "Just a coincidence."

"I'm not willing to accept anything as coincidence at this point. We have to check it out," Brett said. "And we will."

"Should we worry about Sonia, then? Suggest she see a different doctor?" Meg asked.

"Let's not jump the gun," Matt answered.

"We're pretty sure that puffer fish poison is being used, and chances are someone with medical knowledge is involved, but we don't have any evidence that it's Treme." He looked thoughtful. "It's almost unbelievable just how completely the poison mimics death."

"I tend to think Randy Nicholson was dying anyway, and someone simply took advantage of that fact," Brett said. "Treme may be guilty of nothing more than too easily accepting that a patient's known condition was what killed him."

Diego made a vague excuse and left right after dinner. He hadn't said anything, but Brett had a feeling his partner had met someone.

After a while Brett began to feel he had worn out his own welcome. They'd hashed and rehashed the case, but without more evidence, there was nothing left to say.

They'd also talked about other things. Matt was intrigued by the Everglades, and since he knew the area well, Brett had filled him in on all there was to do in the area: air-boating, visiting the Seminole and Miccosukee reservations, and checking out the museums at the Seminole Hard Rock in Hollywood, Florida, and in Big Cypress.

He'd realized then that he'd been talking purely to fill time, and that it was after 1:00 a.m. and he needed to go. He rose, but once again Meg spoke up. "Unless you can't sleep without your own pillow, it's crazy for you to leave. We'll only be heading out again in a few hours."

He thought about the emptiness of his place, something he hadn't really even noticed until these past few days — with Lara. His life certainly wasn't bad. He liked the people he worked with, and they all enjoyed a lot of the same things. Watching the local teams — the Heat, the Dolphins and the Marlins — play. Fishing. Boating. Diving. Camping in the Keys, the occasional weekend in the Bahamas.

But there was really nothing for him at home. Ichabod probably only came over to give him a mercy meow or two.

Lara was looking at him with those eyes that seemed both as blue as the sky and as green as the sea. "I wish you would stay. I should say the more the merrier, but frankly, the more agents running around with guns, the safer I feel," she said.

She was trying to sound flip. Maybe she saw his hesitation.

"I'll get pillows and pull out the sofa," she

told him, taking the decision into her own hands.

"No need. I'm fine with it the way it is," he said.

"Don't argue with me," she said with a smile. "It's no trouble, and I want you to be comfortable."

"And honestly, I can be comfortable sitting in a chair," he said.

"Great, the kids are all in for the night. I'm going to bed," Meg said.

"Sounds good to me," Matt said. "I'll go make sure the gate's locked, then I'm heading to bed, too. Good night, all."

Alone with Lara, Brett felt suddenly awkward. For several long, awkward moments they both sat without speaking.

"Can I get you anything else?" Lara finally asked.

"No, thank you."

"I guess we should get some sleep," she said.

"Yes, I guess we should."

But neither of them moved.

"I think I owe you an apology," Lara murmured.

"Why's that?" he asked.

"I really didn't want you to go," she said. "But I didn't mean to scare you."

"Scare me?"

She was wearing a light summer dress; her legs were bare and tucked beneath her, looking longer and sleeker than they had any right to be. Her hair played around her shoulders like spun gold in the lamplight.

She smiled. "I kind of came on to you last night."

"Did you?" he asked. "I was taught never to assume."

"And what were you trying not to assume?"

"What were you asking?"

She flushed and looked away, picking up her glass, which held an inch of soda and some ice chips. He'd never seen anyone swirl a glass with more sensuality before.

"Well, Agent Cody, call me crazy. I guess *I'm* the one making assumptions now, but I was thinking of sex."

"With me?"

"Okay, now you're being ridiculous. Yes. With you."

"You and me?" he asked.

"Yes, I think that identifies the situation exactly."

He stood, walked over to her and took the glass from her hand. "I thought you'd never ask. It would be my most absolute and total pleasure."

He set the glass down and took her hands,

then pulled her to her feet and into his arms.

"Oh, Agent Cody, now you *are* assuming," she said with a smile.

"No, I'm quite positive I've got it right," he assured her.

He tightened his arms around her and brought his mouth down on hers. She seemed to melt into him, her body molding perfectly to his, sending a searing longing ripping through him. Their first kiss was hard, desperate, all liquid heat and dueling tongues. When they finally pulled apart he started to sweep her up in his arms, ready to carry her upstairs, knocking over everything in their path, completely forgetting for the moment that there were other people in the house.

She remembered, though, and stepped back. "I'll walk up the stairs under my own power — no, I'll run!" And then she was gone.

He was right on her heels.

12

Lara's mind was racing almost as quickly as her heart as she reached her room and waited for Brett to join her.

She couldn't help thinking about the possible repercussions of what she was doing. Apparently she'd spent too much time in politics, where life was all about creating positive consequences and avoiding negative repercussions. Which was this going to lead to? She told herself she was crazy. They were in the middle of trying to solve a terrifying mystery, and he was the agent in charge; anyone in the world would say that this was the wrong time to get involved with someone, and the wrong time to get sexually involved with anyone, especially him. And while her walls were concrete block and stucco, they weren't alone in her house. She wouldn't lie to Meg if she asked what was going on. For all she knew, Meg might already know how she felt.

So what kind of spin should she put on this?

Then Brett walked into the room behind her, and she suddenly realized that she didn't have to analyze or explain herself. She wanted him, wanted this, wanted to be with him more than she had imagined ever wanting a man. She slipped into his arms again. They kissed, hot and delicious, as both of them struggled out of their clothes. Her dress was gone, along with her bra; his shirt followed and she felt her breasts press hard against the burning muscles of his chest. She ran her fingers over his shoulders and down his back. She felt the protrusion of the gun shoved into his waistband. He put his hand over hers, then removed the gun and stepped away to set it on the bedside table. He looked at her in the dim glow of the streetlights that filtered through her drapes. She ran to him and leaped into his arms, and they kissed again, wrapped around each other, half-naked. Finally they fell onto the bed, where she eased her fingers into his waistband, seeking the zipper of his jeans. He reached for it at the same time, and they struggled a little awkwardly, laughed and then he took off his jeans while she shimmied out of her panties. Finally they were together again.

"My God," he murmured, whispering against her ear, and he lowered himself over her, the whole of his body like a fire, a shimmering flame that danced across her sensitive skin. "I dreamed about you," he whispered. "After diving . . . seeing you in a bathing suit."

"How very . . . male of you."

"Yes. And it wasn't even that sexy a suit."

"Gee, thanks," she said breathlessly.

"Well, maybe it was on you."

She didn't know what to say to that, so she only smiled.

"Admit it. You dreamed about me, too."

"What an ego you have!"

"Admit it," he repeated, his mouth moving over her flesh. "You dreamed about me, too."

"Not at first." She trembled, then shuddered. His lips were moving lower on her body. A pit of something like lava seemed to boil inside her, ready to streak through her, awakening every nerve in her body. "Not really."

"Kind of? Almost?" The heat of his whisper tickled her ear.

"I noticed you, I will say *that.*"

"Only noticed?" His kiss landed on her throat. "You weren't the least bit interested?" His next kiss landed on her midriff; his fingers teased her flesh.

She laughed, despite the sensations sweeping through her, or maybe because of them.

"Noticed — and not in the best light," she teased.

He dropped a kiss on her abdomen.

"And there I was, dreaming away," he whispered.

She threaded her fingers through the thick darkness of his hair. "Liar," she murmured. He looked down at her, and she touched his face and said, "But I think maybe, just maybe, there was always something there."

"Always," he said. "We just had to pay attention."

She felt the pressure of his thighs between her knees, and wrapped her arms and legs around him.

Then they looked at each other in simultaneous alarm.

"I'm not on any birth control," she murmured. A flush rose to her cheeks. "I haven't . . . seen anyone in a long time, and . . ."

He winced and rolled to her side. "I never intended to stay," he said softly. "Much less for anything like this to happen." He turned and caressed her cheek. "There are other things we can do."

"Wonderful things," she agreed. "Though

it will be almost like torture."

"Good torture," he said, and smiled.

She leaned over him and pressed her lips to his shoulder, then trailed them along his flesh until she felt the sharp contraction of the muscles in his belly. Then she moved lower, only to feel his grip tighten on her shoulders as he shifted her onto her back, his face above hers, a smile on his lips as he kissed her mouth, and then her throat and her breasts. He moved his liquid caress lower and lower until she was gasping and writhing and trying to escape his hold, but only so she could stroke and kiss him in return.

And then, to her amazement, he leaped out of bed, and for a split second she wondered what in hell she had done.

"My wallet!" he said.

"I'm, uh, sure it's still in your pants. Why?"

"Sex education."

"What?"

"Always be prepared. Stuck in the back, behind the credit cards."

She stared to laugh, and when he dug the condom out of his billfold, they were suddenly as giddy as children.

"A treasure," she said.

"Better than gold."

"And diamonds."

"Way better than diamonds."

"Actually, I don't even like diamonds. Better than . . . all the tea in China, all the fish in the sea, all —"

"The dolphins in the world?" he asked.

"Don't push it," she told him, and they fell together, kissing and laughing.

And then the laughter was gone, and they made love in earnest.

When they climaxed, Lara knew that the reason she hadn't been interested in other men for a very long time was because she'd always wanted it to be like this. She'd wanted someone like Brett Cody.

And when he touched her, everything in life seemed worth the wait, and even the struggle for truth seemed like an easier task.

And when early morning came and they made love again, she prayed she'd been right and together they might actually solve this string of horrors. She was glad when he asked, "We're not making any pretenses, right? I'd feel like an idiot trying to pretend I slept on the couch."

"No pretenses," she told him. And she smiled suddenly. Little did the lovely Sonia Larson know that the little white lie she had told Grant Blackwood at the fund-raiser would turn out to be the truth.

Each of the long rows of bricks set flush in the ground had a number, as did each brick. This cemetery, unlike the one they had visited the day before, was in the middle of the city, down in Kendall, and situated between a fire station and a telecommunications company. There was no impression of grace, no flowing sense of peace here, no feeling of history; it was no Woodlawn or Bonaventure.

Still, it wasn't ugly; it was a park, of sorts. There were trees and trails — and the rows of bricks with their numbers.

This was where the unclaimed, the forgotten, were taken. It was a potter's field.

They had decided it was time to use the city's records to try to find Antoine's final grave.

Brett closed his eyes for a minute. The knowledge that so many people had died unknown, unremembered, was disheartening.

If he closed his eyes, he could pretend he was somewhere else. And, standing there, even in such a place, he almost smiled. Because last night had changed everything for him. Life could be hard and brutal, and he spent his days pursuing evil, so it had been incredibly good to have a night in which he'd felt as if he'd touched something that was exhilarating and purely good.

And waking up to see her face . . .

To touch her cheek, to see her eyes open and a smile curve her lips . . .

Diego cleared his throat, and when Brett opened his eyes he saw his partner frowning at him as if he was afraid there was something wrong.

"What?" Brett asked.

"Your eyes were closed."

"The better not to see," Brett said drily.

It was bright and early, and there weren't many people around, not that many people were likely to come here anyway, even though the highways were clogged with people heading to their jobs. This being Friday, most of them would be looking forward to the weekend.

A man walked by with his dog, despite the no-dogs-allowed sign just outside the gate. But standing there, with Diego, Phil Kinny and the work crew, Brett thought that walking a dog in a cemetery seemed like the pettiest of crimes.

"There was an autopsy, and I have the records," Kinny said as the cranes worked to dig up the poor pine coffin holding the man who had been buried with a number rather than a name. "Cause of death was listed as a heart attack." He hesitated. "There are a number of tests that weren't done because, believe it or not, the morgue works on taxpayer money and there's never enough of it. Certain tests for poisons and other factors aren't done, not when cause of death appears to be obvious." He turned to look at Brett. "I may learn something for you. Then again, I may learn that this man died of a heart attack while walking down the street."

"I know. But paranoia on the streets about zombies is growing. This is the information age. The public knows a lot more is out there than what we've shared with them. Thing is, what used to be word of mouth now becomes word of internet. We've got to get to the bottom of this, Phil, and as quickly as possible," Brett said.

"I'll do my best," the ME promised. "I'll get right on this, and I'll call you as soon as I know something, but I'll be asking for a number of lab reports, and even if I put a rush on them, they'll take time."

When the coffin was in the county hearse and headed for the morgue, Diego turned to Brett. "We going back out on the bay now?"

Brett nodded.

"And the ghost hunters think we'll find a body out there?"

"Randy Nicholson is out there somewhere. Zombie, dead man . . . who knows? The bay is as good a place to look as any."

"I have no problem with spending the rest of the day diving," Diego assured him. "The Bureau and county legal departments are still wrestling with Diaz-Douglas, but they tell me they'll win in the end. It will just take time. I'm with you, certain those people sent an empty casket to the cemetery. They have to answer for it. But the paperwork is killing me. Don't you wish we could go rogue sometimes? We could say screw the law and *make* the bad guys talk. Or not. I don't really see me torturing old Mr. Douglas."

"No, but bureaucracy *is* a pain in the ass," Brett agreed. "Still, if we find Antoine Deveau in this casket, that's another step toward finding out what's going on. I'm really hoping we can find at least part of Randy Nicholson in the bay somewhere, because that will give Kinny three bodies to work with. Matt is with Pierre Deveau now. We're hoping he can identify 'Boss Man' from a sheaf of photos Bryant has been keeping on suspected members of the Barillo family. If he *can,* we can make an arrest and just maybe get him to talk."

"Yeah — if torture was legal. No one in that family talks."

Brett shrugged. "They may not talk, but that doesn't mean they can't be tripped up. And we *have* to solve this one."

The good thing was that no one intended to let up. Even without the paranoid populace, they had the full support of the powers that be.

Murderous zombies were not good for tourism.

They reached Sea Life ahead of their ten o'clock appointment to meet the Coast Guard and headed up to the offices, where Rick, Lara and Meg were waiting. So were their wetsuits, and the two men changed quickly; the rest of their gear would be supplied onboard.

"How's Cocoa doing?" Brett asked, trying not to look at Lara, because it was impossible to look at her and not smile like an idiot.

"She's swimming around and around. It's as if she knows. As if she's waiting for us to get the show on the road," Rick said.

"We should probably head down, then," Brett said. "Lara can start talking to her to calm her down or even get in the water with her."

"Sure," she said.

He noticed from the corner of his eye that she didn't look directly at *him,* either.

He was eager to get out there, praying that they could find a needle in a haystack. He realized he was also anxious for the day to go by and for it to be night again.

The Coast Guard cutter *Vigilance,* again with Lieutenant Gunderson captaining, arrived at precisely ten. Rick and Lara started off in the water, leading Cocoa out of the lagoon.

Brett was grateful to the geeks once again; they'd run the calculations for the night Antoine had been buried the first time, adding in the coordinates where they'd found the other body parts and taking into consideration the different timing, the tides, the currents and the weather.

Their first two dives proved to be futile, but on the third Cocoa chittered away at Lara, trying to lure her down. They were just off a sandbar. Seaweed and sea grasses grew around broken branches of old coral. The water here was deeper than he'd expected, because at one time the area had been dredged to allow for the passage of larger boats. Lara managed to free dive down to about twenty-five feet, but the dolphin still seemed agitated, as if she was trying to lead them farther. Lara went up for air, but Brett, with Rick and the Coast Guard divers, headed down to the area that seemed to be disturbing Cocoa.

He wasn't the one to find the decaying and half-eaten torso, and neither was Rick. It was one of the Coast Guard divers.

They bagged the torso and headed up with it. Breaking the surface, Brett lifted his mask and looked over at Lara. She was treading water without any trouble, even though it was choppy, waiting for them. He could see one of Miami's infamous almost-daily summer storms on the horizon.

He nodded at her without smiling and told her quickly what they'd found. The nod she gave in return was equally serious. The find had been a grim one.

Cocoa broke the surface, squealing loudly, and Lara praised her effusively.

Back on the boat, Lieutenant Gunderson warned them that they had time for just one more dive that day, because the storm was coming in quickly. "That dolphin is amazing, like a cadaver dog," he said.

"Don't get me wrong, I love dogs. But dolphins are much smarter," Rick said.

"How much time do we have?" Brett

asked Gunderson. "Another hour?"

"About that," Gunderson told him.

"Good. We have one more sandbank where we think something might have gotten caught. If we move, we can make it." He looked questioningly at Lara.

She nodded. "I'm game."

They sat drinking coffee until the cutter reached the specified coordinates.

Brett was grateful they'd had time for this last shot. Cocoa led them to an underwater ridge heavily covered with refuse. It was near an embankment popular with boaters, too many of whom threw beer cans and other garbage into the water.

They found most of the rest of what Brett believed would prove to be Randy Nicholson's body strewn among the debris.

Most important, they found what remained of the head.

As soon as they got back on the cutter, Lieutenant Gunderson told Brett that Matt Bosworth had asked him to call when he was back aboard. After he hung up, he told the rest of them what had gone on while they'd been in the water.

First, Pierre had given them a tentative identification on Boss Man.

His name was Jose Acervo, and he was a

known associate of Anthony Barillo. He wasn't in the upper tier of the family business, but he wasn't a peon, either. The way Brett explained it to Lara, Barillo himself was the king, his family were the heirs to the kingdom, the second tier were like the nobility and had real power and the third tier — which included Jose Acervo — was being groomed to become part of the aristocracy. The problem now was to find Jose.

An all-points bulletin had already gone out; all they needed now was for someone to spot him. The scary thing was that he might have heard he was a wanted man and already be in the wind. The area was full of private planes, and it was easy to slip off to the Caribbean or even South America.

On top of that breakthrough, Matt had received a call from a mystery woman who was trying to reach Brett, because Brett had set his phone to forward unanswered calls to Matt, in case something important happened while he was underwater. The woman had been too nervous to reveal her reason for calling when she'd realized that she wasn't speaking to Brett, but Matt *had* managed to trace the call to one of the city's few remaining pay phones.

"It's on Bird, near the Diaz-Douglas

Mortuary Chapel," Matt had told him.

"I'll be damned. Someone there means to talk," Brett had replied.

"I doubt it's Mr. Diaz," Diego said drily when Brett told the group.

"That leaves just one person," Brett said. "Jill Hudson, the makeup artist."

"And she's scared, I'll bet," Diego said.

"I hope she'll call back, but I don't want to count on it," Brett said.

"We certainly can't go see her at the mortuary," Diego said.

"We'll wait for her to leave. And it's nearly four now. We need to get the hell down to Bird as soon as we're back in port," Brett said. He looked at Lara. "When you and Meg are finished at Sea Life for the day, head straight to your place. We'll all meet there as soon as we can."

She nodded. His hair was still wet, his shoulders bronzed and sleek. On one hand, she was anxious for the day to end.

On the other, she wasn't sure he would notice her if she did a naked tango right in front of him.

He was so focused on the case right now, so determined to solve it before things became worse.

Before they had to go out looking for more bodies.

"Of course," she said. "Straight home."

Once they returned to Sea Life, Lara didn't even have a chance to talk to Brett. According to Meg, he and Diego had spoken briefly to Phil Kinny, who'd been waiting to take possession of the remains, then rinsed off in the kids' spray play zone, thrown on their clothes and left, still buttoning up their shirts.

She and Rick had swum the last little way with Cocoa, making sure she was well rewarded for her efforts with love and fish. By the time Lara was out of the water herself and ready for a shower, Meg was waiting for her by the lockers.

"Itching to get back on your computer?" Lara asked.

"That obvious, huh? I need to see if there's a connection between someone at that mortuary and someone who's part of the Barillo family. When it comes to something petty that you think you can get away with, you'd be amazed at what people are willing to do — sometimes for money, sometimes to keep someone else safe or out of trouble, or to cover a debt they can't pay."

"Who do you think it is?" Lara asked her. "I don't know any of them, only what Brett has told me."

"I didn't meet any of them, either. But as

320

far as I've been able to find out so far, no one there has a criminal record. That's why I think someone was bribed or someone close to them was threatened."

"Well, I'm going to hop in the shower. Then I'm going to work on some last-minute preparations for Sunday. It's going to be a big day for us here," Lara said.

"I'm glad my job is to hang with you, because I'm looking forward to it. It's impossible to really pay our soldiers back for everything they do, but what you guys are doing is really wonderful."

By then they'd reached the offices and headed upstairs.

Lara wanted to head straight into the shower, but she needed to get some things first. As she walked into her office, she paused.

There was something on her desk.

She walked over, frowning, puzzled.

It took a second.

And then she realized what it was.

Blue paper had been cut up to simulate waves.

And strewn over the paper were the pieces of a doll, a fashion model doll. Someone had taken the doll and dismembered it, then painted it in red. Bloodred.

The doll had once had blond hair, but

now that was scarlet, as were all the joints where the head and limbs had been ripped off the torso.

There was no note.

There didn't need to be.

The message was clear.

Back off — or wind up in pieces in Biscayne Bay.

13

They had barely parked when Jill Hudson walked out of the back of the funeral home, heading for her car, a white Toyota.

"So much for me bitching about endless hours of surveillance," Diego commented from behind the wheel. "How far are we going to let her get?"

"Far enough to make sure we're not being followed, too," Brett said. "We'll stop her before she gets to her house, though. I don't know what her family situation is, and I don't want to put her in an awkward spot."

Diego kept several car lengths behind Jill as she drove toward Kendall. Eventually she turned in to one of the large malls in the area. That was good, Brett thought; he could catch up with her with dozens of people around, while Diego kept watch to make sure they weren't being watched in turn.

He was glad to find parking just down from her, then followed her in through the food court. He turned quickly and made sure Diego was behind him, nodded and kept pace behind Jill until she entered one of the anchor stores in the center of the mall. She paused to look at a cosmetic company's free-with-purchase advertisement, and he caught up to her there.

"You tried to call me," he said quietly. "You didn't call back."

Jill wasn't schooled in subterfuge; her face turned bright red immediately, and she looked around guiltily.

"We're good," he told her softly. "Want to get out of the main aisle? Will you be more comfortable?"

She nodded and headed toward the men's department, taking shelter behind a rack of coats.

"I think it was Geneva," she blurted out. Then she went silent, gnawing her lip and looking around again. "I don't know why I'm so scared. No one is after me. But that man . . . His body was stolen from the funeral home. I'm sure of it. I'm terrified. I won't even go home alone anymore. I'm here because there are people all around, and my husband meets me here when he gets out of work. He'll probably divorce me. Who wants to be married to a paranoid freak, you know?"

"It's all right, you're not paranoid. I think you're very smart to be cautious right now," Brett said gently.

"But what if no one figures out what's going on? What if dead men keep getting up and killing other people?"

Brett felt tension tighten his jaw. It was sad but true. It often took months, even years, to catch a murderer. And some murderers were never caught.

"We'll find out what's going on and we'll catch this killer, I promise," he said, knowing even as he spoke the words that he should never make the kind of promise he couldn't be sure of keeping.

But it seemed to calm her. She met his eyes and began to talk. "Okay, this is what I know. There was a strange man in the office one day. Mrs. Diaz and I were the only ones there at the time. It was too early for viewing, and both Mr. Diaz and Mr. Douglas were out and Carl wasn't in yet. I asked her about him later — just casually, you know. I asked her if he was looking to bury a loved one. She was so strange, vague. She didn't lie, she just said he was asking questions, but she didn't say about what. I never saw him again. And now everyone has been on edge since you and those other agents came in. And it might not mean anything. I could be maligning a good woman — she *is* a good woman. I like working for her better than Mr. Diaz or Mr. Douglas, because she's so nice. But I have little kids. I'm not going to jail for something someone else did."

"You won't go to jail. Not only didn't you do anything, you're trying to help," Brett said. "Do you know why Geneva Diaz might have agreed to let someone take Randy Nicholson's body?" he asked. "Is there anything else you can tell me?"

"She was upset. I think the man threatened her," Jill said, looking around nervously again. "I really don't want anyone to see me talking to you. I — I think I would have called back. I just didn't have a chance. On the phone . . . That would have been better."

"I'll leave. Where do you meet your husband?"

"At the food court." She made a face. "Funeral directors might make a lot of money, but I'm not rolling in it, I promise you. He's bringing the kids, and we're going to have dinner before we go home. The food court is cheap, and you can choose things that are almost nutritious."

He smiled at that. "Go ahead. Go back to the food court. We'll watch out for you until he comes."

She nodded, looked worried and then smiled. "Geneva really is a good person. I don't know why she would have done it, but if someone arranged for those doors to be open, I think it was her."

He thanked her, and she turned and started walking. He gave her some space, but followed. Diego, he knew, was following him.

A little while later Jill met up with her husband in front of a fast-food Chinese place. Brett thought they were a nice-looking young couple. The kids looked to be about five, seven and nine.

He headed toward the exit, and once he was outside, Diego fell into step beside him. He filled his partner in on what he had learned.

"Divide and conquer," Diego said. "We'll have to get Geneva away from her husband so we can question her. I'll get with legal in the morning. I'm sure they can figure out a way to shut the place down if we don't get some cooperation."

Brett glanced at him. "The media has had a field day with the place. Half of their customers want their loved ones dug up to make sure they're still in their coffins. The place should call us and beg us to do something. At least we've got another lead."

His phone was ringing. Matt. Matt had been keeping an eye on Sea Life. Brett answered and listened, then said grimly, "We're on our way."

As soon as he hung up, Diego asked, "What the hell's going on?"

"Someone threatened Lara," Brett said. "We're heading back to Sea Life."

Lara was surprised to realize that she felt angry rather than frightened. She was supposed to be terrified, she knew. It was clearly a threat. She would be killed because she and Cocoa had found the body parts the killer had thought were gone forever. Well, too bad. She had no intention of letting this sick-minded individual get under her skin.

She told Grady as much when he came in to see how the search had gone. She'd asked Meg and Matt, who'd hurried back as soon as Meg called him, not to tell anyone about the dismembered doll, but they had told her that was impossible. They had to let their fellow agents and the police know, the scene had to be documented and the doll tested for fingerprints and other trace evidence.

Lara insisted that she didn't want her

coworkers to know, and she was even more vehement about not telling the press.

They agreed, but because they couldn't disturb the evidence, there was no way to keep it from Grady when he came by. And once he saw it, of course he was worried sick. His first question after ascertaining that she was physically unhurt was to ask if she wanted to take a leave of absence or even — and he stressed that it was the last thing he wanted — resign.

She assured him that she had no intention of leaving, that she loved her job and everything Sea Life did.

Her heart seemed to leap when Brett returned, along with Diego, but she hid her feelings and made a point of staying across the room from him. She wasn't into pretending, but she didn't think this was the time to go flying across the room and into his arms. It was also important to her for him to realize that while she might not be Meg — trained in the law and with the skills to enforce it — she also wasn't a hothouse flower. She was smart and strong, and she could hold her own, even in this company. She intended to be so. Not stupid — but strong. Eventually, after the agents had studied the scenario and pictures had been taken — dozens of them — Diego bagged up the doll and the paper waves, then left to take them to the crime lab.

"Are you sure you're all right, Lara?" Matt asked her.

"Actually, I'm starving," she said. "How about dinner? We can take the bridge and go to Bayside. There are a ton of great restaurants at the mall."

They were all silent for a long moment, staring at her.

"I think we all thought you might just want to get home," Meg finally said.

"Hell, no. I'm surrounded by FBI agents. I'd like to sit down at a nice restaurant and have dinner," Lara said.

"If that's what you want," Brett said.

"It's exactly what I want. Whoever threatened me is a coward who slinks around. They knew that no one would be in my office. A blind man would have known that the Coast Guard was here and we were going out with them. I think this means your conspiracy theory is right. Someone was bribed — or threatened — to put that display in my office. And if we find out who that was — just like if you find out who let someone into the mortuary — we'll be that much closer to finding whoever's behind this."

Matt said, "In fact, we believe we know

who we're looking for there."

"Two people, one man and one woman," Brett said. "We've had a report that Geneva Diaz met with someone and then began behaving very strangely. We'll be talking to her tomorrow."

"Good. Then, let's eat," Lara said.

She saw Brett lower his head to hide a smile. She grabbed her bag, and he smiled openly at her as he swept out his arm toward the door and said, "As you say, let's go."

As she started past him, he bent down and whispered, "And here I thought you'd be in a hurry to get back to your house."

His whisper alone sent heat shooting through her veins.

Matt and Meg were right behind her, and she wondered if they'd heard, not that it really mattered. If they hadn't figured things out this morning, they were bound to when Brett stayed over tonight and — she hoped — every night from now on.

They had three cars for the four of them, so Matt and Brett took their own vehicles, and Meg drove with Lara. To Lara's surprise, her friend said nothing about Brett. Finally she looked at Meg and asked, "Warnings? Anything?"

"About life? It's brutal out there," Meg said.

"About Brett."

"Well, I knew how you felt about him."

"What? *I* didn't know how I felt about him!"

"You forget how well I know you. Better than you know yourself, sometimes. And I can't think of anyone better for you."

"You just met him," Lara said.

Meg nodded. "Yes, but Matt's known him for years and says he's one of the best. And if Matt said it, it's true."

Lara loved her friend's confidence, but still she hesitated before asking, "Do you think . . . do you think it's just that I'm afraid, and because I'm afraid, I'm looking for a protector and mistaking that for something else?"

"You have Matt and me here. You'd be protected without him. Look, for the moment you're both getting something you need. And I'm not just referring to sex. It's just a bonus that you're sleeping with a guy who has a Glock by his side and knows how to use it. I don't like that doll. I really don't like that doll."

Lara didn't like it, either, but she decided to focus on anger, not fear. "My best friend and her significant other are FBI agents, and — as you pointed out — I'm sleeping with another. Let the bastards try something. If they do, you'll get them."

"We always get them in the end," Meg said.

They chose a restaurant, and Lara suggested that they eat outside, by the water. They agreed, and she noticed that Brett hurried to claim the seat nearest the water. She realized it was actually the most vulnerable side, the easiest route for someone to slip up and surprise them. She noticed, too, even as they discussed the menu, that the others were studying the water. It was a beautiful night, with lights glistening on the water, boats off in the distance, music playing softly and a benign moon smiling down. But even in such a perfect setting, there was an elephant in the room that couldn't be ignored.

Brett seemed bothered by something more than the overall situation, Lara thought. She looked at him, a question in her eyes. "What are you thinking?"

He sighed. "It still bothers me that anyone can get to Sea Life by boat."

"I don't think anyone is after the dolphins," Lara said.

"Someone threatened you because of your role in finding those body parts, so why wouldn't they threaten Cocoa for the same reason?" Meg said.

That thought disturbed Lara. "Do you really think someone would try to hurt Cocoa?"

"Maybe," Brett said.

"We need security there, then," Lara said determinedly.

"How would just anyone know which dolphin is Cocoa? I know that everyone who works with them can tell them apart. They have scars, they're different sizes, whatever," Meg said. "But how would a stranger know which dolphin was Cocoa?"

"They could show up during the day and find out what she looks like and which enclosure she's in," Brett pointed out.

"I wonder if we need to move Cocoa to another facility, just for a while," Lara said. She bit her lip. "From what I've heard, it's a tricky thing to do, moving a dolphin. But Grady must know somewhere she could be taken until this is over." She hesitated, looking at the three of them. "I'm going to stay at the facility tonight."

She knew, of course, that they wouldn't let her stay there alone.

In fact, she was counting on it, since she didn't have a gun or the faintest idea how to use one. Point and shoot, of course, but beyond that . . .

"You know I'll stay wherever you stay," Brett said quietly.

Meg laughed softly at that. "Yes, and we know you'll keep a very close eye on Lara, too."

"I'm wondering if we should all stay there," Matt said thoughtfully. "Until now I didn't really see the facility as being in danger, but the threat to Lara puts a new spin on things. We'll all stay."

"Slumber party?" Meg said drily.

"I wasn't planning on getting that close and cuddly," Brett said, grinning. "But here's the thing. The offices aren't that close to the lagoons. If one of us is guarding the dolphins, someone else will have to be on guard duty in the offices."

Matt nodded. "Shifts down by the lagoon."

Lara felt uneasy. "I wonder if we should have left at all. Rick and Adrianna are in for the night, so if something happened down by the water, they wouldn't even know."

Brett reached across the table, his fingers curling around hers. "Don't panic. I can fix that with a phone call. You guys order — I'll have the roast beef — and I'll be right back."

She looked at him curiously.

"World's greatest partner," he said, then

stood and walked away to make his call. When he returned, just as their waiter was leaving, he told Lara, "Call Rick and Adrianna, tell them Diego will be there in ten minutes. They need to meet him at the parking gate and let him in."

She called Rick's cell. He seemed surprised by the change in plans, but pleased, as well.

"Never hurts to have some big guns around when the world goes crazy, huh?" he said.

"Never," she agreed.

She hung up and smiled at Brett. "Thank you — and Diego, too."

"We might be taking things a step too far, you know," Matt said. "There's a good possibility that it hasn't even occurred to our killer that snuffing out a dolphin would help him in the least."

Lara nodded, knowing he was trying to reassure her. "But maybe the killer is vindictive, too. He obviously knows I'm involved, so he probably also knows it's through Cocoa."

No one argued that. Just as their food arrived, Brett's phone rang. He answered, listened briefly, then said, "Thanks" and hung up. "We're good. Diego is on the job."

They didn't linger, but they did enjoy their

dinner. As soon as they were done, they drove straight back to Sea Life.

Diego's car was there in the lot.

Lara used her key to enter, then reset the alarm once they were inside.

Brett called Diego as she closed the gates. "I told him we're here. He's going to keep first watch by the water."

"That's the kind of partner you keep," Matt said.

Brett nodded. "Seems as if you did okay, too."

"He did extremely well — and so did I," Meg said, smiling. "What watch? We can divide things up however you want."

"I'll take the second water shift," Brett said. "That means you guys can get at least six hours sleep up in the office, so you can take care of that end. After that point, your choice whether you take guard duty alone or together. You'll hold down the fort in the morning until the gates open to the public."

Lara had moved ahead to unlock the doors to the office. Now she stepped aside and asked Brett, "Mind if I head down and thank Diego?"

"No. But I'll watch you from here, and I'm not going in till you're back."

She hesitated. "Don't you need as much sleep as you can get before your shift? And really, I know you're all just humoring me on this."

"The more I think about it, the more I think there could be a real threat to Cocoa as well as you," he said, his tone serious.

She nodded and turned away, feeling suddenly awkward.

As she got closer to the water, she saw Diego. He was seated on the platform in the lagoon beyond the dock, looking out at the water. He stood and turned the minute she got within a hundred feet, his hand on his gun, though he didn't pull it.

"Hey," she said, going out to join him.

"Hey. How was dinner?"

"Really nice. And thank you so much for coming right out here. Without you, we would have had to settle for takeout. You and the others are putting in an awful lot of hours."

"Doesn't matter," he assured her.

"I hope Brett's call didn't interrupt anything important."

He grinned. "No, it was fine."

She tilted her head and stared at him assessingly. "I meant a date."

He laughed. "No, I was just starting to see someone, but it wasn't going to work out, and I knew it. My fault. I was intrigued, just . . ."

"Just not intrigued enough?"

"Just not intrigued enough," he echoed. "Besides, with this thing going on . . . I don't think any of us is really going to rest until we get to the bottom of it."

Lara hesitated, and then sat down on the platform. Diego followed suit. It was a beautiful night, crystal clear. The water stretched out before them, rippling in the moonlight. A pleasant breeze off the bay swept away the day's heat. Palm trees bent gently, their fronds rustling in soft whispers.

"Thank you," Lara said again.

He smiled at her. "No problem. It's my job."

"I don't think anyone is supposed to be on call twenty-four hours a day."

He shrugged. "This isn't exactly your usual job. It's kind of a passion, I guess."

"I guess. As long as I've known Meg, she's wanted to be in law enforcement. She was so thrilled when she got into the academy."

He smiled at her. "I knew from the time I was a kid, too. I grew up in a nice, decent neighborhood, but it started getting rough when I was in my teens. I saw a little girl killed by a stray bullet in a gang shooting. The cop who came was a real dedicated guy. I still remember how when he questioned me, I knew he wasn't going to stop until he caught the guy. And he did, too. I became a cop first, then went into the FBI." Studying her, he said, "I still remember to stop and eat even when I'm on a case, though. Brett, well, he flat-out forgets half the time. Are you the type of woman who can live with that?"

She flushed, looking away. "I wonder if I even know myself half the time, what type of person I really am. I know I . . ."

She paused.

"You what?"

"I know that if he'll let me, I want to hang around your partner for a very long time."

Diego grinned, set an arm around her shoulders and gave her a brotherly hug. "Just be careful. It won't be easy."

"You speak as if you know."

"I'm divorced," he said with a shrug.

"I'm sorry."

"So am I."

"Her loss."

"We'll go with that," he teased. "She's a great person. I've never fallen out of love with her. But if you see her, don't tell her that."

"Will I see her?"

"I doubt it. She moved to Colorado."

"Well, I still say it's her loss."

"It's a tough road. You have to be ready.

You know what I'm saying?" he asked her. "You're not mad?"

"Hey, you're trying to keep my girl Cocoa safe," Lara said. "What's not to like?"

"Anyway, I suggest you go back inside and get some sleep — or whatever," he teased. He glanced at his watch. "Brett is due to replace me here in less than three hours. Plenty of time for . . . whatever," he said with a grin.

Lara stood and grinned back. "All right, I'm off. And, Diego . . ."

"Yeah?"

"Thank you. For everything."

"My pleasure, *mi amiga,*" he said. "Now go."

Lara didn't waste any more time but hurried down the path toward the offices. Along the way she paused for a minute. The breeze was rustling the tree branches; except for the auxiliary lights near the buildings, it was very dark here.

She turned back toward the water. She could see the glow that was downtown Miami. It was a beautiful city at night, with multicolored lights from a dozen skyscrapers or more reflecting off the water.

But here, where the shadows lurked . . .

Anyone could be hiding, watching, waiting . . .

341

She hurried along and saw that, as promised, Brett was waiting for her outside the building. She had the feeling that Diego had called him and said she was on her way. She smiled. And when he smiled back she knew that they were good.

She hurried to his side.

"Diego okay?" he asked.

"Yes."

He grinned. "Come on, then. We have a few hours before I need to relieve him."

She laughed softly. "Your partner suggested that would be more than enough time."

Brett grimaced. "Did he now? That boy may be in trouble one day. I do have a long memory. But . . . where are we headed? Matt and Meg took the break room sofa."

"They're asleep?"

"They sleep lightly, but yeah, they're already catching their z's."

"We'll take the extra room in Grady's apartment," she told him. "I'm sure he won't mind."

She led the way, aware that a feverish flush was already suffusing her skin.

They made it up the stairs and into Grady's guest room. Then they were tugging at each other's clothes and trying to touch one another at the same time, their lips meeting, tearing apart, then meeting again. The only thing Brett paused for was setting his Glock on the bedside table, where it would be within easy reach at all times, she realized.

Seconds later their clothes were strewn in a tangle on the floor and she was in his arms, savoring the feel of his naked flesh against hers. It amazed her how quickly she could forget everything but the feel of his lips against her skin, the movement of his body against hers . . .

His fingers teased at her thighs; his mouth brushed over her breasts. She swept her hands down his back to his buttocks, feeling as if she was sinking in a strange world of molten lava and longing. They seemed to meld together, and yet she was also aware when he entered her, moving with her, filling her with sexual excitement and building fire.

She felt as if she'd been denied too long, and a hunger that eclipsed everything else rose and carried her to a searing — and shared — climax.

Brett whispered against her ear, "My partner did warn you that I didn't need much time."

"He did," she said, laughing.

"But that was only the first course, you

343

know . . . the appetizer."

"In that case, I can't wait for the entrée."

"You won't be disappointed," he promised. "You'll want to taste, to savor. Every touch will be perfection."

"Do tell," she murmured, the tip of her tongue teasing along his flesh. "Something like this . . . ?"

Time lost all meaning. Whether he felt challenged to prove a point or was simply so involved he couldn't stop, Brett taught her a new definition of foreplay, and she hoped she returned the favor. She loved that he could laugh, that they could play and that lying with him seemed the most natural thing in the world. She was curled against him, half-asleep at last, when she heard him sigh as he eased away from her.

"Three hours goes quickly," he said. "As the cliché goes, time flies when you're having fun."

"Wait for me. I'll go with you."

"I'm accustomed to this, you're not. Get some sleep," he told her.

She didn't listen. She was already up and searching for her clothes. She intended to prove that she could be ready for anything in a matter of minutes, and she did it.

He smiled, shaking his head as he looked at her. "Are you sure? This is what I do for a living," he reminded her.

"And Cocoa," she said softly, "this place . . . They're what *I* do for a living."

He nodded, and they headed downstairs together.

Diego rose as they arrived. "Everything's quiet in the lagoon," he assured them. "Your dolphin has been eyeing me suspiciously, though," he told Lara.

She smiled. "You can tell Cocoa from the others?"

"We've been out with her several times," he reminded her. "I know the darker coloration right on her nose and the little scar pattern above her eyes."

"I'm proud of you," she said.

He nodded and looked at Brett, then walked away, waving to the two of them. "I'll be in the comfiest chair I can find," he called. "Because I'm sure the other two are already hogging the sofa!"

As it happened, the sunrise was on their shift. It wasn't as glorious as the burst of color when the sun set in the west, but it was still beautiful. Pale yellow shards broke through the blue darkness, then began to grow, until finally the golden orb of the sun burst above the horizon.

Cocoa made a stunning leap into the sky, a beautiful silhouette against the gleaming circle of the sun. And then she dropped into the water and swam over to Lara, who stroked her and apologized for not having any fish.

Matt and Meg joined them on the platform a little while later.

Soon the day would begin.

And despite the "bloodied" and disarticulated doll on her desk, Lara thought that it was going to be a good one.

Because she was grateful for all life had to offer. And she wasn't afraid.

14

Brett and Diego started the morning by arranging a visit to Dr. Robert Treme. His receptionist informed them that no one saw Dr. Treme without an appointment, and that the next opening was weeks away.

They flashed their badges and the woman reached for the phone. Brett smiled and said they would show themselves in. Then they walked past her down the hallway and into the doctor's office.

Treme looked thoroughly displeased by the interruption. He stood and glared at them for a moment, then sat back down suddenly as if his legs had given way. He looked like a beaten man.

"You signed a death certificate for a living man," Brett informed him. "Who was then stolen from a mortuary and went on to commit murder."

Dr. Treme went white. He was suddenly angry as he leaned over his desk. "Do you know how many lives I've saved? I wasn't the only one there! The nurses saw that he was dead, his family saw that he was dead. By all medical standards, the man was dead!"

"And you know nothing else about cause of death?" Brett demanded.

"What?"

"His heart didn't kill him — poison did. Someone most likely gave him puffer fish toxin. The Haitian zombie toxin," Diego said quietly.

Treme sank back into his chair. He lifted his hands helplessly. "With his heart, I didn't know if Nicholson would make it or not. I told his family that. Don't you understand? There was no reason to test for poison or anything else. The man was dying when he came in, and then he died. Anyone could have gone in there before that point. He was in a hospital, not a prison. Don't you men see what this is going to do to me? I'm good at what I do, but my practice could be ruined if this gets out. As it is, I'll have to face the board. All my life . . . all the good I've done . . . gone. It's a disaster."

Brett looked at Diego. Dr. Treme was guilty of accepting what seemed obvious without thorough testing. But neither of them thought he was responsible for what had happened or had even been aware of it. This visit had only confirmed that earlier impression.

"It was a disaster for another man, too, Doctor," he said quietly. "And that man is dead." He and Diego turned to leave, ignoring the receptionist and her threat to call security on their way out.

"We need to get someone looking into the hospital and everyone who treated Nicholson while he was there, every visitor," Brett said.

"Agreed," Diego said. "I'll call Matt and put him on it."

"Good idea," Brett said as Diego took out his phone.

Their next stop was the mortuary.

Geneva Diaz looked as pleased to see them as if they were the CDC walking in to announce that bubonic plague had arrived.

"What?" she demanded, standing at the door and blocking the entry. "You've already ruined our business. Neither my husband nor Mr. Douglas is here. I suggest you contact our attorneys."

"We could do that," Brett told her, shrugging. "But if I speak with your attorneys, I'll have to ask them why you let someone else into this place. And it *was* you, Mrs. Diaz. We know it."

Her face instantly gave her away, though she denied the accusation, stuttering, "I — I'm not guilty of . . . of killing anyone or stealing a corpse or . . ."

She fell silent.

"How about you talk to us? Do it now and we can make things go as easily as possible for you," Diego said.

"I don't want to die," she whispered, looking around as if someone could have slipped into the mortuary to attack her.

"If you're that afraid, you really need to talk to us so we can protect you," Brett said.

Her shoulders fell. Her perfect-hostess demeanor seemed to fall along with them.

"My husband doesn't know, and neither does Jonathan Douglas," she said. She looked out at the street and then ushered them in. "My office," she said, and added, "Please."

Her office was soothingly decorated, which made sense. After all, it was where people came when they were heartbroken by the loss of a loved one. There were tissue boxes on both corners of the desk; the chairs were beige and plush and comfortable.

Diego and Brett both sat while she walked around behind her desk.

"It was my nephew," she said, not quite

meeting their eyes. "My sister's son. I swear to you, my husband is insisting he's innocent because he is. And to be honest . . . I didn't know what had happened, what had been done, until you came to us." She was quiet for a few seconds. "Until we knew that Mr. Nicholson wasn't in his grave."

"Could you give us some more details, please? Starting with your nephew's name?" Brett asked.

She sighed, still not meeting their eyes. "I knew that Pedro — Pedro Campesino — was in trouble. He started with drugs in college. Cocaine, an expensive habit. If I'd realized earlier . . ." She paused, shaking her head. "He's in rehab now. He came to me when he was at his worst because he had no choice. My sister . . . She's a single mother. Pedro's father was in the army and was killed in Afghanistan. There was no way she could give him the money he needed, so I was his last resort. He owed so much money to the dealers. So much. I was trying to figure out a way to get it when . . ." At last she looked up at them. "When the man came to me."

"What man? Does he have a name?" Brett asked.

"I'm sure he has one," she said drily. "But he didn't share it with me. I thought he'd come in about a funeral at first. I didn't know until we were in this office that he was after something . . . wrong. He told me that he needed to make a copy of my key. He said he'd use it once, that it would have nothing to do with anything that would put me or my family in jeopardy and that if I just let him have my key, he'd see that Pedro was never bothered again. If not, Pedro . . . Pedro would be killed. So . . . I let him have my key. I had no choice. I didn't know — I swear, I didn't know — why he wanted it or what he was going to do. I didn't know someone would be killed. Am I going to go to jail for this? No matter what happens to me, you have to know that my husband and Mr. Douglas are innocent."

"Mrs. Diaz, I believe you. And I believe that your intentions were good," Brett said. "Your nephew is lucky to have you. But now we need your help, and I promise we'll do our best to keep you out of real trouble. We need to figure out who this man is. I'd like you to work with a police sketch artist, and right now I also need you to give me your best description of this man."

She shuddered suddenly. "I don't know. He was the kind of man who I think can kill me far more easily than you could ever protect me," she said flatly.

"But if we can arrest him, you're safe, aren't you? Do you really want to live in fear for the rest of your life? What about your nephew?" Diego asked her.

She lowered her head. "Middle-aged, Hispanic. I'm not sure from where, though. His accent wasn't Cuban, but I'm not sure what it was. Dark hair, dark eyes. Medium height and build. That could be at least half the men in Miami, right?"

There was a knock on the door. Geneva Diaz froze. Brett smiled at her. "It's okay, be casual."

"Yes?" she said.

The door opened and Carl Sage, the mortician, stuck his head in. He looked annoyed and was about to speak when he saw the agents and stiffened.

"Excuse me. I didn't know you were busy," he said to Geneva.

"What is it, Carl?" she asked.

He looked acutely uncomfortable, then finally spoke. "There's . . . a body. I have no instructions, no information regarding this man."

Geneva frowned. "I wasn't expecting a delivery."

"It's not a delivery. I walked in, and he was on the table."

Brett pushed past him and hurried back

to the employees-only area, then burst into the embalming room.

The man on the table appeared to be in his forties, medium height and a medium build. His looks suggested he was Hispanic.

Diego, Geneva and Carl had followed Brett.

Geneva let out a scream.

He turned to look at her, certain that he was about to learn that this was the man who had approached her — the man who had demanded her key.

He was also, Brett was certain from the pictures he had seen, Jose Acervo, the man who had hired Pierre and Antoine, and been responsible for Antoine's death. Twice.

Jose Acervo, a known associate of Anthony Barillo — and not the man Brett had seen with Barillo.

"Mrs. Diaz," Brett said, about to ask, though he was certain of the answer.

He didn't get a chance to voice the question, because Geneva Diaz slumped to the floor.

Diego instantly hunkered down by her and looked up at Brett. "No pun intended, but it appears that Mrs. Diaz has fainted dead away."

Lara wasn't sure why she felt as confident

of her own safety as she did. Of course, by midmorning the place was bustling. It was Saturday, which meant it was a great day for parents to spend time in the sun with their children.

Every swim and encounter was booked. Adrianna's theory was that they were especially busy because Sunday would be totally devoted to the military and Just Say Thanks.

Whatever the reason for the crowds, Lara wasn't the least bit concerned about walking around the place. She decided "safety in numbers" was a reality, not just a cliché.

She was able to put yesterday's threat out of her mind because she was certain that whatever cowardly creep had put that doll on her desk couldn't possibly have anything to do with Sea Life, other than having bought a ticket. Yes, whoever he was, he'd found his way to her office, but it wasn't that difficult. The building was clearly marked as being for employees only, and her name was on her office door.

As she walked around the facility, she was pleased with the way everything for the following day seemed to be falling into place. Several reporters would be on hand, they'd received a nice response from the local community and every one of their military

355

guests had been slotted into the schedule for their experience of choice.

With everything going so well, she decided to take a walk down to the educational building and have a chat with Dr. Amory about what she'd seen at lunch the other day.

When she arrived, classes were underway. Cathy and Myles were talking to a room full of people of all ages, from grandparents to toddlers.

Myles waved to her but continued speaking as she smiled and walked by.

Nelson Amory left the public programs to his staff so he could focus on his research. He was undeniably brilliant, so it was undoubtedly a much better use of his time.

He looked up the minute she walked into his office and flushed. Was he feeling guilty? Or had she only imagined his momentary look of unease?

He smiled and said, "Hello. What can I help you with today, Miss Media? Looking for news for your next press release?"

"Oh, no, I'm not here to grill you," she said. She pulled up a chair and sat down in front of his desk. "Honestly? I came here because I'm worried."

"Worried?" he asked quickly.

She nodded gravely.

Could he have been the one to put the savaged doll on her desk?

"About what?" he prompted her.

"You were at lunch with some heavy hitters the other day."

He shook his head. "Yes, some of our top sponsors. Why should that worry you? I don't owe you an explanation, Lara. You're the new kid on the block here, you know."

She nodded. "I *do* know. And you've all been wonderful to me. I just wanted to ask you to tell Grady if you're considering leaving. To give him time to find someone else."

He looked down, as if his papers were more important than her presence. Then he said quietly, "Don't worry, I'm not leaving."

Lara leaned forward. "Did one of them offer you a job?" She spoke lightly, but she was serious, and she was sure he knew it.

He leaned back. "Taggerly," he admitted. "He wants to develop a protocol for testing a new category of drugs."

"But your specialty is marine mammals. How would you . . . ?"

He nodded. "In my past, I did a lot of necropsies on marine life. Not just mammals. Sharks. I was with a company that did all kinds of work on sharks. They rarely get sick, and cancer is especially rare. Ely thinks — and I tend to agree with him — that

357

research into the shark immune system will transform medicine."

"But you were with Blackwood and Martinez, too," Lara reminded him.

He nodded. "Taggerly is encouraging the others to invest in this new line of research with him. I guess he figured he'd wow us all at once — them with predictions of huge profits and me with the huge salary he offered — and we'd all fall into line."

"But you really didn't accept?" Lara asked.

He stared at her, irritated. "If I'd accepted, I'd have turned in my resignation already."

"Was the salary really that huge?" she asked.

"My God, you're nosy. Must be from hanging around with the FBI all day," he muttered.

He looked at her squarely. "I have to admit, I was tempted. But I've had jobs in that kind of research before. I've analyzed enzymes, cells, brains, blood systems . . . I've tried to measure the effects of naturally occurring chemicals, how certain animals live so long, why others die so young. Truth is, I like it here. I like Grady. I love the dolphins and all our other animals. But the dolphins most of all. Their intelligence is virtually unmatched in the animal kingdom, and yet they still love interacting with people. Look at how much Cocoa loves to work with you! It's fascinating. So yes, I turned down the job. And I never said anything to anyone here *because* I turned it down. I'm here, and I'm staying here. Poor but happy, instead of rich but miserable."

Lara smiled at him. "That's great," she said.

"Poor is great?"

"As long as it comes with happy," she said. She stood, hesitated, then said, "And by the way, I'm sorry for being so nosy about the salary."

"It's all right. I'll be nosy myself soon enough. As I said, I've been fascinated with Cocoa's determination to win your approval."

"Is that what she's doing? Trying to win my approval?"

"Yes."

"I thought she was just trying to be friends."

He grinned. "Same thing, I guess. But dolphins are like people in a way. When they like someone, they want to please that person. Cocoa's determined to please you. I think it's important, and something to be studied. As is her ability to find and bring you things in the water other than objects you've specifically asked her to locate."

"Body parts," Lara said.

He nodded gravely. "Body parts," he repeated, and shivered. "Let's hope the cops get this guy — and quickly."

"Amen," she murmured.

She thanked him and headed out of the office. No, she couldn't believe that he had left a butchered doll on her desk. Look how honest he'd been with her.

Then again, was she truly capable of knowing?

She left the building via the classroom. She waved to Myles and Cathy, then felt them watching her as she kept walking.

Of course. She'd interrupted their class. And she'd gone to see Dr. Amory. Maybe they were wondering what she'd talked to him about.

And maybe she was just being paranoid.

No, she wasn't.

Someone had warned her to keep out of the water. To stay out of the Miami zombie case.

As she walked back to her office, she caught various bits of conversation coming from the crowd.

No, they hadn't abandoned Sea Life in horror.

But they were talking about body parts in the water.

And zombies.

This time, when the questions flew, when the medical examiner arrived, when crime scene techs flooded the place, Brett had no trouble believing that Geneva Diaz had absolutely no idea how a corpse had ended up in their embalming room — the corpse of the man who'd had her key.

When Jonathan Douglas and Richard Diaz arrived, both of them now eager to help with any investigation, Geneva cried and confessed what she'd done to both men. Oddly, the truth seemed to make things easier for everyone at the mortuary.

Phil Kinny told them that he would know more details postautopsy, but he was quite certain that Jose Acervo was truly dead.

He wouldn't be coming back to life to usher anyone else into heaven or, in his case, hell.

"I'm guessing that cause of death will turn out to be stabbing," Kinny told them after his initial on-site examination of the remains. "You can see that he was stabbed several times. I won't know the order of the wounds until autopsy, but they were to the heart, stomach, kidneys, spleen and liver."

Kinny looked at them from the far side of the body. "Come see me tomorrow. It's Sunday, when even the Lord said we should rest, but this case is too important to wait. Come in and I'll show you what I've got on the bodies of Antoine Deveau, Randy Nicholson, Miguel Gomez and your Mr. Acervo here."

"We'll be there," Brett promised him.

The body was removed, but the crime scene techs stayed on.

Richard Diaz was clearly worried for his wife; he was dismayed that she had done what she had, but he felt that the failure was his, as well. "She should have come to me. She should have felt that she could tell me anything," he said over and over.

Brett and Diego offered the Diazes protective custody until the case was solved, but Richard preferred to handle things himself, planning a trip that would take them out of the area for the immediate future.

Since Douglas and the rest of the staff had no direct connection to the crime, they would be provided with police patrols and an officer on mortuary premises for at least the next several weeks.

Jill managed to get Brett alone for a few minutes. "What happens if you don't find whoever is doing all this? What if it goes on

362

for months . . . years? Just how long will the police protect us?"

"Jill, I can only tell you again, we *will* find him. This is too big. Too many people are involved, and we have so many officers from so many different agencies working on this that we can put a lot of pressure on the whole enterprise. Whoever's behind this, he'll make a mistake, and then we'll get him."

She nodded. "We'll just have to be very careful, I guess." She started to walk away, then turned and asked, "You will make sure we know if . . . if there's a reason for us to watch out for something or some*one* in particular, right?"

"Yes," he said. He shouldn't have, of course. But she'd helped them immeasurably, and since he couldn't personally watch over her and her family, the least he could give her was peace of mind.

When she left, it was finally time for him and Diego to head out and meet back up with Matt and Meg, and try to put the pieces together.

"We're fucked," Diego said as soon as they were outside.

"Fucked?"

"That guy was our best lead. If we'd found him alive . . ."

"He wouldn't have said a word. He would have gone to jail before he ratted out his boss, who in this case might be Barillo or might be someone else entirely. Anyway, we're meeting with Kinny tomorrow, so let's see what he has to tell us."

"Let's hope to hell it's something useful."

"No matter what," Brett said, "I think we're going to pay a visit to an associate of Acervo's."

"Barillo?" Diego asked.

Brett nodded grimly.

"He's denied everything. He made a point of confronting you face-to-face to deny everything."

"But Acervo was a known associate of his. I want to see what he has to say."

"You're worried," Diego said. "You're worried about Lara."

Brett managed a smile. "Yes — and no. Meg won't leave her. And I honestly believe that the man pulling the strings will make a mistake, and soon. And then all this will be over."

Diego was quiet. "Money's involved in this somewhere," he said. "We already knew that, though. After Kinny and Barillo, we're going to start looking at money."

"Who the hell has more money than Barillo?" Brett asked.

Diego smiled. "Lots of people. Lots of *rich* people. This is Miami, *mi amigo.* Lots of people here have money."

When Sea Life closed at five o'clock, people jumped into action to make everything spick-and-span. Everyone was excited about the next day. The entire staff was set to arrive early to be ready to greet the massive numbers of soldiers and supporters who would be coming.

As things wound down and staff started leaving, Lara wandered back out to the lagoon to check on Cocoa. There were still people around, and it was daylight, so she wasn't worried about her own safety. The dolphin swam over to the platform and allowed Lara to stroke her. Then she backed away, chattering, and Lara turned around quickly, her heart suddenly pounding, expecting to see someone coming up behind her.

The sun was still up but sinking slowly, and at first she saw no one.

And then she did.

Miguel Gomez was standing there, watching her and Cocoa, a slight smile on his face.

"Hello, Miguel."

"Hola, senorita."

"Join me," she suggested.

It didn't even seem odd to her that she was speaking to a ghost.

He came and sat with her. "That dolphin is very special, is she not?" he asked.

"Yes, she is."

"She sees me," he whispered.

"I think so."

"Have you found out . . . how this happened? To me, I mean," he asked.

"No, but we're making progress."

He nodded. She felt his sadness as if it were something in the air that washed over her.

"I wish I could help," he said. "I wanted to live the dream, and we did, for a while. But now . . . I'm here. And Maria . . . I want so badly to see her, to know that she forgives me . . ."

"I'm sure she does," Lara said.

He looked at her anxiously, as if desperately hoping she could say something that would prove the truth of her words to him.

And suddenly she realized that she could.

"My friend . . . the FBI agent. You know him, too. Brett Cody. He's seen Maria. She knows it wasn't really you."

He seemed to brighten. "This is true?"

"Cross my heart," she said, smiling.

He shook his head. "Why can't I see her?"

he whispered.

"Maybe you will," she said. "Maybe soon. Maybe when we find out what happened to you."

She didn't know that, of course. But she felt she had to say something to reassure him.

After a moment he said, "I hope so. For now, I am just . . . here."

She looked at him and said, "Miguel, someone threatened me. They went up to my office and put a broken-up doll there, warning me. Since you're here, perhaps you could watch and see if anyone does something like that again."

He frowned. "People come and go from that building all day."

"You see them, right?"

He nodded.

"Who?"

He lifted his hands. "All the people who work here."

"Did you see anyone else? People who *don't* work here?"

"I don't know what happens all the time," he told her. "I come a lot to the water. To watch the dolphins." He pointed to Cocoa, who was watching them from the water. Cocoa and the other dolphins often watched people. It made Lara wonder just what they were thinking, if they were as curious about human behavior as humans were about theirs.

He smiled. "I think she performs for me sometimes. Just for me."

"She certainly might," Lara said.

He smiled at that, and continued to watch the dolphin for a minute. Then he turned to her. "I will watch for you," he said. "I will help solve this if I can. I promise you that. I tried to be a man for my family when I lived. I loved my wife, and I was so lucky to have a wife who loved me, too, so dearly and so deeply, for so many years. I will watch for you. And I will know who comes and goes from now on."

"Thank you, Miguel," she told him.

She smiled, pointing to Cocoa, who had decided to entertain them with a high-flying flip.

"Look, Miguel," she said. "I know that was for you."

But when she turned back to look at him, he was gone.

15

"So this man, Jose Acervo, he's really dead?" Lara asked.

Brett nodded, enjoying being out to dinner again, despite the circumstances. They'd chosen another restaurant on the water, though this one offered a certain amount of privacy despite the fact that it was Saturday night and the area was in full swing. They'd headed to South Beach in his Bureau car. He hadn't used the restaurant's valet service because he'd learned early in his career to have his car available at all times, but his federal plates allowed him to park in places the average driver couldn't, unless they were looking to incur a fine.

As they ate, music spilled from a dozen clubs. Miami's beautiful people were out, the women in short skirts and ridiculous heels, along with tourists in flip-flops and T-shirts. They'd actually decided on the beach because of the crowds; it was easier to talk in private when the noise around you didn't allow for anyone outside your intimate circle to hear what you were saying.

Diego was taking the first watch at Sea Life again while the rest of them escaped for a few hours.

"We're getting close — closer anyway," Matt said. "The fact that Acervo was killed — and left at Diaz-Douglas as a . . . warning, I suppose — is telling. Someone was afraid that we would find Acervo and get him to talk about what's going on. I wonder if the killer thought Geneva Diaz would be so terrified by the arrival of the corpse that she would make sure he was buried quickly to avoid her secret coming out. Any word on whether the crime scene techs found anything useful?"

"Not yet," Brett said.

"Well, I discovered something pretty interesting today," Matt said. "I pulled up all kinds of information and statistics, and I emailed all of it to you and Diego," he told Brett. "And based on what I found, I can tell you that I don't think this began with Miguel Gomez, or Randy Nicholson or Antoine Deveau. About three months ago, the body of a young woman washed up on a beach up in Broward. There had been severe damage to her head."

"I remember that, actually," Brett told him. "The theory was that she'd fallen overboard and been killed by an engine propeller. She was eventually ID'd as an illegal, finally claimed by an uncle after he received his legal status in the country."

Matt nodded. "Fishermen out in the Florida Straits brought up a body about four months ago. A man. Same thing. Head bashed in. They never did discover who he was. The assumption is that he was an illegal, trying to make landfall so he'd be allowed to stay in the country. No one ever claimed him, needless to say."

"That's the problem here. So many people take off from Cuba or Haiti in rafts and boats, desperate to make it to land anywhere they can. A lot of them don't make it, but a lot of others do and then end up part of the criminal underworld, because that's the only option open to them."

"A whole slew of unwilling human subjects for medical experimentation?" Meg asked thoughtfully.

"Maybe," Brett said. "But what's the connection to our zombies?"

"That's the interesting thing," Matt replied. "They'd been struck on the head. Sure, people are murdered often enough by being struck on the head. But with everything that's going on, I'm thinking we ought to be testing for puffer fish poison. And," he added with a shrug, "who do you choose, who's your ideal victim, if you're doing something criminal? Someone with no name. A forgotten person. People die — they *drown* — when boats go down at sea. They don't usually wind up with their heads bashed in."

"But I still can't figure out *why* someone would do it," Lara said.

"Because he can?" Matt asked.

Brett thought about the question. "I don't know. Unless we really do have a would-be Papa Doc Duvalier out there, someone who really believes he can create an army of zombies who'll do anything they're programmed to do?"

"Is that really possible?" Lara asked.

"Possible, maybe, but certainly not feasible here," Brett said. "I think that local law enforcement is more than capable of stopping an army of what amounts to automatons."

Lara sat back, frowning. "You think someone has been actively kidnapping people — starting out with people no one would notice were gone, or at least wouldn't dare report? And then they upped the game when they weren't caught?"

"I certainly think it's possible," Matt said.

"I'll go one step further and say I firmly believe they set out kidnapping the forgotten people and experimenting on them," Brett said.

Lara turned to him. "You've got me thinking. I went to talk to Nelson Amory today. He was out with three of our high-powered sponsors a few days ago. Meg and I saw him when we went to lunch with Sonia Larson. Their conversation looked . . . heated. I had the feeling he might be accepting a job offer from one of them. Today I flat-out asked him what was going on. If he was going to work for one of them, I thought he needed to tell Grady. In fact, Ely Taggerly *had* asked him to leave Sea Life and go to work for a new pharmaceutical company Ely is starting up to look at what Dr. Amory says is a whole new class of drugs. Apparently he used some of his time at Sea Life events trying to gather some funding for his project. So here we are talking about a zombie drug made from puffer fish, and now there's a Sea Life connection to pharmaceuticals. It might not mean a thing, but it seems worth thinking about, at least."

"You think Ely might be looking for something — some magic drug — that's found in the brains of the dead?" Meg asked. "That's . . . gruesome."

"Very gruesome," Matt agreed. He looked at Lara. "I'm not sure how that fits with zombies going around killing people, but who knows? You could be on to something."

"A cure," Brett said. "Someone might be looking for a cure for something. A brain disease. Alzheimer's. Parkinson's. Any one of the dozens of neuro diseases out there."

Lara cleared her throat. "So," she said, looking at Brett, "let's say that you're all right and this started out with someone kidnapping illegal immigrants trying to get into the United States. The forgotten people, as you say. They performed experiments on their brains, which they covered up when disposing of the corpses by smashing in their heads. Then . . ."

"Then," Brett picked up, "they took Antoine Deveau. They knew he was illegal and that Pierre couldn't raise a stink, because he was illegal, too. And given that we're talking illegals, there may be more people missing than we'll ever know. So Antoine 'dies' and they have a funeral, and when they bring him back they send him to kill Pierre. Maybe they were trying to see if he still recognized his brother after what they'd done to him. Who knows?"

"And then," Meg continued, "they gradu-ated to cruising the hospital to see if they could get away with fooling the doctors with their toxin. At least they had *some* scruples. They looked for someone who was dying anyway and found Randy Nicholson."

"What about Miguel and Maria Gomez?" Lara asked.

Brett felt his muscles tighten. "Miguel was on purpose. They knew that he'd contacted the FBI. They wanted to torture him before they killed him. And even if he didn't know what he was doing, they wanted his final torture to be killing his own wife, the woman he loved. I'm hoping tomorrow we'll find out more about how it was done, how the drug actually works." He took a drink of his water and went on, "We stopped in to see Dr. Treme, too. We're pretty sure he wasn't complicit in any way, and it seems unlikely he had anything to do with a body being found in the bay. He made a mistake, one that's going to cost him. But we're pretty sure he wasn't involved in any criminal way."

"So we're back to the Barillo family?" Meg asked.

"Or someone with ties to the Barillo fam-ily — and money," Brett said. "Diego and I are going to see Phil Kinny tomorrow. He has some ideas that might add to what we've been talking about here. We're going to pay a visit to Anthony Barillo, too." He turned to Lara. "After that threat yesterday, I was thinking that maybe you should come with us tomorrow, so we can make sure you stay safe."

She smiled at him. "Not tomorrow. It's Just Say Thanks day. I'll be running around like a chicken with my head cut off."

"Mike the chicken," Brett said.

"What?" Meg asked.

Brett shrugged. "Look it up. Diego told me about it. Back in the 1940s a chicken lived for months with most of its head missing."

Meg and Matt stared at him.

"I've heard about Mike the chicken. Our zombies still have their heads, at least," Meg said.

"Until they don't," Lara added very softly.

Brett looked over at her and felt his body grow tense. Apparently there was something to chemistry after all.

He hated knowing that she had to go to work tomorrow, but she wouldn't be alone. Meg and Matt would be there.

Not to mention hundreds of retired members of the American military.

He wanted to argue that she should leave

the event to someone else and be with him. It was that primeval need every caveman felt to protect his woman. But he didn't say anything. It was pure ego to think that he could be a better protector than Meg and Matt. Not to mention that it was wrong to take something away that meant so much to her — and to so many others, as well.

He'd actually intended to be there himself, but there was no waiting on this case. He and Diego had to follow these new leads.

"Tomorrow," he told her, "you have to be careful. Very, very careful. Please."

"Tomorrow," she assured him, "I'll be safer than ever. The place will be flooded with people — including the media. I can't imagine a situation where there could possibly be more help at hand — if help was needed, which I'm sure it won't be," she said. "I'll be surrounded by the military, for heaven's sake. And of course I'll have Meg and Matt with me at all times."

"I know," he said.

She smiled. "And I'll also have Miguel Gomez." She paused and touched his arm. "He was there this evening when I went to see Cocoa. She sees him, too. He's lost and so sad. I really pray that there's a heaven and that he'll find Maria there."

"I believe that they're meant to be together

forever and that they *will* meet again," Brett assured her. And, he realized, he *did* believe it.

"Have you seen her again? Maria?" Meg asked him.

He shook his head. "But I haven't been home in days except to grab a change of clothes. She only shows up at night, or when I'm just waking up, actually."

"Miguel definitely wants to help," Lara said with a smile, "and he's going to be watching out for anything strange now, too."

After dinner they returned to Sea Life, where Brett and Lara went down to the docks to see Diego.

Brett caught him up on the conversation they'd had at dinner, and Diego nodded gravely. "Mike the headless chicken," he said. "And to think you mocked me."

"You have to admit, it sounds pretty strange," Brett admitted.

"You two better go get your sleep — or whatever," Diego said. He winked at Lara. "After the 'whatever,' you should have plenty of time to rest."

"He must be speaking from experience," Brett told Lara. She laughed softly, linking an arm through his, and they left Diego there on the platform. He'd apparently formed his own relationship with the dolphins. Brett looked back and saw two of them swim over and let Diego stroke their backs.

Back at the house, he and Lara tiptoed past Meg and Matt, who already seemed to be asleep on the couch. Up in the guest room of Grady's suite, they turned to one another by instinct and fell swiftly into a frenzy of lovemaking, as if they really did have only minutes.

He wondered if making love to her would ever get old.

No, never old. Just more comfortable, easier, with more time to laugh and tease.

But it would always be amazing.

As he drifted to sleep, he thought of Miguel. And he wondered if this was how Miguel had felt about Maria when it had all begun for them.

Lara had done more work on the Just Say Thanks day, with press releases and appeals to their sponsors, than on anything else since her arrival at Sea Life. She'd approached it with every bit as much passion as she ever had brought to her political campaign work and enjoyed it more.

They always hoped for contributions to help keep the place afloat, but they didn't have to kowtow to lobbyists, nor were they expected to provide payback beyond the occasional gala dinner and special opportunities to interact with the dolphins.

Far better than politics!

But Just Say Thanks day was the best, because it was all about giving back to those who had given so much themselves.

She was with Rick and the trainers when they had their 6:30 a.m. meeting, and she was with Grady twenty minutes later when he spoke with the rest of the staff, including the interns.

She caught Dr. Amory watching her as they all listened to Grady talk about the importance of the day. When Dr. Amory smiled at her and gave her a thumbs-up sign, she returned it. She saw in his face that what he'd told her the other day had been true.

He loved Sea Life. He didn't mind being a happy poor man.

When it was almost time for the Just Say Thanks people to arrive, she was thrilled to see that her efforts had paid off. Ely Taggerly, Grant Blackwood, Mason Martinez and Sonia Larson had all, as promised, shown up to make the day special for the vets.

Grant flirted with her — the man just couldn't help himself, she thought — but she easily kept a safe distance.

The locals and tourists had also come out in droves to say thank-you to the veterans, and that made her even happier. Their show of support was bound to bring smiles to a lot of faces.

When the buses drove up with the soldiers and their counselors, she felt an incredible rush of pleasure at being part of something so special. She stood at the entrance, the head of their welcoming committee.

There were several hundred people lining the paths behind her, waving American flags and applauding as the soldiers entered the facility. She glanced down the line; Sea Life sponsors, from the high flyers to those who donated what few dollars they could, were mingling with all the other guests. Sonia Larson was applauding enthusiastically, a look of tremendous appreciation on her face. Lara was also glad to see Meg just a short distance away, keeping an eye open for anything out of place and potentially dangerous.

The soldiers started getting off the buses and making their way through the gate. Some walked easily while some needed canes or crutches. Still others were in wheelchairs.

Some had prosthetic arms or legs — or

both. Some looked down, faces reddening, as if embarrassed by the show of appreciation. And some smiled and laughed, fist-bumping the children standing by the path and thanking those who'd come to thank them.

Once all the vets were inside the gate, they headed in groups down to the docks and the different lagoons, where the trainers would work with them. Lara helped with directions and made sure everyone knew where they were going.

She also talked to reporters and made certain that they only talked to veterans who had agreed ahead of time to be interviewed. She left one reporter with Grady, then took a minute to hang out by Cocoa's lagoon, where Rick was taking a group in to swim with her as another group made their way out of the water.

Lara was pleased to see that her favorite dolphin was ready to show off. Even as the soldiers readied themselves to go into the water, Cocoa greeted them with a spectacular leap and a chattering sound that sounded almost like "Welcome."

Lara paused then, and felt a wave of gratitude and emotion nearly overwhelm her as she noticed a wheelchair by the dock. It was piled high with the artificial limbs the men and women couldn't wear into the water.

She turned to see if she could help the group whose swim had just finished, but she didn't need to. One of the soldiers using a crutch was already standing by the wheelchair, handing out limbs.

"Hey!" one of the others called to him. "Wrong leg. Give a marine *one* task and he blows it!" he teased.

"That one might make you taller, GI Joe," the marine called back.

They were young, she thought. All so young. And it occurred to her that too often there was no choice in life but to fight, and so many times the fight took the young and beautiful of the world.

"Lara," Adrianna called to her from the platform. "Want to help piggy-back a soldier?"

She was startled; she'd had no idea she might be asked to help out in the water.

"Me?" She felt a moment's genuine fear. What if she did something wrong?

"Cocoa knows what to do, but she likes to have someone she trusts with her."

"I'm not wearing a suit yet."

"There are extra suits like mine in my locker," Adrianna said.

Lara thought Adrianna's outfit, which was

more like a T-shirt and shorts than a bathing suit, looked both comfortable and flattering.

"Come on in!" one of the soldiers called, and suddenly it was a chant.

"Okay, I'm coming! Just let me grab a suit and I'll be right back," she said.

She realized she was still scared, but this was also something she really wanted to do.

Meg nodded to her. "I'll be watching the lockers," she said quietly.

Lara hurried back to the lockers, heading to the left side where the trainers kept their things. Adrianna's locker was open, with a pile of suits neatly folded and ready for use on the upper shelf. Lara grabbed one and shut the door, and the locker next to Adrianna's popped open. Evidently the lock on it hadn't caught.

She started to close it, then paused.

There was a small tube of paint lying on the floor of the locker.

Red paint.

Like the color poured all over the dismembered doll she'd found on her desk.

For a moment she froze. Then she felt her anger kick in, and she looked quickly through the locker, trying to determine whose it was.

None of the lockers had nameplates, and

the contents — a newspaper, a water bottle, a towel — didn't tell her anything. She bent down and carefully picked up the tube of paint, using her shirt to hold it so she wouldn't disturb any prints.

Then she went ahead and changed, leaving the paint wrapped in her clothes in Adrianna's locker. She closed the door and wished she had a lock, but she figured it would be safe for the next thirty minutes or so. She would tell Meg about it right away, and get it to her as soon as she could. Since she suspected the perpetrator had thought the paint would never be found, she thought it was highly likely that they might find fingerprints on it.

She had a smile on her face when she headed out the door.

And she felt a steely determination that no one was going to mess with Sea Life.

"I've now had the opportunity to compare the brains and tox screens of each of our dead men, so I'll speak as plainly as I can," Kinny told Brett and Diego. "Certain chemicals that the body makes — dopamine, for one — can be given in doses to patients suffering from various diseases of the brain and nervous system. There are a number of dopamine systems in the brain, managing neural and muscle control. It's logical to think other chemicals — including man-made chemicals — could have different effects, effects that could be harnessed in some way." He paused, shaking his head. "I believe that someone was directly injecting certain chemicals into the brains of the dead men to destroy their mental capacity, their ability to reason, and leave them open to nothing but his direct commands. I haven't been able to figure out the exact compounds that were used, because they were slightly different in each case. What, exactly, the experimenter has been trying to do, I'm not sure. But while the victims meant no more to him than cockroaches do to you and me, I don't think that creating a zombie army is what he was trying for. I think the murders were simply part of the experiment."

"So your theory is that someone was experimenting with mind-control drugs for a reason we don't understand. He used some kind of poison to create the perfect simulation of death, then injected the 'dead men' with other chemicals to destroy their ability to think and to control their behavior, keeping them alive long enough to kill someone else? Someone close to them," Brett asked.

"Yes, as far as it goes. It's the end game that eludes me. But here's the thing. There are traces of chemicals that improve motor skills and mental well-being in the mix, as well," Kinny said. "Given the degradation of the remains, I can't be positive, but it does seem that puffer fish poison was used to simulate death so the actual experiment could begin, but I don't think it was key to the experiment itself. All I know is that we have a budding Dr. Frankenstein on our hands."

"So we're looking for someone with medical know-how?" Diego asked.

"Indeed we are. Possibly a biochemist," Kinny said.

"And here I thought everything led to Barillo," Diego said.

"Maybe it still does. The man has a medical degree, and one of his sons is in med school," Brett said.

"I forgot about that. And he's probably got doctors in his employ."

"Not to mention his mansion might as well be a castle. I think we're going to take a trip to see *Dr.* Barillo right now," Brett told Diego. "Thanks for the help, Phil."

Diego waved to Kinny on the way out. "First zombies and now Frankenstein," he

387

said. "What will we discover next? The *chupacabra*?"

Lara saw Meg watching from the platform while she was in the water with Cocoa and one of the vets who was waiting for his dorsal tow.

The young naval officer was minus his left arm; despite that, he could probably swim better than she could. But she knew Cocoa, and Adrianna was trusting her to help both dolphin and vet enjoy their experience, and Lara liked to think that even if she wasn't actually a trainer, she did have a special bond with the dolphin.

Cocoa certainly made her look good, going above and beyond and giving the officer a great swim around the entire lagoon. When she had safely returned him to the platform area, she made a stunning leap right over Lara's head, delighting the entire crowd.

When Lara emerged from the water, she was on a high. It had been an unbelievable experience.

Shaking hands with so many of the servicemen and women, laughing and as wet as they were, she felt a sense of camaraderie unlike anything else in her life so far. It was a far cry from what she had known in politics, that was for sure.

She hadn't had a chance to tell Meg about the paint she had found earlier, because as soon as she'd left the locker room she'd been surrounded by soldiers rushing her down to the water, and now, just as she was about to say something, Meg got a call on her cell. Lara pointed to the locker room and mimed dressing. Meg nodded and went back to her call.

Lara hurried into the showers marked Women. There were several stalls separated by nothing but thin plastic curtains. She could have hurried back to the privacy of the office, but she wanted to hurry. Quickly stripping down, she stepped into the hot spray.

A few minutes later, when she turned off the water, she heard something just outside.

The whole facility was crawling with people. Many of the veterans and counselors were women. Maybe one of them had wandered in to change.

But the noise had been furtive, a strange scraping sound, as if someone had inadvertently brushed against the wall.

"Hello?" she said.

No answer.

She could scream, of course, and a hundred people — including Meg — would come running. It was ridiculous to feel afraid.

But she did.

Someone had been in there, watching her. She felt incredibly vulnerable, standing naked and wet in the tiny shower stall.

And for all she knew, someone was standing just outside the curtain, waiting to attack when she emerged.

She hesitated for a second longer. There was no weapon in the shower, unless she could force her attacker to slip on a bar of soap. There was nothing to do but open the curtain and look outside — and be prepared to scream blue blazes if someone really was out there.

She jerked the curtain open, ready to face an attack, but the room was empty. From outside, she could hear cheering and laughter, signs that the day was the huge success she'd hoped for.

She grabbed her towel, dried off, then hurried to retrieve her clothing.

Immediately, she realized that something was gone.

The tube of bloodred paint had disappeared.

And then she knew. Someone *had* been in there with her. Someone who'd somehow known what she had found.

Someone who knew what it meant and had no intention of being incriminated.

16

"Mr. Barillo isn't receiving visitors," a voice said over the speaker.

Brett and Diego were in their car in the driveway at Anthony Barillo's waterfront estate. A call box on a pole to the left of the great iron gates protecting the estate warned "All visitors must request entry."

They had requested.

Someone at the other end had listened to them identify themselves, and then, sounding bored, the detached voice had replied.

"You know, sometimes it seems as if people just don't like us," Diego said, shaking his head. "This could get depressing."

"We'll get in," Brett said firmly.

Diego smiled. "Of course we will."

"You tell Mr. Barillo that Special Agents Brett Cody and Diego McCullough are out here. He came to see me, and now we're coming to see him."

The voice started speaking again.

"I've informed you once, Mr. Barillo isn't —"

"You go tell your boss what I said, and I suggest that you do it quickly, instead of trying to send us away before checking with Mr. Barillo," Brett said firmly.

There was silence on the other end and then he heard another voice, this one aggravated. "What do you want?"

"To speak with Anthony Barillo."

"Are you trying to arrest my father?"

"I'm trying to speak with him."

"Then —"

Brett glanced over at Diego. Then they heard a third voice — older, gruffer, accented and deep.

"What is it, Jeremy? Who is there?"

"Agents Brett Cody and Diego McCullough, Mr. Barillo," Brett said. "I'd like you to do me the courtesy of inviting me in for a conversation."

"Open the damned gate," Barillo said.

The gates swung open. Brett entered the long driveway that curved in a horseshoe shape in front of the house. Barillo had two acres on the water, an estate purchased from a popular music mogul twenty years earlier. The lawn was perfectly manicured and expansive. The porch was tiled in rich mosaics. The front door was etched glass.

When they got out of the car, Diego nodded toward two men in suits standing on the porch, one on either side of the door. They were wearing earwigs, and while their arms were folded across their chests, Brett was certain that they were armed. Their faces were impassive.

Brett didn't expect trouble, however. It would be bad business for Barillo to let his men have a gun battle with federal agents in his front yard.

"Good afternoon, gentlemen," Brett said, exiting the car and heading to the door.

One man nodded grimly and opened the door for Brett and Diego.

They entered a large foyer leading to a huge room with ceilings that appeared to be about twenty feet high. A curving staircase led to an open balcony above them, and halls to the right and left led into the rest of the house. Brett had heard that the place had over ten thousand feet of living space.

A woman in a tight-fitting business suit and high clicking heels hurried toward them. "Mr. Barillo will see you in his office."

She swept a hand to her right and led them forward, opening a carved wooden door at the far side of the entry.

Anthony Barillo was there, standing

behind his desk.

Brett thought that the desk — and the room — seemed to dwarf him. On the one hand, it was a typical office, with a desk, computer, bookshelves, an elegant globe in the center of the room and several chairs arranged before the desk.

On the other hand, the windows behind the desk looked out on the water and a yacht that was at least fifty or sixty feet in length berthed at an even longer dock.

"Gentlemen," Barillo said.

His voice still sounded rich, but Brett detected a light rasp to it. As Barillo sat, his hand shook slightly. "Sit, please. To what do I owe the pleasure?" he asked drily.

Brett and Diego looked at one another and took the chairs facing the desk and the view. They'd already decided that Brett would be asking the questions. Diego, who was even now angling his chair so he could see the door in his peripheral vision, would be listening and watching their backs.

This place was actually a small fortress — no matter how well camouflaged it was as an elegant home. Brett had seen other criminals with similarly pleasant-looking homes that housed entire arsenals.

"Mr. Barillo, I admit to being in a quandary," Brett said. "I assure you that neither of us is wearing a wire, so I hope we can speak frankly. We both know that you're a businessman. All kinds of business. You're almost a small country unto yourself, with your own army. And desertion from that army amounts to treason. We know this. But you made a point of coming to me to tell me that you didn't kill women, that you were innocent of Maria Gomez's death, and that you didn't even kill her husband, a former employee of yours. But now, Mr. Barillo, things are getting very complicated. You see, a man disappeared from a funeral home. A man named Randy Nicholson, who supposedly died in a hospital from heart failure. Except that he wasn't really dead."

"It's my fault a hospital makes mistakes?" Barillo asked.

Brett ignored that and said, "I believe he was poisoned, that someone administered puffer fish toxin to simulate death. I think someone who works for you — someone in your 'family' — found out about Randy Nicholson's condition and figured he'd be a nice specimen for your experiments. Easy to slip into the room and poison a guy with a heart condition. And there you go. He's 'dead.' Then he disappears from a funeral home. And the man who arranged that? None other than Jose Acervo. Another member of your fine family. Or should I say, a *late* member of your family?"

Barillo was good; he kept his features impassive. But there was something in his eyes. Something that told Brett he had been blindsided.

He hadn't known that Acervo was dead.

Barillo stared at him. "I knew nothing of this," he said, confirming Brett's suspicions. "Yes, I knew the man. I even called him a friend. But I can't be held responsible for the criminal activity of others. This thing . . . This whole thing with Miguel and Maria . . . I am innocent. I am grieved to hear about Jose Acervo, as well as the death of Mr. Nicholson. But I don't know anything about any of these things."

No, Brett thought, Barillo hadn't known — until now. But now that he knew, he was suspicious of those around him.

Because someone was using his power and his private "army."

Diego nudged Brett's foot with his own, nodding toward the windows.

A half dozen of Barillo's men had gathered on the lawn and were staring steely eyed into the room.

Brett thought that he had discovered what he needed to know, for the moment anyway, so there was no point in tempting fate —

397

and Barillo's bodyguards — by pushing further.

He rose. "Thank you for your time, Mr. Barillo. If you think of anything that can help us solve Mr. Acervo's murder, we'd greatly appreciate hearing from you."

Barillo rose, as well. He was visibly shaky.

"Gentlemen," he said, nodding. "Cecelia will see you out."

Brett thanked him. He glanced at Diego. He realized that neither of them had known that the smartly dressed young woman who had led them in was Barillo's daughter.

When they reached the car, Diego turned around and waved at the phalanx of bodyguards who had come to watch them leave.

"I feel like we just visited the Hispanic version of the Godfather," Brett said. "I have a revision on an old theory here. Maybe, oddly enough, I think someone made him an offer that he *could* refuse, but someone in his circle of power decided to accept it." He shook his head. "We're still back to *why*?"

He thought about the meeting they'd just had. And he thought back to the night Barillo had come to his house. He looked at Diego and said, "*I know.* I know what they're doing. Or trying to do." He paused.

"At least I think I do. I think I know how it began, and why. But what I don't know is who's behind it, or what power he wielded that let him take control over Barillo's men, or how he managed to blackmail, threaten or bribe so many people. Now we just need to figure out who he is."

Lara knew she needed to tell Meg about the paint, and the person who'd been watching her in the shower, but with so many people still at Sea Life, half of them needing her for one thing or another, finding a free and at least semiprivate moment was turning out to be impossible.

When she emerged from the shower, she was immediately approached by a reporter from a national news show. No sooner had she finished the interview than Sonia approached her, full of enthusiasm for a new line of clothing to benefit Just Say Thanks. As frustrated as she was by being unable to talk to Meg, Lara had to admit it was a great idea, and she was thrilled that Sonia had thought of it.

Meg was never far away, of course, and Lara wondered if her friend knew she needed to talk to her.

She probably did. Since they'd been kids, they'd had that bond.

But as the day wore on, the opportunity still eluded her. She began to wonder if she should just tell everyone to move aside, she needed to talk to the FBI. But she realized that whoever had taken the paint had undoubtedly disposed of it where it would never be found by now, so time wasn't of the essence. She might as well focus on her job making sure everything ran smoothly and the veterans had the wonderful time they deserved.

And today *had* been as wonderful, thanks to everyone at Sea Life who had worked so hard to make sure every detail was taken care of. She wanted to see it through to the end, say goodbye to the veterans and applaud for them as they left.

She was near the gift shop exit when Sonia came over and gave her a huge hug. "You've just changed my world. I can't wait to start designing my new line. And," she added, beaming, "to date one of the soldiers I met."

Lara smiled. "There's nothing like a man in uniform," she teased.

"Forget the uniform. There's nothing like a man in almost nothing," Sonia said. She frowned suddenly. "I almost forgot, I'm supposed to tell you that Adrianna needs you at the back right lagoon. I just ran into what's-his-name from Education."

"Myles Dawson, the intern? Or Dr. Amory?"

"The young one, Myles," Sonia said.

"What's going on, do you know?" Lara asked.

Sonia shrugged. "They had all the dolphins in the back lagoon for the last show. I was there, and it was fabulous. Cocoa was the star. Adrianna gave people things to throw in the water at the same time, and then she told Cocoa which one to get. She never missed! But now Cocoa doesn't want to go back to her own lagoon. Myles said Dr. Amory is down there now, too, but Cocoa is ignoring both of them."

"I'm on my way," Lara said.

She glanced over at Meg, who was talking with Ely Taggerly. She pointed to the far lagoon, and Meg nodded.

Lara headed directly for the far right lagoon, but when she paused along the way and glanced about fifty feet back, she saw that the last of their guests were hovering by the gift shop and exit. Grady was smiling as he shook hands with Mason Martinez. Everyone looked happy.

She rounded the bend that led to the platforms at the back.

"Lara!"

She heard the speaker's anxiety and turned.

The ghost of Miguel Gomez was keeping pace with her, reaching out as if he could stop her, but of course he couldn't.

She stopped walking and asked, "What's wrong?"

"I've been watching, just like you asked me to. That man — the teacher — he followed you before. He went into the locker room, but then he came back out right away and threw something in the lagoon."

Lara paused. "Myles?" she asked. "Young guy about my age?"

Miguel nodded.

She realized that if Myles had stalked her into the locker room — afraid she might have found the paint — this was a trick, and she had Miguel to thank for saving her. She turned to thank him, but he was gone.

She was on the dock that led from the center of the facility out to the platforms at the far lagoons, and she quickly turned around — and saw Myles standing behind her, just at the beginning of the dock.

Watching, she thought, to make sure she went out to the lagoon. He was definitely alone, and now she was torn between hurrying out to the lagoon to see if someone else was there and striding back to tell him what she thought of him.

Going out alone would be foolish; she could prove a point, but she could also get herself killed.

She headed toward the man, feeling her fury increase with every footstep. He saw her, and then he must have heard something, because he turned and his eyes widened.

Lara smiled; the bond she shared with Meg — not to mention Meg's training as an agent — meant her friend was standing between Myles and the rest of the facility. He was sandwiched between them, with nowhere to go. His only possibility of escape was to jump in the water, and even then he wouldn't have gotten very far.

Lara reached him first. "What the hell were you planning, sending me out there?" she demanded.

He frowned in confusion. "Adrianna is out there," he told her. "She and Dr. Amory are having a conversation with Cocoa. She doesn't want to listen."

Meg was directly behind him at that point, but she stayed silent and waited for Lara to speak.

"Want to tell me why you were snooping around the women's shower?" Lara asked.

"Why I was — No!" Myles protested. "I

wouldn't."

"You were seen. There was a witness. Just as there was a witness when you decided to put a chopped-up doll on my desk," she accused him. He hadn't been seen, of course, not then. But *he* didn't know that.

His face went red.

"Meg, would you check out the end of the dock?" Lara said. "I don't think Myles will take off. He has nowhere to go, because when people who are part of this get caught, they wind up dead. Don't they, Myles?"

He just stood there, jaw locked, a sea of misery and confusion in his eyes.

"Move a muscle before I get back," Meg warned him, "and you'll be guilty of resisting arrest, and then God knows what we'll have to do to you to capture you."

She walked past Lara, simultaneously drawing her Glock from the holster at the small of her back and slipping her cell phone from her pocket.

Lara stared at Myles.

"It was a joke. It was just a joke," he said.

"The doll? A bloody doll, dismembered like the bodies we found? A nice blond doll, just like me? *That* was a *joke*?"

He looked away.

"Who told you to do it, Myles?" she asked, thinking of Brett's idea of an unwitting conspiracy. "How deeply are you into this thing?"

"I'm not in on anything. It was a joke. Okay, it was a bad joke. But you're Little Miss Perfect, coming down here with a full-time job in two seconds, everyone fawning all over you. Smart, beautiful and everyone loves you — including the damned dolphins. Then you turn into Miss Supersleuth. I just wanted to scare you, show you you're not so special."

Lara heard footsteps behind her and turned quickly.

Meg was coming back.

Lara looked at her, arching a brow questioningly.

"Adrianna and Dr. Amory are down there waiting for you, hoping you can get Cocoa to listen to you," Meg said.

"But — but he *did* it. He put that doll on my desk," Lara said.

Meg inclined her head toward the path. When Lara turned to look, she saw Matt approaching. Obviously Meg had called him, and he'd come quickly from wherever he had been.

"Mr. Dawson," Matt said. "I think you need to come with me."

"Because of a doll?" Myles said, his voice cracking.

"Because of a whole lot of dead people," Matt responded. "I can put cuffs on you, or we can walk out of here nicely together. It's your choice."

"I don't know anything." Myles insisted. "I didn't do anything except chop up a doll. That isn't illegal."

Matt started toward him.

Myles backed away, hands up. "I'll walk out! But you're crazy. You can question me all night, but I just wanted to scare Lara, maybe make her quit. That's all, I swear." Then he gave up talking and walked away with Matt.

Lara and Meg watched the two men go.

"Thanks," Lara said, and let out a soft sigh. "I suddenly thought that if I kept going, I'd find someone waiting there for me with a gun or a knife or something."

Meg shook her head. "They really are trying to get Cocoa back to her lagoon."

"I'll see what I can do. What will Matt do with Myles?"

"Take him to headquarters. Call Brett and Diego."

"What do you think? *Was* it a joke, or did someone bribe or threaten him into doing it?"

"I don't know," Meg said. "I honestly don't know. Let's hope that one of the guys can get the truth out of him," she said. "For now . . ."

"Cocoa," Lara said.

As they walked, Meg asked her, "What happened? What made you suspect Myles?"

"I didn't, not at first. I found a tube of red paint in a locker this morning when I was changing. I took it and wrapped it up in my clothes, and I was going to tell you about it, but I never got a chance. Later, I heard someone when I was in the shower, and when I came out, the paint was gone."

"But how did you know that Myles took it?"

"Miguel," Lara said, and she smiled. "Miguel was watching."

"Parkinson's, ALS, I don't know," Brett said under his breath as he drove. "But it's got to be something neurological."

"What are you talking about?" Diego asked.

"Did you get a good look at Anthony Barillo? Did you see the way he shakes?"

"He shakes. So what? He's weak, he's old."

"Not that old," Brett said. "He's somewhere in his early sixties. To be as frail as he is, to shake the way he does . . . Something's going on."

"You've lost me."

"I think someone's trying to save Anthony Barillo, and that's what these experiments are all about."

"So you think he — whoever he is — is killing people to save a life?"

"I do," Brett said. "And I don't think Barillo himself knows anything about it, so I'd say someone right under him — his brother, Tomas, most likely — is pulling the strings."

"Why Tomas?" Diego asked. "I mean, Tomas stands to take over a giant crime empire. He might want his brother dead."

"Barillo's still his brother," Brett said.

"Your mind is far too twenty-first century," Diego said. "Throughout history, brothers have killed brothers for power and control. Cain and Abel, for a start."

"One of Barillo's children, then?" Brett said. "One of his sons is in med school. Whoever it is, he's close enough to the seat of power to have access to money, so if he doesn't have medical knowledge himself, he can just buy someone who does."

"They could all be in on it," Diego acknowledged.

Brett was thoughtful for a moment. "With Little Haiti right here, it's easy enough to get the recipe for the traditional zombie toxin. He probably started out experimenting on animals, but that couldn't tell him enough. He needed to test his theories on human beings. Where to look first? In the ranks of those who could disappear without consequences, unnoticed or noticed only by those who didn't dare take action. Perhaps those who were desperate enough to seek haven in the United States by crossing the Florida Straits on rafts and inner tubes if they had to. But they weren't always available. So he turned to the streets and people like Pierre Deveau. I don't think he was interested in creating zombies for their own sake but in exploring how to affect the brain, with the goal of outsmarting the disease, or even bringing Barillo back from the dead with his facilities intact. He might even have been disappointed that his zombies were willing to kill their own family and friends, because that meant he'd failed in his goal.

"At some point he got braver and expanded his experiments into a hospital. I think at that point he was simply curious to see how well his potion could feign death, and he must have been very pleased with the results."

Brett's phone rang just then. He saw that it was Matt and used the car's built-in Bluetooth to answer. "Hey, Matt. I'm in the car with Diego and we've got you on speaker."

"I'm at HQ, and I've got the Sea Life intern, that kid Myles from the education department, in an interrogation room. He's the one who put the doll on Lara's desk. He claims he did it to scare her and get her to quit. Apparently he resents the fact that she's the golden girl while he's been trudging along unappreciated. I thought I'd let him cool his heels, then send you in."

"How did you find out it was him?" Brett asked tersely.

"Lara found him out," Matt said. "With a little help from Miguel, as it turns out."

"A ghost fingered him?" Diego said. He looked over at Brett, but he didn't seem as surprised as Brett would have expected, given that he'd never actually talked to his partner about seeing Maria and Miguel.

"Long story, but Lara found the paint and ended up confronting him. She lied and told him there was a witness, and at that point he folded pretty quickly."

"Is Lara there with you?" Brett asked, trying to tamp down his anger that she'd been in danger and he hadn't been there to protect her.

"No, she and Meg are still at Sea Life, finishing up after the event today. I'll see you at headquarters."

Diego didn't say anything after Brett hung up. Finally Brett looked at him and asked, "You don't think all of this is crazy?"

Diego looked at him and smiled slowly, shaking his head. "I'm half Cuban and half Irish. Hell, if a leprechaun walked onto the scene, I'm not sure I'd be surprised. So what the hell. If a ghost can solve our case, I'm all for it."

17

"Cocoa is being as stubborn as all get-out," Adrianna said, aggravated. "I could leave her back here overnight, which I may have to do, but Tampa, Luke and Bartholomew are already here. She'll want to play as rough as they do, and I'm worried she'll get hurt."

Lara hadn't told them that Myles had been taken down to FBI headquarters. For one thing, at her request, no one at Sea Life, except for Grady, knew about the doll, so there was no easy way to explain that Myles was gone and why. Anyway, it didn't really matter. The day was over, and she would worry about tomorrow when it arrived.

Adrianna's attention was all for the dolphin.

"She's not listening to me, either," Lara told Adrianna after ten minutes of fruitlessly trying to coax Cocoa back into her own lagoon. "I'm sorry. Can Rick help?"

"He's with the last of our sponsors," Adrianna said, shaking her head. "He likes to pull the 'head trainer' card when the big money is around. Besides . . ." she murmured, then hesitated. "The truth is, he doesn't work as well with Cocoa as you do. Want to swim with her, see if that works?"

"I guess, but you'll have to open the gates so I can go from lagoon to lagoon."

"I'm worried the others might get in the way, so we'll go around the long way. Through the bay," Adrianna said.

"You really think she'll follow me?" Lara asked.

"She followed you all over the bay the other day," Adrianna reminded her.

Dr. Amory was still standing on the platform, so Lara turned to him. "What do you think?"

"I think you're the most interesting research opportunity I've seen in ages," he told her, grinning. "I think you need to give it a try so I can observe."

"All right, I'll grab my suit and be right back."

When Lara turned to go, Meg followed. "I'm not letting you go anywhere alone," she said.

"I'll change in the office," Lara said. "Nice and safe."

"We'll have to find an opportunity for you to wear that suit Sonia gave you," Meg told her.

"Sounds great," Lara said. "Meg, what do you think about Myles Dawson? Is he just a nasty jerk, or is he part of this?"

"Hopefully the guys are finding that out right now."

Back at the office, Meg waited while Lara changed. When they left, Lara noticed that there was still a group gathered near the exit by the gift shop, talking with Rick and Grady. She wondered how they could hear each other over the anthems and military songs that had been playing all day but seemed really loud now that the crowd had thinned out to almost nothing.

She and Meg made their way to the sandbar that led to the farthest platform.

Dr. Amory was nowhere in sight, and Adrianna was standing on the platform as if frozen, staring out at the water.

"Hey, Adrianna!" Lara called. "I'm back!"

Without saying a word, Adrianna fell face forward into the water, as if she'd been pushed by an invisible hand.

"What the hell?" Lara said.

"Get behind me," Meg ordered, forging her way around a tangle of sea grape trees and ragged brush that had taken hold on the sandy spit. Her Glock was in her hand, and Lara followed her as the path curved toward the dock.

"We have to go help Adrianna!" Lara said.

And then she tripped over something.

A body.

"So you just don't like Lara, is that it?" Brett asked, sitting across the table from Myles Dawson.

Dawson looked at the small digital recorder sitting between them. "I like her fine," he said.

"Then, why would you play a trick like that on her?" Brett asked.

Myles slumped back and sighed. He lifted his hands. "You don't understand. I've worked there for three years now. I'm still an intern. I teach classes. I play with kids. I smile and haul fish for the trainers. Hell, I get people coffee when they ask. It was past time for them to hire me and bring on some other sucker as an intern. Instead, they paid a fortune to hire Lara."

"So you just wanted to scare her away? Why? Your job is nothing like hers."

"Really? She was hired to do media. Next thing you know, she's a star trainer and consultant for the FBI. She'll be running Education soon enough. Dr. Amory thinks she's the best thing we've seen since he doesn't know when. He wants to work with her and Cocoa. If she starts working with Amory, I'll never be full-time."

"And you're sure — you're absolutely sure — that no one put you up to your 'prank'?"

Myles looked back at Brett, baffled. He lifted his hands again. "What? I'm so stupid I can't even have an original idea?"

Brett leaned forward. "People have died, Myles. Do you want to be convicted for being an accessory to murder?"

"Me? Murder? Good God, it was a prank!" Myles protested.

"You ever have a drug habit?" Brett asked him.

"What? No!"

"Were you ever caught stealing? Doing anything you shouldn't have done?"

"What do you mean?"

"Do you have a record or anything else someone else could hold over your head if you didn't do as you were told?" Brett asked.

"No. No, no, no! What I did was stupid and I shouldn't have done it, but I did it on my own," Myles said, looking as if he was about to cry.

"And no one — no one — suggested in even that vaguest way that you should have

416

done it?" Brett pushed.

Myles shook his head. "Do I need a lawyer?"

"You're not under arrest."

"But you just said —"

"We're just talking here, Myles. And I'm really hoping that you really will talk to me."

Myles seemed to sink into himself even more. "You must know everything there is to know about me. Big Brother is watching and all that. I don't have a record. I admit I don't always recycle, but that's it. I just . . . I just got so jealous that I wanted Lara to go away! Can't you understand that?"

"Do you know of anyone else who dislikes her?" Brett asked.

"There must be other people who resent her, but I have no idea who they are. Rick, Grady, Dr. Amory and everyone else seem to think she's more of a natural with the dolphins than they are. Maybe Adrianna! I mean, she's never said anything to me, but she must get sick of hearing Rick praise Lara all the time."

There was a rap on the door. Frowning, Brett got to his feet and went to answer. Matt was standing there with a sheaf of papers in his hand.

"I think I'm just getting somewhere," Brett said. "Any chance this can wait?"

"Not a chance in hell. I just got the hospital's list of every visitor who was there on the day of Randy Nicholson's death. Trust me, you're going to want to see it."

As Meg kept running toward the spot where Adrianna had tumbled into the water, Lara, with her heart in her throat, bent down and saw that the body she'd stumbled over was Dr. Amory's. He was crumpled on the ground, half-covered by one of the sea grape trees. There was a bloody gash on his head.

"Dr. Amory?" she said, testing for his pulse. He looked as if he had taken the curve too quickly and tripped, hitting his head on a tree root.

She was relieved to find he had a pulse. She started to rise to cry for help, but then she heard the blast of gunfire.

She ducked, shocked by how loud it had been. They must have heard it even back by the gift shop. At least that meant help would come quickly.

Was Adrianna still in the water, or had Meg gotten to her before the shot?

A voice came from somewhere past the sea grape trees. "Your friend is shooting at me, Lara. Make her stop. If you do, I'll let you go down for Adrianna. She has about another minute and half, I imagine, before it's lights out forever. My dart only gave her a little prick, but it's enough to keep her from doing a thing to help herself. There's a wonderful study on puffer fish poison. Seems way back when Cook was exploring, he and his men all grew sick after a meal in the South Pacific. Pigs on board, fed the remnants of the meal, all died. Turns out they'd been eating puffer fish. Scientists ran some weight calculations and determined that the dosage the men received was sufficient to harm but not to kill them, but it was more than enough to kill their pigs."

"A hundred soldiers heard that shot and will be out here in about two minutes," Lara said.

Ignoring her, he said, "And then there's Meg. She can't see me, but I bet she can hear me." He raised his voice. "You *can* hear me, can't you, Meg? I can pop a dart into you any time I want, and it won't be a small dose."

"Lara, don't!" Meg warned. "Don't do anything he wants — he'll just kill us both anyway."

Lara stood, her legs shaky, her hands trembling. She knew that these people had no problem killing, but she needed to help Adrianna.

She walked around the bend in the trail

to the platform. She couldn't see the man who'd been talking to her, and she didn't have time to waste looking. She dived into the water, found Adrianna's body and she dragged her back to the platform.

"Now, Meg," the man said, "I have you in my sights. Help Lara get Adrianna out of the water. Oh, throw down that gun first."

"Like hell I wi—" Meg began.

Something whistled through the trees.

Meg ducked, and the dart went past her and dropped into the water.

"Toss the gun!" he said.

"Do it, Meg," Lara pleaded.

Meg, stony faced, looked at her. And dropped her Glock by her feet.

"Oh, no. That's not good enough. Kick the gun away from you."

Lara met Meg's eyes and could tell she didn't want to do it. But whoever was watching them was calling the shots.

She thought that she could hear Meg's voice in her mind.

We've gotten out of messes like this before. We'll get out again.

"Do it, Meg," Lara pleaded. "Kick it away."

Meg did. Then she reached down and helped Lara get Adrianna onto the dock.

Lara dared to look back. Help was

nowhere in sight. How had they missed the shot from Meg's Glock?

The music. It was the music.

"Meg, Adrianna needs help — now!" They bent over the woman together, Meg counting and Lara trying to breathe life into Adrianna's lungs.

"It's time to go," the voice said.

"Go where?" Meg demanded tersely.

"Ten steps, other side of this little sandbar."

Lara was sure she knew that voice, and she tried to place it. There was something so familiar about it, and yet . . . different.

"I'm not sure Adrianna is okay yet," Lara said between breaths. "God only knows what you pumped into her."

"Not enough to kill her, though perhaps the water took care of that."

At that exact moment, Adrianna coughed.

"Come — now! Or she'll be dragged into this, too."

Lara looked at Meg. Neither of them moved.

"I can down you both in two seconds."

"Then, do it. You're planning on killing us anyway," Meg said.

"Don't you want to buy time?"

"Yes, we'll buy time," Lara said, looking at Meg and then nodding meaningfully at

Adrianna, who was sputtering but breathing.

If she regained full consciousness, the killer would undoubtedly carry out his threat, and then she would end up dead, too.

"Do you want me to shoot her after you went to all that trouble to save her?" the man asked.

Lara stepped over the platform and started across the little sandbar. Meg followed her.

A small boat with three occupants was waiting on the other side. A fourth man was waiting to hop aboard. He had to be the man who'd been watching. Threatening them.

She saw who it was. And she knew him. But she didn't understand why he was involved.

Life — and apparently death — could be deceiving.

"They were all at the hospital? Ely Taggerly, Grant Blackwood *and* Mason Martinez?" Brett said, heading out to the car.

"Taggerly was there to visit an employee, a man named Jackson Baum. Martinez was visiting a sick sister. And Blackwood was having some tests done," Matt said. "We have officers tracking down both patients now, making sure the men actually visited them, and we're verifying that Blackwood did indeed get those tests. And," he added, "I've already sent officers out to Sea Life. But —"

"We have to go," Brett said. "We need to get there. Whether or not they're guilty, all of those men are there. Now. And while the doll may have been a vindictive prank, someone may still want Lara dead for her part in retrieving those body parts." He was already striding down the hall toward the exit.

As they hurried out of the building, Matt said, "Meg is there, and she's a great agent."

Brett nodded distractedly. "Money. I did say whoever was behind this had to be someone with money."

"We'll get there, but let's stay grounded. This isn't proof that any of those men are guilty," Diego reminded him. "This just tells us that they were at the hospital the day Randy Nicholson died."

They'd reached the car. Brett had his phone out, trying to reach Lara.

No answer.

"Give me the keys, *amigo*," Diego said.

Brett tossed them over; Diego was an ace driver, and he knew he wouldn't be able to focus on the road. "Lara isn't answering," he said.

Matt frowned, sliding into the backseat, his phone out, as well. After a minute he frowned. "Meg's not picking up, either."

"They had their big event for the vets today," Diego said. "They're probably just busy. They probably can't even hear their phones."

Brett glanced at his watch. "It should be over. It's after five." He looked at the other two men. "Taggerly is old and runs a drug company. Martinez has focused his entire business on getting people to lead healthful lives. And Blackwood . . ."

"Is a rich asshole," Diego said.

"You think one of them is hooked up with the Barillo crime family?" Matt said, his tone skeptical.

"This could have created all kinds of strange bedfellows," Brett said. "In the meantime, we've got to reach someone there. We have to find out what's going on."

"Try the main number," Diego suggested.

"That will probably get us some kid in the gift shop," Brett said.

"I'll call Grady," Matt told them. "I got his cell number from Adam before I came down here."

Matt made the call, and Brett did his best

to listen to the conversation. He could hear distant noise coming from Matt's phone — music, he realized, and it must be loud if he could hear it over the phone — but he couldn't make out what Grady was saying.

"Good to hear it went so well," Matt said. "Listen, Grady, we need to make sure everyone there is safe." A second later, he said, "Yes, yes, there are police cars on the way." There was more noise from the other end. "Grady, listen to me. Are your sponsors still there? The big-money guys?" He put his hand over the phone and said, "They're still around somewhere. He's asking Sonia Larson if she's seen them."

They were already on the causeway, and Diego was sliding around other cars with ease, definitely ignoring the speed limit.

Brett couldn't tamp down the sense of deep unease that filled him.

Nothing had changed except that now he knew those men had been at the hospital. And he was certain that the "zombie" experiments had begun because someone was looking for a cure, someone who had connected with one of the higher-ups in the Barillo empire. Someone with money.

And Lara wasn't answering her phone.

"Ask him about Lara," Brett said. "And Meg."

Matt did, telling Grady that both women had gone down to the back lagoon and why, and that they might still be there.

"Grady says that the cops have arrived and told him they're checking out the place for safety."

"Tell him to get the cops down to that lagoon now," Brett said. "They're at the far lagoon? No one can see them there, right?"

"Grady," Matt said, "this is important. Ask the cops to head straight to the back lagoon and make sure everyone out there is fine. We'll be there in a matter of minutes. Get one of them to call Brett or me right away. Thanks, Grady."

There was a knot in the pit of Brett's stomach as Matt rang off. Something was wrong; he could feel it.

He was pretty sure that Matt did, too.

"One of those bastards is in with the Barillo family," Brett said. "The real family. He's promised to cure Anthony Barillo."

"We can't know that. Not just from a hospital visit," Matt said.

"We're there," Diego announced.

He'd barely said the words before Brett was out of the car, running toward the gate. As he ran, he heard sirens in the background.

The entry through the gift shop was still

open; he burst through it.

The Navy anthem was playing as he tore through the store and ran straight to the path out to the lagoon.

When he got there, he found utter chaos, cops on walkie-talkies, people milling around. Brett reached the first cop. "What's going on?" he demanded, flashing his badge.

"An ambulance is coming. There are two people out by the lagoon."

"Women?"

"A man and a woman. He got a good bash on the head, possible skull fracture. We're not sure about the woman."

"What about Lara and Meg?" Brett asked, then realized this man wouldn't have any idea who he meant. He started running again, his steps crunching on the gravel of the path until he reached the long dock that led out to the sandbar island at the far lagoon.

Matt and Diego were right behind him when he got there. Grady and a cop were kneeling down beside a body. He quickly realized that the body was Dr. Amory.

Grady looked up at him, his features solemn. "Someone hit him. Hard. And Adrianna . . . She's breathing, but barely moving, just staring at the sky."

"Lara?" Brett said. "Lara and Meg?"

"I don't know," Grady said. "I just don't know."

Paramedics were running down the path toward them, carrying stretchers.

"The woman on the dock has probably been injected with puffer fish poison," Brett told them, fighting to control his panic.

Where the hell were Meg and Lara?

He knew the answer right away.

Because he saw Miguel Gomez. The ghost was walking up and down by the platform, pointing.

Pointing out to sea.

A boat. The place had always been vulnerable from the bay.

"We need the Coast Guard," Matt said.

"I'm getting Lieutenant Gunderson. This is his area," Diego said.

Brett couldn't wait for the Coast Guard. "Grady, you've got a boat?"

"Yeah, a little Donzi."

"Speedboat? Perfect. Where?" Brett asked.

"There's a small dock on the other side of the lockers," Grady said. He pulled a massive ring of keys from his pocket. "It's this one," he said, and handed the whole thing to Brett.

"I'm going with you," Matt said, turning to Diego with a question in his eyes.

"I'll handle things here and come with the

428

Coast Guard," Diego said. "Who the hell are we after?"

Brett looked quickly at Grady. "Who was with you at the end, Grady? More important, who wasn't?"

Grady appeared surprised. But even as he gave his answer, Brett turned to run for the Donzi. He was surprised; the answer hadn't been who he had expected.

The boat was a twenty-five-footer with a small cabin holding a tiny kitchen, horseshoe table and sofa.

Lara and Meg found themselves seated at the table while the vessel sped away from the dock. It was surprisingly fast, but she supposed she should have expected that.

Grant Blackwood could afford anything he wanted.

She hadn't recognized his voice because the Southern charm had disappeared when he'd spoken to them at the dock; there had been no trace of his liquid accent. And when they'd gotten on the boat he'd produced a gun with a massive silencer, and he kept it pointed at them now, smiling all the while.

"Good thing you decided to come along. Unlike your Dr. Amory. Decent guy, even if he didn't accept Ely Taggerly's offer. He was a smart man, and he could have gone far with us. I didn't mean to hit him so hard. And Adrianna . . . Well, I'd have killed her without much regret. She was no one to me."

"So why haven't you just shot *us*?" Meg asked him.

"Because I have something else in mind. Poetic justice of a sort," he said, then turned to Lara. "I *am* sorry about this, but, Lara . . . You and that damned dolphin. You just had to find those body parts and bring down the whole FBI. Well, I'm sorry, but yours are going to be the next ones they find. You found the dead in the water? Now you'll *be* the dead in the water."

Another man — one of the crew who had manned the boat while Blackwood cracked Dr. Amory's skull and poisoned Adrianna — came down to the cabin. He was about forty, Lara thought, Hispanic, medium build, with dark eyes and hair.

"You're a Barillo, aren't you?" she asked. "You look like your father. I've seen his picture in the paper."

The man looked at Blackwood. "She knows."

"You know, sometimes you're an idiot. She doesn't know anything — or didn't, till you confirmed her suspicion. It's a good thing it doesn't matter anymore, isn't it?"

Blackwood asked.

"Tomas Barillo?" Meg asked.

"The same, *chica*," he told her, sweeping into a bow. He looked at Blackwood. "She's FBI. Talk about being an idiot. The FBI will never let this go, not once you kill one of their own."

"The FBI can chase their tails forever, just like they've been doing all along. Once they lose cadaver girl here, they'll have nothing," Blackwood said. He slid next to Lara on the seat and laughed. "Such revulsion! Not all that much different from the look you gave me at the party when I asked you to take a walk, huh, little girl? Leave it to Sonia to let me know about Special Agent Cody. I wouldn't have killed you for that, though. But you just had to keep finding evidence. All those body parts . . ."

"I had to keep finding them because you kept providing them," Lara said, surprised that she could talk, stunned that she wasn't terrified. She was going to be killed. And Meg — who was powerless because she had asked her to drop her gun — was going to die with her.

She looked at her friend. Meg wasn't betraying fear. She wouldn't, either.

Meg was looking at Tomas Barillo. "I understand what you're trying to do," she

431

said. "Your brother Anthony is dying of some neurological disease, and you're trying to find a cure."

Tomas lowered his head, grinning. "You think I did this to save my brother?" he asked. "Yes, I need to keep him alive. But just barely. I need people to see him and *think* that he is alive and well."

"A puppet figurehead, while you take over his empire?" Lara asked.

"Bingo," Tomas said. "Lovely *and* smart. What a waste. We could play awhile, you know, Blackwood."

"No. No time for play," Blackwood said. "Stop letting the little head rule the big one."

"Why are you part of this?" Lara asked Blackwood. She really did want to know. She also realized they were about to kill her and Meg, and it wouldn't hurt to play for time. "You're rich as Midas, and you earned all your money legitimately. You have everything."

Barillo started to laugh. "Everything? Let me tell you something. My partner here, Mr. Grant Blackwood, has been diagnosed with a neurological disease that will first steal his muscles, and then his organs, and then . . . he will die like men die from puffer fish poison. He will know that he is wasting away, that he will be nothing but a lump of meat."

"Shut up, you mongrel bastard!" Blackwood said. "Let's do this! Ladies, get up and out on deck."

"Why should we make it easy for you?" Meg demanded, staying where she was.

"Let's see. I can drop you into the water to drown whole, or I can blow up your kneecaps first. Maybe the sharks will eat you before you have time to drown. I don't care which. Your choice."

Meg looked at Lara, and Lara could read her mind.

Do what he says. Every second of life buys us more opportunity to escape.

Lara rose and pretended to catch her suit on the table.

"Move!" Barillo said.

"I'm trying!" she said.

He ushered them both up on deck. There was a third man there — he'd been captaining the vessel.

They hadn't come as far as she had expected.

Lara could see other boats closer to shore and, in the distance, downtown Miami. Sea Life wasn't all that many miles behind them.

It wouldn't be an easy swim, but if he just threw them over the side . . .

"Get the rope," Blackwood commanded Barillo.

Barillo swore in Spanish but didn't move.

"We're going to hog-tie you, little ladies," Blackwood said, his accent suddenly heavy again. "Hog-tie you and leave you to the water until you're nothing but bones." He looked over to his partner. "Damn you, Barillo, get the rope!"

"Get your own damned rope," Barillo said.

The two men were facing one another, testosterone blazing. Lara was closest to Blackwood, and as far as she knew, Barillo wasn't armed.

She didn't really know what she was doing, but she also knew that they didn't have any choice but to take this one chance. Hog-tied, they would die.

She prayed that Meg was reading her mind as she suddenly slammed herself as hard as she could against Blackwood's gun arm.

The gun went flying, and she and Meg threw themselves over the rail into the water.

They went deep . . . deeper . . .

She saw bullets whizz by in the water, close . . . so close . . .

There were dozens of boats out on the

water. Brett tried to think of what kind Grant Blackwood would have chosen.

Nothing obviously expensive. Something very fast, though. He looked out and dismissed several right off the bat.

"We're looking for something the average boating enthusiast could afford," Matt said, a pair of binoculars trained in the distance. "They must be holding them inside," he murmured, a strained expression on his face. He looked at Brett. "I don't know how the hell he disarmed Meg."

"Threatened her with someone else's life," Brett said flatly. He let out an oath of utter frustration. "I don't know which damned boat to follow. That's been his strategy all along. Kill the forgotten. Blend in with the everyman. Where the hell . . . ?"

His voice trailed off as the water beside them suddenly burst upward in a majestic display.

It was Cocoa. She was soaring in front of them, surging ahead.

She was guiding them.

Showing them which way to go.

"She's right — just ahead!" Matt said. "There! There's a man shooting into the water. Hell yes, it's Blackwood." He turned to Brett, who had hit the throttle hard.

"The guy next to him is the man who

came to my house with Anthony Barillo."

"Tomas," Matt said. "It's Tomas Barillo. Faster! They're shooting. They'll hit one of them soon if . . ."

If they haven't already.

The words hung unspoken between them.

There was no way out of it.

Lara was a good swimmer. Not the strongest ever, but good enough. So was Meg.

But even if they'd been Olympic athletes, there was a point when a human being had to breathe. They had both kicked down deep — thirty feet, at least — but they were still close to the boat.

But now her lungs were burning as if they were about to burst, simply explode.

She had to have air. And she knew that when she surfaced, she would be seen, and for Grant Blackwood it would be like shooting ducks in a carnival gallery.

She was at the point when a bullet seemed better than drowning when something huge whisked by her in the water. It took her a second to realize that it was Cocoa.

As the dolphin swerved back toward her, Lara turned and saw Meg about ten feet away, about to shoot back toward the surface, too.

Lara didn't know if Cocoa could possibly understand what was needed.

But she did.

Lara grasped the dolphin's dorsal fin and motioned toward Meg. She didn't know if it was the correct hand signal; she simply didn't know what else to do.

But Cocoa did.

She whisked her elegant, long body through the water to Meg's side. The second Meg had also clasped Cocoa's fin, the animal thrust her powerful body forward.

They were rising and drawing away from the boat at the same time.

The two men aboard the boat were so busy looking into the water and shooting that they didn't realize anything else was going on until the captain shouted something and immediately threw himself over the side of the boat.

Brett didn't think twice about ramming the vessel; he knew that Grady would readily sacrifice his Donzi, and he didn't give a rat's ass about the other boat.

"We could give a warning — Oh, fuck it!" Matt said, bracing for the impact.

He jerked the wheel, and the Donzi slammed sideways into the other boat with bone-jarring force, but Brett barely felt it.

As the two boats splintered, he felt a bullet graze his shoulder.

Blackwood had turned and was already shooting again, hiding behind the wall of the small cabin. Brett saw Matt leap onto the other boat's deck and head for Barillo; meanwhile, another bullet soared past his head as he followed Matt's lead and boarded the other boat. He had to find cover.

At least now the men were firing at him and Matt, two people who could fire back.

Brett rolled and got to his feet, sloshing in water as he made his way toward the cabin. Blackwood was still firing in the direction where he'd been. All he had to do was circle around behind Blackwood and take him by surprise.

The boat was listing heavily. Brett had nearly made it all the way around the cabin when a wave sloshed over the side and the boat began to capsize. He tried to catch himself, but he was thrown into the water, and his Glock went flying.

He pitched downward and instinctively scissored his legs hard to head back to the surface.

Blackwood had been thrown into the salty waves just as he had — but Blackwood still had his gun.

The man smiled at him and aimed.

He never fired.

It was as if a gray torpedo rammed the man, hard and sure. Blackwood seemed to fly through the water, his mouth opened in a scream of pain.

A dolphin!

Cocoa was there, saving his life.

He shot up to the surface for a breath. Twenty feet away, he saw Blackwood surface, gurgling and screaming in pain, thrashing desperately to stay afloat.

He would go after Blackwood. But not until . . .

"Brett!"

It was Lara, just a few feet away, swimming strongly toward him. He drove toward her and threw his arms around her, and they both began to sink as he caught her to him for a fierce, salty kiss, then kicked hard, propelling them both back up.

"Meg?" he asked anxiously.

"Fine," she assured him. "Blackwood?"

"Still alive. I'll go get him," Brett said. "I'd like to kill him."

"Don't do that," Lara said. "He got involved because he's dying from something neurological, too. Let him rot away with it. Serves him right for thinking he could kill others to cure himself."

He left Lara treading water by the ruins

of the two boats and made his way to Blackwood. The man bellowed and tried to move away, but he was clearly in pain and finding it hard to breathe; Cocoa had evidently broken several of his ribs.

As Brett shook his head and closed in on the man, he saw that the Coast Guard cutter, with Diego and Lieutenant Gunderson at the bow, had nearly reached them.

"Grant Blackwood, you are under arrest," he said, and gripped the man in a lifesaving hold.

Blackwood truly deserved to live until he met the agony of his natural end.

EPILOGUE

Brett had never really thought of his house as a home, but in the weeks since the arrests of Blackwood and Tomas Barillo, Lara had taken to staying at his place.

And since Grady had insisted that she take a short break from work, she had been able to make it something like her own home, too.

Little things changed the place.

Like the flowers she liked to have in the house, the pictures of the parents she'd lost and the aunt who had raised her, pictures of her and Meg and more. There was also the scent of her soap and shampoo and perfume, lingering lightly and teasingly on the air.

And major things changed it.

Like waking up to find that she was beside him. And realizing why he'd cared so much about Miguel and Maria. They'd had what he'd always wanted: the knowledge that you wanted to wake up that way every single day for the rest of your life.

Because his house had become a home, he had Grady, Rick and Adrianna over, along with Diego, Meg and Matt, on the day that Adrianna and Dr. Amory were released from the hospital. He felt they deserved the best explanation he and his fellow agents could give.

They had a barbecue with fish and meat, salads, corn on the cob and key lime pie for dessert. And afterward they sat in the back and watched the sun set and the moon rise as they talked.

Grady shook his head in puzzlement. "How on earth did Grant Blackwood meet up with Tomas Barillo?"

"At the hospital," Brett said. "Grant was in the process of discovering that he was going to rot away for the next few years and then die. Tomas Barillo was there with Anthony, learning that his brother might not have long to live and stewing in the knowledge that he himself didn't command enough respect from the rank and file to take control once his brother was dead. It would be nice to think that Tomas just wanted his brother to live. He didn't. He was afraid that when Anthony died, the 'family' would fall apart, leaving him with nothing.

"Blackwood knew about experiments that had been going on, using monkeys, in which researchers were working on cures for Parkinson's, MS and other neurological diseases. They'd had some success making use of the body's own chemicals to at least ameliorate some of the symptoms."

"Tomas Barillo had hired chemists and biologists to look into uses for puffer fish toxin," Matt said. "They're all under arrest now, but most of them were kept pretty much in the dark. They must have suspected that some of their work was being used in less than legitimate ways, but they were being paid — and they were afraid. Their motto was pretty much 'act stupid, receive a nice income and live.' It's self-defense when you see people being killed all around you."

"Just how many people did Tomas and Blackwood kill?" Adrianna asked.

"We'll never know for sure," Brett said.

"Because they won't tell you?" Grady asked.

Brett sighed. "No, Blackwood is silent and mean as a snake. But Tomas Barillo is talking away — dealing for his life. He's implicated just about everyone. They arrested Anthony Barillo today with what his

443

brother gave us. His empire is going to crumble to dust. But those bastards have been at it awhile. They don't even know how many people they've experimented on — and killed — since they started."

"But why make zombies out of people and then program them to kill?" Rick asked, shaking his head.

"It turned out to be a byproduct. One of the concoctions they put together killed, but slowly. And it wiped out the portion of the brain that had to do with rational function. They were basically programmed. I think that having them go after their own loved ones was an attempt to see how much of the original personality remained, and given that all the 'zombies' seemed willing to kill their nearest and dearest, the answer seems to be 'not very much.' So in the end, they still didn't find the cures they were looking for," Brett said.

"I'll never be able to understand how anyone could be that cold and that cruel," Grady said.

"They put two powers — money and the urge to rule — together and ended up with a force that was truly terrifying," Diego said.

"My heart breaks for all the victims who will never be properly mourned," Lara said.

"We should say a little prayer for the forgotten."

They were all silent for a minute, paying tribute in their own ways.

Grady sighed. "And the man was a sponsor at Sea Life. I hope what he did doesn't overshadow everything we're trying to do."

Brett looked at Lara, and she shrugged and said, "Blackwood had convinced Taggerly to form a new company to focus on neurological research. He knew about relevant research Dr. Amory had done in the past and convinced Taggerly to try to lure him away. But neither Taggerly nor Dr. Amory knew what was going on."

"Of course not! Not that I would have left under any circumstances," Dr. Amory said.

Grady looked grim for a minute, but then he brightened. "We're going to be okay," he said. "We have a famous lifesaving dolphin after all. With the wonderful way Lara has written about her and handled everything with the media, we're going to be golden. And," he added, "thank God we didn't lose anyone at Sea Life."

"Well, technically. But that snake Myles won't be darkening our doors again," Dr. Amory said.

"Sea Life is like a family," Adrianna said. She looked over at Meg and Lara and smiled. "I can attest to that. You two risked your lives for me."

Lara smiled back at her. "My life wouldn't be worth much to me if I'd hadn't at least tried."

"Ditto," Meg said. "And I'm not just saying that because it's my job."

For a minute they were all silent again.

Then Grady let out another sigh. "I'm heading out, folks. Long day tomorrow." He turned to Lara. "You'll be back after your break?" he asked.

Lara nodded. "I'll be back," she promised. "I love Sea Life."

Rick, Adrianna and Dr. Amory followed Grady's lead. Good-nights were said. They were awkward and a little emotional, but nice.

Diego hovered by the door. "I need to get going, too," he said. He grinned at Brett and Lara. "Apparently only one of us gets to go to the Caribbean for a week."

"You're off the week after," Brett reminded him.

"Yeah, yeah, whatever," Diego said.

"Don't go yet," Lara said, taking his arm. "We want you to see something."

Together with Meg and Matt, they returned to the backyard.

There was a tiled bench that looked over

the yard. The moon was full and the night was warm, without a hint of the rain that so frequently plagued the South Florida summers.

There, on the bench, together at last, were the ghosts of Miguel and Maria Gomez.

Arm in arm, they sat together, content to watch the moonlight.

"I see them," Diego said softly. "And I'm glad they got their happy ending."

When just the four of them remained, Matt told Brett, "You know, there's a place for you in the Krewe, if you're interested in moving up to DC."

Brett looked at Lara, and she smiled. "Well, my best friend *is* a Krewe agent. It looks like a really good job. Right now, though, I still have a dolphin who deserves a lot of fish."

Brett turned to Matt and shook his head.

"The offer remains open," Matt said. A few minutes later he and Meg went up to bed.

Lara started to pick up the few remaining glasses, but Brett went over and stopped her by slipping his arms around her.

"It really is beautiful to see Miguel and Maria together that way," Lara said. "I just wonder . . . will they leave? And go — I hope — to heaven?"

"I don't know. I know that if they stay, it will be together. I believe, though, that they will go on, and that they'll stay together."

"I believe that, too."

"It's a forever kind of a thing," he said.

"Kind of what I feel for you," she told him.

He smiled. "Same here. So I guess tonight begins our forever, don't you think?"

She nodded gravely, and then a fiery light touched the blue-green beauty of her eyes. "Forever should be fun and really sexy, huh?"

"Absolutely."

She nodded, turned and headed up the stairs.

He watched her and thought of Miguel and what he'd once told Brett.

I knew — I just knew. And it didn't matter how long we'd been together or what others thought. I knew that I would love her forever.

"Thank you, Miguel," Brett said softly.

And then he followed Lara up the stairs.

ABOUT THE AUTHOR

New York Times and *USA Today* bestselling author **Heather Graham** majored in theater arts at the University of South Florida. After a stint of several years in dinner theater, back-up vocals, and bartending, she stayed home after the birth of her third child and began to write, working on short horror stories and romances. After some trial and error, she sold her first book, *When Next We Love*, in 1982 and since then, she has written over one hundred novels and novellas including category, romantic suspense, historical romance, vampire fiction, time travel, occult, and Christmas holiday fare. She wrote the launch books for Dell's Ecstasy Supreme line, Silhouette's Shadows, and for Harlequin's mainstream fiction imprint, Mira Books.

Heather was a founding member of the Florida Romance Writers chapter of RWA and, since 1999, has hosted the *Romantic*

Times Vampire Ball, with all revenues going directly to children's charity. She is pleased to have been published in approximately twenty languages, and to have been honored with awards from Waldenbooks, B. Dalton, Georgia Romance Writers, *Affaire de Coeur, Romantic Times,* and more. She has had books selected for the Doubleday Book Club and the Literary Guild, and has been quoted, interviewed, or featured in such publications as *The Nation, Redbook, People,* and *USA Today,* and appeared on many newscasts including local television and *Entertainment Tonight.*

Heather loves travel and anything have to do with the water, and is a certified scuba diver. Married since high school graduation and the mother of five, her greatest love in life remains her family, but she also believes her career has been an incredible gift, and she is grateful every day to be doing something that she loves so very much for a living.

The employees of Thorndike Press hope you have enjoyed this Large Print book. All our Thorndike, Wheeler, and Kennebec Large Print titles are designed for easy reading, and all our books are made to last. Other Thorndike Press Large Print books are available at your library, through selected bookstores, or directly from us.

For information about titles, please call:
   (800) 223-1244

or visit our Web site at:
   http://gale.cengage.com/thorndike

To share your comments, please write:
   Publisher
   Thorndike Press
   10 Water St., Suite 310
   Waterville, ME 04901